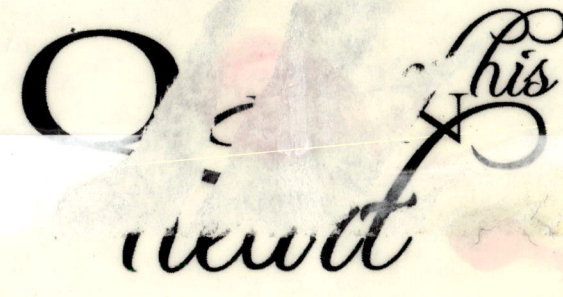

LENA HART

QUEEN OF HIS HEART
Copyright © 2014 Lena Hart

ALL RIGHTS RESERVED.

No part of this book may be reproduced or transmitted in any form or by any means, including electronic or photographic reproduction, in whole or in part, without express written permission, except in the case of brief passages embodied in critical reviews and articles.

ISBN-13: 978-1-941885-07-9

DEDICATION

~~~

To CGB—thanks for the memories and the lessons learned.

And to all my readers and fans—I truly appreciate you from the bottom of my heart.♥

The Queen of Hearts lives a life of love—and though she may fall, she is strengthened by that which is a part of her.

♥

chapter 1

Satin bed sheets slid along her bare legs and fell to the awaiting floor.

Judith Bell awoke with a soft breath, missing the cool material that left her heated body exposed. The smooth, crimson sheet had been like an intimate caress, brushing languidly against her freshly shaved legs.

She sighed. Unfortunately, the departing material hadn't been the only thing that had pulled her from her deep slumber. The steady throbbing between her legs was a delicious reminder of what still lingered in her slowly fading memory. Judith squeezed her thighs together, trying to dull the ache that a pair of piercing dark eyes and sensual lips had aroused.

Damn Carlos Moreno.

Now he was invading her sleep.

In her dream, his eyes, the color of onyx, had held many promises, while his lips had been places she would only dare to dream of...

Rolling onto her back, Judith released a shuddering

sigh.

Since he had started working at Royal Courts two months ago, he had not been shy about his interest in her. Every week, he'd made it a habit to ask her out, whether it was for lunch, dinner, or a family gathering. Of course, she would always decline, not wanting to lead him on. But the way he spoke and looked at her when others weren't around said her forced disinterest didn't bother him. He flirted outrageously, some of it serious, most of it bordering on ridiculous, but each time it made her smile inwardly. However, she was careful not to show him her weakening resolve. It would only encourage him and he didn't need any more confidence.

Her unwavering attraction to the tall, dark Latino was something she was steadily trying to rid herself of. Not only because they worked together, which was a motivating factor in itself, but because Carlos Moreno was too…intense. There were times when he reminded her of a wolf, with his thick, black eyebrows and the trim facial hair covering his jaw and around his lips. He was rugged and had the look of a man who kept a wild animal inside just waiting to be roused.

She didn't want to be the one to awaken any animalistic instincts in him—or in any man. Getting involved with someone who harbored such passion behind cool, piercing dark eyes and a lazy smile, was not someone Judith wanted to entertain or encourage.

Yet, even now, from just one dream—just one thought—her nipples hardened and pushed against the soft, thin material of her rose pink cami.

Judith pulled a pillow over her face and groaned

into it. She was happy with her quiet, solitary life and a relationship with a man like Carlos could be dangerous. He could easily charm her into places unknown and before she knew it, she would fall. Hard. And she couldn't let that happen.

She might get lonely at times, but the thought of letting a man get close to her like that again almost sent her into a panic.

Besides, there was only room left in her heart for one special guy.

The familiar dip in the bed forced Judith's eyes open. She shoved the pillow aside and turned toward the loud purring that came from beside her head. Her bright orange, long-haired Siberian mix stared down at her with pale gold eyes and released a loud meow, this one snappy and demanding.

She groaned. "Okay, Prince, I'm up," Judith muttered, rolling out of bed.

Clad in old pajama shorts and her camisole tank, she padded out of the bedroom without her glasses. The sight in her left eye was clear enough for her to navigate her way to the bathroom and she made it just in time to keep Prince out. His loud meow came clearly through the door and she shook her head. Every morning was always the same routine, yet she still couldn't help but laugh. Prince tended to get feisty when he didn't get his way, but she had to set some boundaries for him.

The rescue shelter she had taken him to, after she'd found him left alone in an old cat carrier behind the dumpster at her last job, had estimated his age to be between three to five years old. He was big enough for her to agree, but after a quick examination, they concluded that he was no more than two years old. Despite his size, she had to remember that he was still a young kitty.

Scraping sounds came just below the bathroom door and a quick glance downwards revealed large paws poking through the small opening at the bottom.

"I'm coming, I'm coming," she grumbled.

She finished up and headed to the kitchen, Prince following closely behind. It had been nearly a year since she'd adopted the abandoned cat. Though she had been hesitant about bringing a strange animal in her new apartment, she hadn't been able to part with him after she'd taken him to the shelter. His loud cries the night she'd found him had been heart wrenching, and when she'd found out that the shelter she'd taken him to euthanized unadopted animals, she hadn't been able to leave him there.

Every living being deserved a chance at life and the thought that someone had purposely left him out to die filled her with a burning rage.

Based on the faded name "Charlie" printed on the worn tag around his neck, it was apparent that he had lived in a home before his owners decided to toss him away like trash. There had been no chip or other identifiers on him, which luckily made her adoption of him quick.

The transition for Prince into his new home, however, had not been as easy. He'd been wary of her and his new dwelling in the beginning, but now he strutted and pranced around her small apartment like a little…prince.

Judith poured his breakfast into his ceramic dish as he circled around her legs with a purr that sounded more like a low growl. She couldn't tell if it was just his long fur, but looking down at him, he appeared to be getting much wider.

"I'm going to have to put you on a diet, sir," she said, placing the small bowl down in front of him.

Prince ignored her and dug his head into it. When it came to food and affection, he was a total glutton. Sitting at her small kitchen table, Judith also dug into her breakfast.

It was still early, which she liked. Mornings were her favorite time of the day. It gave her time to eat a proper breakfast before work, though many might not consider cold cereal part of a balanced meal. Her days at Royal Courts had become unpredictable lately, especially Mondays, and there were times she would miss lunch altogether. Though she enjoyed working at Royal Courts—and it certainly beat waiting tables at a snooty Italian restaurant—being an executive assistant to the co-founder and CEO wasn't something she wanted to do long-term. Until she could figure out what she wanted to do with her life, now that dance was no longer an option, being an assistant would have to do.

Judith placed her empty bowl in the sink and got ready for her first day back to work after a nice, quiet weekend. In the shower, thoughts of Carlos Moreno once again intruded. Lately, everything she did reminded her of him. Even simple, everyday tasks like taking a shower. Fantasies of his soapy hands lathering her wet body flooded her mind. What would it feel like to have his hands caressing her body, his lips kissing all over her?

Judith groaned, shoving the perilous thoughts away. If Carlos had set out these past few weeks to make her aware of him, he had succeeded. A relationship between them could never be, yet her defenses against him were weakening every day. But it wasn't his friendship he was offering and she couldn't accept anything else.

Now, if only her body would follow her head, and ignore his corny pickup lines along with his flattering endearments, he would be easier to handle. Then again, it was her head conjuring up dreams and fantasies of him.

Traitor.

The small rebuke didn't stop her body from clenching with frustration. She quickly rinsed off then jumped out of the shower.

Wrapped in a thick towel, she sifted through her underwear drawer. Judith eyed the red and black lace bra and matching panties she had bought a few weeks ago then pulled them out. She had been feeling particularly bold that day and had made the impulsive buy, though she had yet to wear them.

Today, however, she was feeling rather brave. Ripping the store tags off, she slipped on the sexy underwear. She turned to her tall vanity mirror, trying to ignore the long, dark scar that slanted across her abdomen and the other tiny marks that painted her torso and waist. Most times she managed to forget the dark scars that marred her body. Thankfully, they weren't rutted and over time, they had smoothed over her skin and she could barely feel them. But it was when she was forced to look at her body that they became glaring.

Turning her attention to the new underwear, which was more comfortable than she expected, she nodded, pleased with her purchase. The bra even made her average-sized breasts appear fuller, and she felt daring and sexy. This was something Carlos would certainly notice.

Glancing at the clock on the nightstand, she began to pick up her pace. Time was getting away from her and she wasn't keeping up. She slid open her closet doors and pulled out her favorite black, sleeveless blouse and red, high-waist skirt. It hugged tightly around her hips and butt, accentuating her figure nicely. Though the skirt was tighter than it should have been, it wasn't indecent—or uncomfortable. Yet.

Prince wasn't the only one who needed to be put on a diet. She would either need to start working out again or toss out the tin of peanut butter-chocolate pieces she kept in the kitchen. She balked at the thought.

Work out it is then.

She carefully inserted the contact lens in her right eye and made her way out of the apartment, stopping long enough to give herself one last assessment in the hanging mirror beside the front door. Her dark caramel skin glowed against the black blouse. She didn't wear much make-up, but she applied her usual cherry lip gloss and a bit more mascara than usual. She debated whether she should clip her thick, dark brown hair up or let it hang down her shoulders for a change.

She left it down. Carlos would probably like it down...

This is not for him, she chided herself, turning away from the mirror.

Deep down, however, she recognized the lie. She knew exactly who she was dressing up for. And in that brief moment, she didn't care.

Her eyes landed on Prince, who lounged on his favorite spot on the corner of the sofa. His limbs were tucked beneath him as he regarded her with eyes full of judgment.

"Don't look at me like that," she muttered. "It's *not* for him."

But a shameless part of her scoffed at her feeble insistence. That same, wicked part of her wanted Carlos Moreno to eat his heart out.

chapter 2

*D*amn.

Carlos Moreno's heart thudded in his chest as he watched Judith bend over an open drawer behind her desk. She continued her rummaging while he enjoyed the view of her red skirt hugging around her hips and ass as if it was just as much in love with her curves as he was.

As Chief of Security, he spent most of his day stuck in his office going through paperwork or dealing with critical issues in the department. But Carlos also liked to stay on the move, checking out the facility, making sure everything was as it should be when he got in each morning and before he left for the night. He'd just been completing his walk-through for the morning when a red skirt molded around lush curves had caught his attention.

Leaning against her desk, he continued his admiration. "I don't have a library card, but I hope you don't mind me checking you out."

She stood up with a muffled screech, almost

dropping her small bundle of supplies. The action jostled the brimming coffee mug near her keyboard.

"*Mr. Moreno, you scared me*," she shrieked.

He stifled a grin. "I'm sorry, I didn't mean to." But he'd enjoyed the view too much to truly regret it.

She was looking especially good today in that sexy black top and that leave-little-to-the-imagination skirt. From the steady beating of his heart, down to the heaviness in his groin, he ached to touch her. He wasn't surprised by his body's reaction from just looking at her. It had been this way from the moment he'd laid eyes on her two months ago.

But damn if she wasn't playing hard to get.

She placed the items on her desk and he noticed the way the collar of her blouse shifted, revealing the smooth brown curves of her neck and cleavage. He noticed a lot about her. Like the gentle way she moved, her fresh, sweet scent, the soft and breathy pitch of her voice. He also noticed the way she tried to suppress her smile when he did his damnedest to make her laugh and the way her face softened right before she replaced it with her cool, aloof mask whenever she saw him.

"May I help you with something, Mr. Moreno?" she asked in a clipped tone, her expression blank.

Carlos wasn't deterred, though. He knew she felt this strong pull between them, but for whatever reason, she hid her attraction behind a facade of professional detachment.

Carlos made an exaggerated show to think about her question then blurted, "If I said you had a lovely body, would you hold it against me? I won't mind if you do."

She shook her head, her brows pulling together in a slight frown. "I don't have time for this, Mr. Moreno. Mr. Carrone is not in the office yet and I have a lot of work to get back to."

"Okay, I won't keep you. I just wanted to tell you that you look very beautiful today. But then again, you look beautiful every day."

He hoped she didn't take it as another line because he was being sincere. She could have been wrapped in a paper bag and he would have found her captivating. She usually kept her hair pinned up, but today it hung down around her shoulders, framing her pretty, round face. The frown fell from her face and just as he expected, she glanced down briefly before looking back up at him.

"Thank you," she muttered.

He smiled at her coy response. "You're welcome, *muñeca*. Now you're supposed to tell me how pretty I look today."

The corner of her lips twitched, but she said nothing. He sighed. *Patience*, he reminded himself.

"Why don't you let me take you out to lunch today?"

She shook her head again. "I can't. Today is going to be a busy day for me."

"Dinner then?" Carlos prompted but he already knew the answer to that. Before she could refuse, he added, "It's my birthday this week," he said, "so why don't you let me buy you dinner tonight."

She hesitated for the briefest of seconds and he took that as a good sign. His birthday had actually been last week, but that was a minor detail.

"I'll think about it," she said after a while.

That was a start, he thought wryly.

But if he let her think too long on it, it would take another two months before they even had their first date. He knew with every ounce of blood that pumped through him that she found him attractive—even if it was just a little—yet she was reluctant about getting involved with him and he couldn't understand why.

In the beginning, it had been different between them. He had come on as Royal Courts' new security chief just shy of two months and she had been friendly and courteous toward him, even gracing him with one of her dimpled smiles from time to time.

Though, he wanted them to become more than two employees who greeted each other in passing. As soon as he'd seen her sitting prettily behind that wide desk, an electric charge had passed between them, and she'd forever had him. But his attempts at courting her had only caused her to shut down. He admitted he may have come off too strong, but he couldn't help it. He was a healthy man with a healthy appetite and when he saw something he wanted, he went after it.

That, however, had forced her to retreat further. So he'd changed his approach, keeping it casual and letting her see his charming and playful side. Sometimes he succeeded, and she would relax. He would even manage to draw an occasional smile out of her when she thought he wouldn't notice.

But most times, he would wince inwardly at the cheesy pickup lines. He hadn't used those ridiculous lines on a woman since he was in junior high, but if making an ass of himself was what he needed to do to get a smile out of her, he would do it.

"Can I help you with anything else, Mr. Moreno?" she asked evenly.

Apparently, making an ass out of himself hadn't completely softened her attitude toward him, but at least the walls she had erected between them seemed to be slowly cracking. And he wouldn't be content until he managed to get a smile out of her this morning. Even if it was just a small one.

He absently rubbed his shins. "Actually, I could use a Band-Aid."

She eyed him suspiciously. "For what?"

"My knee. I accidentally scraped it falling for you."

She rolled her eyes and bit her lower lip, but that didn't stop it from curving slightly.

He straightened from his perch on her desk. "There it is, *muñeca*," he said. "There's that beautiful smile."

She shook her head again but, to his surprise and delight, her expression softened into a full smile. He marveled at the way the tiny dips formed on her smooth, round cheeks. Lately, she rarely smiled at him but when she did, her face lit up and transformed, captivating him until he thought of nothing else but doing it again, wanting to see nothing but joy on her beautiful face.

And it was her sweet smile and gentleness that had first drawn him to her. Like now.

He came toward her and her eyes widened in surprise—and awareness. The way her dark amber brown eyes dilated, the way her lips parted and she slowly inhaled as he neared—all soft and breathy—said she was more than physically aware of him. Though she tried to keep her reaction contained, he picked up on every nuance. She was that expressive.

Passion and longing simmered behind those large, baby-doll eyes of hers, yet he saw a kind of hollow sadness that he wanted to wipe away forever.

She stared up at him transfixed as he drew near, never taking her eyes from his. Reaching around her, he picked up the coffee mug, the action bringing them closer together and he inhaled deeply. She smelled good—like what sweet dreams probably smelled like.

Heavenly.

And he wanted some of that sweetness for himself.

No. Not some. He wanted it all. But he would bide his time and hold on to his patience.

He pulled back and moved the warm drink to the opposite end of her desk, away from the computer. She exhaled slowly and he didn't miss the faint disappointment in her expressive eyes before she looked away, busying herself with a stack of papers.

He stared down at her bent head. "Dinner tonight, Judith," he urged quietly. "Don't think too much about it. It's more fun if you just say yes."

Carlos left, not at all disappointed by her lack of acknowledgment. His instincts were right and eventually he would break through her resolve. He didn't know what it was about her, but he knew they were meant for each other. He could feel it. She, however, chose to fight it.

Her delicate innocence elicited a protectiveness in him that made him want to fold her into his arms and shield her from whatever it was that brought on that quiet sadness he could see in her at times. Hopefully, with his love and patience, he would be able to break down her walls, and draw out the passionate woman she so obviously kept buried inside.

****

"Hey, Judith. I have presents for you."

She looked up as the young mail clerk dropped a stack of envelopes onto her desk. Though she didn't really socialize with any of her co-workers at Royal Courts outside of work, she would occasionally grab coffee with the young, aspiring musician in the mornings while he filled her in on the latest office gossip. Three months at Royal Courts and still, she couldn't place all the names and faces, but she enjoyed the little distractions.

Today, however, didn't leave them much time for any of that. The amount of work Judith had on her to-do-list in preparation for the resort's week-long branding meetings, which kicked off early tomorrow morning, had been more than she'd anticipated.

She should have taken Carlos up on his lunch offer, though there hadn't been time for lunch anyways. She had skipped the meal and was starting to feel the effects. After his little visit that morning, she'd been working non-stop, yet was still behind in preparing the materials for tomorrow's meetings. Someone from marketing should have been here helping her, but wasn't surprised when no one showed.

Judith sighed as Brian continued loading her desk with envelopes. Mondays always brought lots of mail.

"Thanks Brian," she muttered, gathering and sifting through the pile. It mainly consisted of internal stuff—

invoices, memos, and the like. She pulled aside a large, thick envelope from the heap and frowned. It was addressed to her, but the return address listed back to the office.

She never got mail at work—she never really got mail period. It had to come from another department.

Before she could tear the large envelope open, the phone rang and she answered it with her standard, routine greeting. "Royal Courts executive office. Judith Bell speaking."

A low, deep voice came through the receiver. "Your brain must be tired 'cause I know I've been running through your mind all day."

Judith didn't bother to restrain her smile.

He's too much.

"Hello Mr. Moreno."

There was a lightness in her tone she couldn't contain and she was grateful he wasn't there to see her grinning like an idiot. She couldn't deny that she was glad to hear his voice and he *had* been on her mind throughout the day. He'd asked her out to dinner tonight and for the first time, she seriously considered it. For his birthday, she told herself. Just to be nice.

"Hello *muñeca*," Carlos said, his voice taking on that intimacy she was fast becoming accustom to, along with the endearment.

She had looked up the word once and wasn't sure if she liked it or not. *Muñeca. Babydoll*. It was slowly growing on her, but one thing was for certain, she liked the way Carlos said it.

"So, what time should I pick you up tonight?"

She had been primed to say yes to dinner with him

all day, had actually been excited about it too. A quick glance down at the pile of letters and she knew she couldn't. There was too much to do. Not only did she have her work to complete, she was also filling in as the temporary assistant for Mr. Kristensen, her boss' business partner who was back in the office from his travels. It was fast approaching five and both co-founders were still in their meeting. Usually, they came out with a request or task for her and she couldn't guarantee she would be able to leave at a reasonable hour tonight.

Carlos must have taken her silence as a refusal because he began cajoling her.

"C'mon, Judith. I don't have any cooties and I promise I won't bite." He paused before adding playfully, "But if I do, I promise to let you bite back."

She stifled a laugh. He really was too much.

"It's not that," she started. "It's just…tonight's no good." She took a deep, unsteady breath. "How about tomorrow?"

He was silent for some time, clearly just as stunned as she was by her unexpected offer. She briefly closed her eyes. Anticipation and confused mortification entwined inside her. *What am I doing?*

"Don't play with me, girl," he growled low.

She laughed nervously at his indignant tone. She may have surprised herself by her bold suggestion, but she definitely wasn't playing him.

"I'm not," she assured him. "Dinner. Tomorrow. For your birthday," she added.

He released a heavy sigh then chuckled. "Man, you know how to make a man work. I thought I would have to start writing poetry and shi—stuff."

"Hmm, poetry?" she teased. "On second thought..." This was the first time she had let herself be playful with him and it felt nice.

"Oh no, *muñeca*," he rushed out. "We're having our date tomorrow night. No take backs."

"No take backs," she agreed. "I promise." She hung up the phone, unsure if the nervous giggle that suddenly burst out of her was from apprehension or excitement.

The heavy beating of her heart told her it was the latter.

Giving in to him hadn't been all that bad. If anything, it felt as if the lid over her bottled emotions had finally been loosened and the pressure and tension was starting to seep out, making room for something new and exciting. It was all nerve-wracking, but she wouldn't deny herself an evening alone with him any longer.

She was startled out of her thoughts when the door to Mr. Carrone's office opened and Mr. Kristensen stepped out. She waited for the fair-haired executive to approach her with a request. Since he spent most of his time traveling, they weren't in any hurry to get him his own assistant. Instead, he rushed past her, not sparing her a glance as he concentrated on his cell phone.

Judith breathed a sigh of relief and returned her attention to the mountain of mail piled on her desk.

It took her longer than she expected to sort the important mail from the junk. The large, padded envelope once again caught her eye and she pulled it toward her. Tearing it open, she removed the contents inside. A thick folder, a short note, and a flash drive. Nothing else.

The message on the note was to the point.

If you want our help, call this number. 6pm sharp.

Below the mysterious message was a phone number with no name. Judith frowned. *Help with what?*

She flipped open the folder and after a long look at the photos neatly tucked inside, she let it slip from her numb fingers. It landed on her desk with a soft thud and for a moment, she couldn't move. She had only caught a glimpse, but it was enough to bring a shudder down her spine. With trembling fingers, she closed the folder and sat there, waiting for her heart to stop its frantic beating.

How?

The Agency had promised her that her records would be concealed—that no one would be able to find her.

Yet someone had.

She stared down at the folder, desperate to know who had sent it. But going through it in hopes of finding that answer would require her to look through the photos and relive that horrible night five years ago. She wouldn't do it.

She couldn't.

Putting those dark memories behind her had taken a long time, though there were still nights when they seemed to find their way to the surface and would linger.

The brief note stared up at her and she reread it. Did she dare call that number? Whoever had sent her this knew more about her than anyone should, and that made them dangerous. An overwhelming sense of distress began to settle in at the thought of starting over. According to the Agency, that was the only option if ever her identity was compromised.

But she didn't want to start over. She liked her life now. It was quiet and perhaps monotonous but it was *hers*. She also had Prince. Would she be able to take him with her?

And there was Carlos... She would never see him again.

Judith shoved the folder back into the envelope and tucked it into her drawer. She needed to sort everything out. But not here. Not now.

It was difficult, but she managed to control her nerves long enough to get through the rest of the afternoon.

"Have a good night, Judith."

She blinked up from her monitor as David Carrone walked past her desk, his computer bag slung over his shoulder. She should have been drafting an important memo, but had been staring blankly at the screen in front of her. How long had she just been sitting there?

"Good night, Mr. Carrone."

She watched as the tall, dark-haired CEO disappeared around the corner then glanced at the time. It was a quarter to six.

...call this number. 6pm sharp.

Judith waited a heartbeat then reached into the drawer and grabbed the large envelope, ignoring the warning bells that were sounding off in her head about the huge risk she was taking. But she needed to know how this person had found out about her, what help they wanted to offer her, and more importantly, why they felt the need to conjure up memories she had long since buried—along with the girl pictured inside.

Though the office was now quiet, she couldn't risk making the call at her desk. It was too open. She made her way to the opposite end of the executive floor, where the offices were isolated and empty. As she neared, she realized the only office with a telephone connection was the office Mr. Kristensen was temporarily using and she mentally kicked herself for not bringing her cell phone.

Slipping into the large office, she shut the door and made her way behind the wide desk. She sat down and stared at the phone as if she expected it to come to life. One minute. She would give the person one minute to explain themselves, then she would hang-up.

At exactly six, she picked up the phone and dialed the number. With every ring, she lost a bit more of her courage.

It finally clicked, but there was nothing but silence.

"H-hello?" she called out, not sure if someone had picked up.

"I'm happy you decided to call, Judith."

Her hands tightened around the receiver until her bones ground into it. Whoever she had expected, it hadn't been a woman. She didn't recognize the voice, but there was something vaguely familiar about her accent.

"Who is this?" Judith asked quietly.

"Who I am doesn't matter, hon," the woman said. "What I can do is help you with your Kenneth Tate problem."

Judith sat up, alert. "What do you mean?" she asked, gripping the phone tighter at the mention of her ex-fiancé. "He hasn't been in contact with me." The protection order she had against him kept him from doing so. Not that he could from his prison cell since he couldn't possibly know where she was.

"Well, hon, when he gets out next week, I'm sure that'll all change."

Judith nearly dropped the phone. *Gets out? Next week?* She had hoped he would serve all nine years of his sentence.

Her mind raced. She'd been keeping track of every day, waiting for the moment she would be notified of his release, praying he would forget all about her once he did.

"I can tell from your silence, you didn't know." The woman almost sounded sympathetic, but there were traces of satisfaction over her ignorance. "His request for parole was granted. Looks like your fiancé's coming home, hon."

There was a ringing in her ears that began to grow louder. Judith had to remind herself to breath. She was safe. He couldn't find her.

Could he?

The strange woman was a stark reminder of that he possibly could.

At her continued silence, the woman added, "Take a look in the folder if you don't believe me. There's a copy of the parole board's approval."

Judith didn't touch the folder. Instead, she stared down at it. The photos hidden inside were another harsh reminder of what Kenneth Tate was capable of and how dangerous he could be.

She could feel the walls of her quiet, serene life tumbling around her. Her stomach churned at the thought of things going back to the way they had once been. The late night phone calls, the constant love letters and looking over her shoulder every time she left her apartment.

She couldn't live like that again.

"But," the woman drawled, "I can make it so that he finishes out the rest of his sentence. You want that, don't you?"

Judith wanted Kenneth Tate to spend the rest of his life behind bars, but that wasn't going to happen. Though the judge had sentenced him with the maximum, Ken had only gotten nine years. And that wasn't enough—not for what he had done to her.

"Who are you?" Judith asked again. "Why do you want to help me? What do you want from me?"

The woman was silent for a moment. "I just need your help getting a simple file out of Royal Courts."

Judith hated the paralyzing fear that was consuming her at just the thought of Kenneth Tate. It would always be a part of her, like a sheath of dead skin she would never be able to shed. This strange woman was playing on her fear, but she was also offering to help keep a monster right where he belonged and Judith would take it. No matter the cost.

"How?"

"The flash drive," the woman began slowly, "do you have it?"

Judith pulled the small device from the large envelope. "Yes," she said hollowly.

"Good. Now all I need you to do is connect it to your computer and I'll take care of the rest. That's all."

The woman made it sound so simple, but it wasn't. Judith would be committing a felony. At the very least, she would be putting Royal Courts at risk—along with her status with the Agency.

"Why do you need the file?"

The woman laughed. "I don't plan to shut down the place, if that's what you're thinking. In fact, it doesn't even belong to the resort."

Judith chewed her lower lip. That didn't answer her question, but did it matter? She either did this or she hung up the phone right now. There was no telling what harm the woman was capable of once she had her hands on whatever this file was. Judith may not be well versed in technology, but she knew the damage could be astronomical.

Did she really want to risk everything on the uncertain word and protection of this woman?

"It's only a file, hon," the woman added at her prolonged hesitation. "No one will even know it's missing. I promise. And let's face it, you need our help as much as we need yours. Unless you believe Kenneth Tate has been fully rehabilitated within our wonderful prison system, as he's managed to convince everyone else."

Judith closed her eyes. Ken could possibly be a changed man now, but the last words he'd calmly uttered to her as he'd sped down the deserted highway still echoed in her head.

If I can't have you...

She shuddered at the memory. Ignoring her

apprehension, she reached for the flash drive and stared down at it. "You promise he'll stay in prison?"

"Don't underestimate our abilities, hon," the woman said in a voice lined with amusement, "Or our connections. After all, we managed to find out all about you, didn't we?"

Judith shivered again, fear and anxiety creating a heavy knot in her stomach. "I'm not at my desk," she began. "I'll have to call you back—"

"Any computer will do," the woman interrupted sharply. "This is a one-time call. We either do this now or not at all." The woman paused then added, "I don't mean to sound harsh, hon, but time is really of the essence."

Judith glanced at the blank screen of the open laptop on Mr. Kristensen's desk. She gingerly ran her fingers over the computer mouse pad and was relieved when it flared to life.

Unfortunately, it was locked.

"I don't have the password for this computer," Judith said earnestly.

"That's okay," the woman said, seemingly unconcerned. "Just put in the flash drive."

Judith inserted the flash drive into the first port she found. "Okay, it's in," she whispered.

"Good, now a message should come up prompting you to press any key to recover the password. Do it."

The black window came up with the message and Judith quickly pressed the space bar. A series of numbers and characters started to scroll rapidly across the small window.

"What's happening?" Judith asked, frantic.

"Don't worry. This should only take two, three minutes. Once the password is displayed, just exit out of that window and enter into the system."

She released an unsteady breath when the code appeared.

Tulips01.

She didn't know why that stuck with her but it did. Following the woman's instructions, she entered it. The home screen appeared and another window popped into the monitor.

"It's now asking me to run a program," Judith said hesitantly.

"Excellent." The woman's voice was laced with satisfaction. "Now hon, the next few steps will be very important so I need you to pay close attention to everything I say."

Judith's heart pounded as she followed the woman's instructions. The computer screen suddenly flickered and right before her eyes, the mouse icon began to move on its own.

"What is it doing?" Judith couldn't keep the panic from her voice.

"It's just me, hon," the woman assured her. "I've just taken over for a while. It'll be done soon. You're doing great," she added as an afterthought.

Judith didn't feel great. Her stomach still churned as she watched as program windows and folders opened and closed rapidly. Everything was surreal and Judith prayed that it would all be over soon. This was not what she'd expected. This was supposed to be a simple copy and paste, right?

But numerous folder and program windows

continued to open and shut at a rapid speed. It was like watching a computer hijacking in progress. Except, she'd practically given the hijacker the keys.

Not having control over what the strange woman was accessing only added to her anxiety. What if she took more than just a *simple* file?

"Are you—?"

The words froze in Judith's throat as a soft rustle came to the door. She flipped the lid of the laptop down as the office door pushed open. It took her a millisecond longer to register the phone still in her hand before she slammed it down. Her heart had practically lodged itself into her throat.

To her immense relief, it was just a cleaning lady.

"Sorry, miss," the woman said, looking just as startled to find her sitting there. "I thought this office was empty."

Judith hurried to her feet. Was guilt written on her face? "It's okay," she rushed out, trying to keep her voice even. "I was just heading out."

"No, no," the other woman said adamantly. "You take your time. I can come back later."

Once again alone, Judith inhaled jerkily. Bracing herself on the edge of the desk, she leaned forward and tried to steady her breathing and calm her nerves to keep her legs from buckling beneath her. Her arms trembled from the tight grip she had on the wide desk, but she couldn't force herself to relax. Taking another unsteady breath, she closed her eyes briefly. When she opened them, her gaze instantly landed on the phone.

Oh, shit.

She grabbed the receiver and redialed the last

number. An automated message came through the line.

Oh, no.

The thought that she may have gone through this nightmare for absolutely nothing, almost sent her into an anxiety attack. Did the woman get what she wanted?

Judith redialed the number. Again, the automated message picked up. She slammed the phone down. She needed to get out of here. The longer she stayed in the executive's office, the more likely she would be discovered.

Judith stuffed the folder back into the large envelope and dashed out of the office. It wasn't until she reached her desk that she realized she'd left behind the most important thing in this whole ordeal.

The flash drive.

Oh, damn it.

chapter 3

What have I done?

Judith shoved the large envelope into her desk drawer and sank down in her seat. Her throat tightened as panic like she'd never felt threatened to suffocate her. She rested her head on the desk, trying to calm her racing heart.

Calm down, Judith. You made this mess. Just go back and clean it up.

The little pep talk didn't help to calm her nerves. Murphy's Law had her by the throat and there was nothing she could do. Everything that could go wrong was rapidly spiraling in that direction—and if that direction was south, that was surely where she would find her sanity.

Well, what did she expect?

The magnitude of her mistake was fast becoming glaring. No, *mistake* was an understatement.

She had just committed a crime.

Whether the woman had gotten what she'd been looking for, Judith didn't know. Just like she didn't know whether the mystery woman would even honor her agreement.

Judith scoffed hysterically at herself. *Honor? Agreement?* She'd just consorted with a stranger to commit a crime. One who knew way too much about her and her past.

The thought of having to look over her shoulder, of having to wonder about every dark shadow or strange letter, was enough to send Judith into another panic. Mentally—and emotionally—she didn't think she could endure living like that again.

But what she wanted didn't matter now. She wasn't safe anymore and she had to be prepared for what was to come. First...

I need to get that flash drive!

Judith barely made it down the long hall to the large executive office before an amused voice came from behind her.

"Glad to see you didn't brush me off tonight for some other guy."

Judith whirled around with a low squeak.

"Whoa, take it easy," Carlos said with a slight frown. "I didn't mean to scare you."

"Sorry," she rushed out. She had never been more horrified and happy to see someone in her life. "I didn't hear you coming."

There was a sort of charming awkwardness in his dark eyes. "Sorry for sneaking up on you. I guess I'm doing a lot of that lately." He glanced down the long hall. "But what are you still doing here? I thought everyone on this floor had left for the day."

She cleared her throat, trying to dislodge the lump

that was rapidly forming there. "Uh, yes. Um, I mean, no, I just had... There was something I needed to get for the, uh, workshops tomorrow."

Her words were a jumbled mess and he regarded her with obvious confusion. They stood near the supply closet and she latched onto that.

"It's in here," she added, motioning to the closed door.

His dark eyes bore into her, but she didn't see suspicion or doubt in them. Only a deep concern. For her.

"Are you okay, *muñeca?*" he asked slowly.

She stared up at him, overwhelmed with despair. *No, not really.* The worry in his eyes was enough to have the lump return. This time from profound guilt instead of panic.

Could she trust him?

It wasn't worth the risk, so instead she took a deep breath and simply nodded. She tried to formulate her thoughts and put them into coherent words this time.

"Yes, I'm fine," Judith assured him with a wide, strained smile. "I just... I got so busy today. I missed lunch and now can't seem to think straight."

At least that wasn't a complete lie. There was no food in her stomach and no rational thought left in her brain—not enough anyway to have stopped her from making the biggest mistake of her life.

"You need to take care of yourself," Carlos said, concern still clouding his eyes. "Don't let Carrone work you to the ground."

Despite herself, she was warmed by his gentle reprimand. He cared.

"I'm fine, really. I just need to grab a few things, then I'm heading out soon." She turned the door knob of the supply room as she spoke and to her dismay, found it locked. Glancing over at Carlos, she let out a weak laugh.

"I guess they've started locking these after hours," she muttered, though that little assessment was a complete guess. In her three months at Royal Courts, she'd only been in the supply room once or twice.

With a grin, Carlos pulled out a set of keys. "The perks of working in security," he said, unlocking the door.

He pushed it open and she walked past him inside. Following her into the small, dimly-lit room, Carlos let the door close behind him with a finality that was jarring.

Judith ended her quick search for the light switch and resigned herself to using the downlighting to navigate through the room. Rows of tall shelves lined the small space and she walked through the nearest set, looking for something suitable to carry out of there. But being isolated in the dark room with Carlos Moreno wasn't helping her cognitive functions.

"What are you looking for?" he asked, coming up behind her. "Maybe I can help."

Her eyes fell on a stack of notepads and she reached for them. "Uh, I think I found it," she rushed out.

Unfortunately, she missed the box of envelopes that was stacked right above them. At her forceful jerking, the large bundle threatened to come down on her head.

"Careful," Carlos said sharply, reaching over her to

catch the items.

He shoved the packs back into position and the action brought him firmly against her. His warm, well-muscled chest pressed solidly along her back and she wanted nothing more than to lean against him, to have him wrap his strong arms around her and hold her close.

"Nothing got you, did it?"

Her face heated up as she shook her head. She was grateful he'd saved her from that embarrassing mishap—and that he wasn't a mind reader.

"No, I'm fine."

She turned around, but he didn't step back. They both stood there looking at each other. There was no way she could stop her body's response to him now—and no way could she hide her unrelenting attraction. Not when he looked at her like that.

Stark desire blazed in his deep, penetrating eyes, but there was also a tenderness and affection in them that made something in her belly flutter.

He reached out and brushed his thumb slowly across her cheek. "What's a good girl like you doing in a dirty mind like mine?"

Judith glanced away from his intense gaze. He'd obviously intended for it to be a joke, but with what she'd just done not too long ago, coupled with the slow throbbing between her legs from his light touch, he was far from the truth.

She was no good girl.

He must have mistaken her guilt for coyness because he brought his fingers under her chin and lifted her face to his. Her breath caught in her throat at the fierce tenderness of his gaze. In that moment, lost in the deep, dark sea of his eyes, she forgot about everything and everyone but him.

He rubbed the pads of his thumbs slowly across her lower lip. "You're so beautiful," he said. Then a small, forced smile tugged across his mouth. "You made me forget my line."

She smiled despite herself, not knowing how to respond to that. She felt beautiful. *He* made her feel beautiful.

"Can I kiss you, *muñeca?*"

Judith's heart skipped, but he didn't wait for her response. Leaning down, he brushed his lips lightly across hers. Once, twice...then again. His touch was light and sweet. Her reaction was anything but.

The soft caress sent a charge through her, igniting a fire that had been smoldering for far too long. The fervor raging through her was unlike anything she'd ever felt before. In that moment, a firestorm of desire erupted inside her. With an unsteady breath, she threw her arms around his neck and kissed him back.

She came alive again.

And he didn't miss a beat.

Crushing her to him, he slanted his head and devoured her lips with his. She returned his kiss with all the pent-up passion and need surging through her.

Their bodies strained against each other as his erection pushed firmly along her belly. Clutching at his shoulders, she arched against him, wanting—no, *needing*—to get as close to him as she could. He thrust his tongue into her mouth, and she gently sucked at it, licking, teasing, and taking all that he gave.

She craved him. Craved his touch and his heat.

With an arm wrapped tightly around her waist, the other gripping the under curves of her butt, Carlos pulled her firmly to him and they ground against each other.

She wanted to feel all of him, and he obviously wanted the same thing. He shoved solidly against her and they fell back against the supply shelf, rattling a few items to the ground, but never breaking contact.

He walked them farther back into the supply room, where the illumination of the downlighting couldn't reach them, and set her on the smooth surface of the high counter. Her tight skirt constricted her movements some, but she managed to spread her legs slightly. She cradled his hips, loving the heat and hardness of him pushed against her.

Dragging his lips away from hers, he trailed soft kisses down her neck. His trim facial hair grazed against her sensitive skin, leaving traces of heat behind. Small shivers coursed through her as he began sucking strongly at a tender spot just above her collarbone. She gasped softly, unable to stop the low moan that escaped her lips.

Still clutching at his shoulder, she brought her other hand up to his hair and ran her fingers through the short, wavy strands. They were softer than she'd imagined and she clutched her fingers around his dark hair as he moved his lips up to the underside of her jaw, still kissing and gently sucking on her delicate skin.

"*Quiero probarte, muñeca,*" he rasped close to her ear.

Everything in her trembled at his husky words. She

didn't know what he'd said, but the words stirred something deep inside her.

He moved to another spot on her neck, gently nipping again at the tender flesh and she released a shuddering breath, her grip tightening around his hair.

Bringing his lips inches from hers, he stared down at her with eyes as dark and rich as his low, baritone voice.

"Can I, *muñeca?*" Carlos asked, his hands sliding down her waist until they gripped her hips. "Taste you?"

Judith gazed at him through lowered lids, her fingers now clenching and unclenching around his rigid shoulders. She loved the way he kissed her, loved the way his tongue slid along hers. And she wanted him to do it again.

He flicked his tongue lightly across the lower edge of her mouth and she instinctively sucked in her bottom lip.

"Say yes," he prompted, his grip tightening around the soft curves of her hips.

"Yes," she breathed.

He brought his head down to hers again for another fiery, all-consuming kiss. His hands moved down to her thighs and made their way underneath her skirt, pushing the tight material up her legs. She tore her lips from his, still holding on to his broad shoulders as he began tugging at her lace panties.

It took her a moment to register what he intended.

"Carlos…?" she gasped softly. What should have been a shocked exclamation came out more like a whimpering question.

"Just a taste," he whispered thickly.

Her hips lifted slightly, allowing the delicate material to be pulled away from her body. There was a strong pulsing inside her and she wanted him to ease the insistent throbbing. She wanted it badly.

The red panties slipped to the floor and he gently pulled her hips forward until she was on the edge of the counter. Judith leaned back against the wide cork board as he hiked up her skirt. The cool air in the small room rushed between her heated flesh and the sensation of being completely exposed only heightened her desire and anticipation.

She didn't have to wait long.

He came down between her legs and she reflexively tightened them around his head. The warmth of his tongue flicking against her heated flesh shook her to the core and she clenched her eyes shut. She was too lost in the body-tingling, pelvic-tightening pleasure he was building inside her and barely aware of her precarious position on the edge of the counter.

With a sharp inhale, she lifted her hips toward his swirling tongue. He licked and sucked on the sensitive flesh, the grate of his coarse facial hair on the inside of her thighs sending her close to the edge.

Her nipples hardened and pushed against her bra and she wanted his mouth there too. Wanted him to suck and lap over the hard peaks just as eagerly. Instead, he stabbed his tongue inside her, whirling around her like he couldn't get deep enough.

"Oh, my God. *Carlos!*"

Cupping an aching breast with her palm, she squeezed tight as a low, rough moan escaped her lips.

He devoured her like a man starved.

Moisture pooled out of her as he continued to lap, lick, and savor that secret part of her. She was powerless to stop the quivering that started from her teeth and coursed down to the ends of her toes.

Judith shook and shuddered. His grip on her hips kept her from slipping off the counter, and she gripped his hair as if he was an anchor keeping her from sinking into the dark sea of pleasure that waited. She fell anyway.

She threw her head back as a sharp cry burst from her. Tightening her trembling legs around him, she convulsed into tiny pieces.

The spasms went on forever, her belly clenching and unclenching with each tremor. Her fingers were still tangled in his dark strands as soft whimpers escaped her. He gently kissed her trembling flesh, then her thighs, soothing her down from her mind-numbing peak.

Balance was once again restored within her quivering body, and she slowly opened her eyes. He rose to stand between her listless legs, and placed soft kisses on her exposed neck. The rigidity in him was the only thing keeping her from melting onto the floor. She placed a trembling hand on his neck then slid it down to his chest. His heart thudded against her palm.

"That was lovely," he murmured, his breathing coming out fast. He brought his mouth down to hers and she could faintly taste herself on his lips.

To her surprise, that excited her. She wrapped her legs around him and looped her hands over his neck, wanting to deepen the kiss, to get even more of him.

He tore his lips from hers. "Baby, we have to stop," he said gruffly, his breathing still labored. "Or I'm gonna come inside you right here. And the first time we make love, we'll both be on a big, warm bed. Completely naked."

He'd spoken so matter-of-factly and she stared at him, saying nothing. She couldn't. From the dark, fierce look in his eyes, there was no question. It *would* happen.

At that moment, she couldn't deny it. She wanted him over her, inside her. She wanted all of him.

He reached out and brushed a strand of her hair behind her ear. Unfortunately, their cocoon of pleasure was disrupted by a loud beep and a muffled voice. "Harper to Moreno."

Carlos pulled out the handheld radio from behind his belt and brought it close to his mouth. "Yeah?"

A male voice crackled through the black radio. "We need you in the Lab. There's strange activity coming off Kristensen's hardware."

Those words brought reality crashing back down on her. Judith tensed then shoved Carlos away from her. He moved back, but kept a steady gaze on her.

"I'll be there in five," Carlos said into the handheld.

"Ten-four."

Judith jumped down from the counter and leaned against it, her legs barely steady enough to hold her. She avoided his curious stare as she began clumsily arranging her clothes.

Where are my panties?

Carlos clipped the radio back into his belt and reached for her. She jerked back and he frowned.

"What's the matter?"

"Nothing," she muttered, sliding her gaze from his.

"Then why won't you look at me?"

She shook her head, still keeping her head down. How could she face him, knowing what she had done—and what he would soon find out?

She didn't dare go back to Kristensen's office now.

Carlos brought his hand under her chin and lifted her face to his. His gaze was filled with tender affection and warmth. Her heart began to flutter.

"Don't feel guilty or ashamed, *muñeca*."

She knew he was referring to what they'd just done, but he couldn't know what those words really meant for her. Tears blurred her eyes for the mistake she had let herself get talked into. What would he think—and do—when he found out?

"I've never done this before." She'd never let fear steal her integrity, and the thought that she had let her terror of Ken have such a strong hold on her, almost made her sick.

"I know, baby," Carlos said, stroking her cheek. "Neither have I. Believe it or not, I don't go around doing things like this in supply rooms. But with you...I can't help myself."

She blushed, her gaze falling to the unmistakable bulge in front of his jeans. She'd been referring to more than just *that, but* let him think her guilt largely stemmed from her loss of control, which wasn't a complete departure from how she felt.

Never had she experienced anything so remarkable and intense that her body still trembled with it.

"There's something between us," he continued. "I

feel it and I know you do too. Don't you?"

She glanced away and tried to pull away again, but his arms shot out, trapping her between him and the counter.

"Don't you, *muñeca?*"

Staring into his dark, penetrating eyes, she nodded jerkily. She did feel it—more than she cared to admit.

His expression softened at her admission, but there was no gloating or satisfaction in his eyes. There was no more denying it anymore. He saw right through her.

And that fact was frightening.

****

Carlos stared down at Judith, wanting to erase the uncertainty in those large brown eyes. He hadn't meant to take it this far, but he'd been unable to help himself. She was a gentle, sexy little thing, yet with one kiss everything had changed.

When she'd pressed against him and kissed him back, it had been like a volcano had erupted, with her turning into burning lava in his hands. All his senses had become in-tune with her, and he couldn't have left the dark supply room without sampling her.

And she tasted good.

The scent and taste of her still lingered on his lips, but it wasn't enough. His cock strained against the zipper of his jeans from not getting to do more. He glanced down at himself to see how obvious it was and caught a glimpse of her red panties tucked beneath the counter. He reached down and grabbed them, enjoying the soft, lacy texture, smiling. So this was what she wore underneath those professional skirts. Sexy. If he wasn't careful, he would develop a panty fetish.

He held out the silky material to her and for a moment she simply stared at it. Then her eyes widened and she snatched it from his hand.

"*Oh God*," she muttered, crumpling it in her hand.

He wanted to laugh, but she was obviously mortified and he didn't want to humiliate her further.

"Don't be embarrassed, *muñeca*. Nothing we do should embarrass you." Propelled by a force stronger than his will, he leaned down and kissed her. The smooth softness of her lips did something to him. He'd never felt like this with any woman.

"We're going to be great together," he murmured, loving the way she bit her lower lip.

"I…I h-have to go," she said, pulling away from him. She went around him and dashed out of the supply room.

Carlos ran his hand over his face and let out a heavy sigh. He didn't go after her. She obviously needed time to get used to what he had already known for quite some time now.

That they belonged together.

There was no way he was going to let her ignore that, but he wouldn't push her on the matter. Not yet. She was already nervous and embarrassed about what they'd done, though he only had himself to blame. He'd been greedy, taking more from her than he'd intended and more than she expected. Yet, he had no regrets.

Maybe fooling around in the supply room hadn't been the best way to start their relationship, but he wouldn't take back that moment for anything. There was something powerful between them, even she couldn't deny it, and it was only getting stronger.

He did regret having to stop but he meant what he'd said. The first time he came inside her, he wanted them naked, flesh to flesh, her moans filling the air and her smooth, curvy thighs trembling around him.

He'd been careful to move them in the back of the supply room, away from the single security camera in front. Not many of the cameras included audio and this one was no exception. He didn't want anyone else besides himself to hear her moans of pleasure.

He also needed to put an end to his erotic musings and head over to the security room. Walking around with a painful erection just wouldn't do.

Carlos made a quick stop by the shelves and grabbed the wrapped bundle of notepads before he left. In her haste, she'd forgotten to grab them. Again, his fault.

Maybe it was best he kept his distance from her at the job. His infatuation with her was starting to cloud his judgment, making him do things he would have never done before. And he was clearly distracting her from her work. He wanted them to be together, but not at the jeopardy of either of their careers.

He stopped by her desk to drop off the bundle and to his relief, found she had left. He would have felt like shit if she had been there later because of him.

By this time, Carlos should have been done with his rounds of the facility, but he now needed to see what the situation was down to the casino resort's new cyber security and surveillance room.

He made his way to the Lab and into Pete Harper's small office, which was crowded with computer equipment and a large white bulletin board hanging behind him, covered in notes. The bald, slender black man looked up just as Carlos walked in.

"Moreno, we have a serious problem," Pete blurted.

Carlos frowned. "What is it?"

"We found a Trojan virus," Pete began. "It was downloading data from the server, but then it stopped. It's still pinging but we managed to quarantine it and found that it's coming from Kristensen's hardware."

Carlos tensed at the news. Though it was a relief that they had managed to isolate the virus, it could have already done a lot of damage to the company's system.

"Did you terminate it?"

Pete shook his head. "Not yet. We wanted to find out where it originated before we had it cleaned. I don't think any of the company's information was compromised. Looks like the virus had just come in because it only downloaded thirty percent of the server's content."

"Do a sweep of the entire server," Carlos said. "Then terminate it. Send out an email letting the staff know that we're performing a regular maintenance update tonight and that the server will be temporarily unavailable."

Pete nodded. "And what about Kristensen's computer? If the virus came from his hardware, it could still be in there."

"Can you locate it?" Carlos asked. Since the executives' laptops held very important company files and information, each computer was equipped with GPS tracking. Before Carlos alerted the two owners, he wanted to at least confirm that the computer was still at the hotel.

"It looks like the laptop is still in the North Tower," Pete said. "Probably in his office?"

Carlos nodded. "I was just up there and didn't see anyone suspicious, but I'll go back and check it out. In the meantime, get the sweep done ASAP."

With that, he quickly made his way back to the North Tower, where the executive and administrative offices sat. Walking through these halls would never be the same for him again. Memories of what had transpired not too long ago in the supply room were etched in his mind. He remembered every searing, erotic detail.

Pushing the distracting thoughts aside, Carlos walked into the large office. On the wide desk, was the executive's laptop. The flash drive sticking out of its side was unmistakable. He made his way around the wide desk and carefully lifted the lid with the tip of his thumb, not wanting to taint any possible evidence. The light at the end of the flash drive began to blink rapidly before a black window appeared on the screen requesting to run a password retrieval program.

He cursed.

Under his watch, someone had snuck in and put this here. Whoever it was had obviously been spooked before they could finish whatever it was they were doing. Unless releasing the virus had been their goal.

Carlos cursed again.

Pulling out his radio, he requested all the security footage be pulled from the executive floors. He was grateful for the few structural and technological changes he'd suggested be made, which allowed the security and surveillance teams to monitor large areas around the resort and casino floors. Though, the person had still managed to slip right under their radar.

His next call was to David Carrone. He picked up on the second ring.

"Yeah?"

"Carrone, we have a problem," Carlos said into his cell phone.

There was a short pause and he picked up on a woman speaking in the background. If his boss was annoyed by the intrusion, he kept it well hidden.

"What is it?" David asked evenly.

"Looks like we had an intruder in the offices tonight." Carlos quickly filled him in on what Pete had told him and what he'd just discovered.

"Shit." David's frustration was palpable in the one word.

Who could blame him? The man had entrusted him to ensure something like this never happened, yet Carlos had let his lust override his responsibilities. While the intruder had been releasing this dangerous virus into the company's systems, he'd locked himself in a supply closet with no thought to anything except satisfying his hunger.

Carlos sighed. Of all nights, why did it have to be tonight?

"Where are you now?" David asked.

"Still in Kristensen's office."

"Wait for us there," David said. "I'll be right down."

Carlos ended the call and stared down at the flash drive.

Who the hell had gotten in here?

chapter 4

Just pretend nothing happened.

Judith repeated those words in her head as she got off the elevator and made her way to her desk. Coffee hadn't been enough to ease some of her tension, but it certainly helped to wake her up.

From the letter to the phone call to Carlos'...kiss, Judith was surprised she hadn't dissolved into a puddle of nerves.

What she and Carlos had done last night had been more than a mere kiss, however. Something her body wouldn't let her forget. Now that her greedy body knew the kind of pleasure it was missing yet could be receiving from Carlos Moreno, it wanted more of him. It certainly didn't care that she was in the middle of a crisis—one big enough to land her in jail if they ever found out what she'd done. With the flash drive she'd so stupidly left behind, that was a possibility she couldn't ignore.

Last night, alone in her apartment, time seemed to drag as she sat up worrying herself into insanity. Judith could count with three fingers the hours of sleep she'd managed to get. Most of her night had been spent replaying everything that had happened yesterday. She'd agonized over not going back for the flash drive, but after the alert had come through Carlos' radio, she purposely steered cleared from that side of the office. But with the cameras, and the cleaning woman who'd seen her, they could easily narrow their list of suspects down to her and then what would she do?

Lying awake in her quiet apartment, she'd entertained the idea of calling Mary Cross from the Agency. The woman had been instrumental in placing her at Royal Courts after Judith had quit her back-breaking job waiting tables and had found herself stuck in a series of temp jobs. Perhaps Mary Cross could help her find something else. But then the questions would come, Judith was certain, and she wasn't prepared to answer any of them.

She would just have to carry on as usual until she could find out what to do—or say—next, but staying at Royal Courts was too much a risk.

As she approached her desk, she was surprised to find her boss' door open. Normally, she was the first one in the office. Though, she had a later start than usual, it was still pretty early.

Placing her bag and coffee cup down on her desk, Judith went to the open door and peeked inside.

David Carrone lounged behind his large desk, his gaze locked on his computer. There was a shrewd intelligence behind those clear gray eyes with no trace of the shameless playboy he was rumored to be. He, in fact, was always friendly and professional toward her, and she liked working for him. He challenged her, offering her assignments beyond her basic administrative duties, which she appreciated.

His dark brows were pulled into an intense frown and she hesitated calling out to him.

Just pretend…

"Good morning, Mr. Carrone."

He glanced up and she inwardly breathed a sigh of relief when his furrowed brows relaxed. His obvious frustration wasn't directed toward her, but she still tugged at her high-collar, his intense scrutiny making her a bit uncomfortable. She hoped she looked professional instead of strange in the dark, high-collar blouse. It was nearly a hundred degrees outside, making the blouse a ridiculous wardrobe selection. But she had no choice. Her neck this morning had been riddled with hickeys. The little red marks ranging from pale pink to crimson red against her brown skin. What make-up couldn't cover, she hoped the collar would. Just thinking about the small love bites, made her face flush.

"I'm glad you're here Judith," he said. "Come in. It's going to be a busy day today."

Judith came fully into his office. "Do you want me to move our morning status meeting?"

Every Tuesday morning they would have their usual standing meetings, where they discussed upcoming work and projects. Lately, the main topic during their weekly catch-up meetings had been focused on the October charity gala. Though it was a little over three months away, he had pulled her in to help with the event early on, which she was excited about. It was a nice break away from scheduling meetings and booking travel, and she also got a chance to see the layout and preliminary designs of the Queen's Palace, Royal Courts' new major event space.

"Let's move it to later this afternoon," David said. "We have enough on our plates this morning and there are a few things I'd like your help with today. The most pressing are these invoices."

With barely steady hands, Judith grabbed the manila envelope he held out to her, not quite paying attention to the words that came out of his mouth next. Her mind had gone back to the same envelope she had received yesterday. The one that she still kept tucked in her purse, knowing she had to get rid of it soon, yet not ready to destroy it.

She was suddenly eager to leave his office, but David continued rattling off a short list of tasks he needed her to attend to that morning. Her to-do list was steadily growing and it wasn't even eight thirty yet. She couldn't forget the branding meetings that she still had to finish prepping for, which was due to start in the next half hour.

"Is there anything else?" she finally asked when he fell silent.

He shook his head. "Just be sure those invoices get back to finance, signed, by noon."

Before she could say anything, his phone rang and he reached for it. Judith took that as her cue to leave, which she did quickly, shutting the door behind her to give him some privacy.

On her desk, she found a bundle of notepads she must have missed when she'd placed her bag and coffee down.

She couldn't help the small smile that tugged at her lips. *Carlos.*

He must have left them there for her last night, after she'd practically bolted out of the office. Her smile faltered when she remembered what had caused her frantic urgency to be as far from him and Royal Courts as she could get. How was she supposed to face him today?

"Hey Judith, do you have time for a coffee break?"

She glanced up to find Brian coming up to her desk. "Sorry, but I'm super swamped this morning." Though she enjoyed their occasional coffee breaks, Judith certainly couldn't spare what little time she had that morning on gossip.

Brian, however, was determined to spark it. He was practically bubbling over to tell her the latest news.

"Did you hear what happened last night?"

Judith kept her expression cool and shook her head, hoping the anxiety and mortification wasn't plain for the young man to see.

"There was a break-in to one of the executive offices last night," he said, his voice pitched dramatically low. "Nothing was taken supposedly, but from what I heard the guy tried to hack into the system and caused the servers to crash instead."

Judith's heart pounded in her chest. *Guy?* Did they wrongly catch someone for this? She sincerely hoped not. She wouldn't be able to stand the guilt.

"Can you believe this?" Brian exclaimed when she still hadn't responded. "Someone tried to shut the company down!"

Her stomach flipped. She could only hope that Brian read her stunned silence as shock to his news.

"How—uh, where did you hear this all from?" she managed to ask. "It's barely nine o'clock."

"I have a friend in security," he said with a small shrug. "No one could believe it when one of the co-founders showed up and stayed here all night while his computer was being worked on."

She forced lightness into her voice. "Do they know who it was?"

"Nope, I don't think so. Can you imagine how pissed that must make them?"

"Yeah, it's crazy," she murmured mechanically, glancing at her boss' closed door. She wondered what thoughts had been going on behind those cool gray eyes this morning.

On second thought, she didn't really want to know.

As soon as Brian left, she sat back on her seat and blew out a breath.

What a mess.

Her once quiet, simple life had gone from having spoonfuls of ice cream with Prince to being blackmailed into committing a crime and getting hickeys from Carlos Moreno.

Everything was happening so fast and she again seriously contemplated putting in her notice. The idea had plagued her last night and now it seemed like her only viable option. If they ever found out it had been her, how was she to explain the paralyzing fear that had made her do it? The thought of Ken's impending parole wasn't far from her mind and left her almost sick with worry. When he got out, would he come after her?

If that woman had found her, then so could anyone. Even Ken. That wasn't a risk Judith wanted to take. She would do anything to keep her monster in his closet, and starting over seemed like her best course of action.

Eventually, she would just have to forget Carlos and learn to put him behind her.

Her heart fell at the thought.

Deep down, she didn't want that. She didn't want to think of never seeing him again, or starting her life over. She had gotten accustomed to this one and didn't want it to change.

Pushing the miserable thoughts aside, Judith let everything about yesterday—the letter, the phone call, the flash drive, Carlos' *kiss*—fall from her mind. She glanced up and noticed a pretty woman walking toward her desk, a visitor's pass clipped on her green blouse.

"Hi, I'm Nina Conners from Holstein & Levy," the woman began with a friendly smile. "I'm here for this week's branding workshops."

Judith immediately recognized the name. Royal Courts' new publicist. Though she had helped set up the woman's travel from Boston, they had only spoken on the phone. Judith forced her anxiety deep inside her, along with the rest of her fears and worries, and returned the woman's smile.

"We're glad to have you with us this week, Ms. Conners," Judith greeted politely. "How was your trip?"

Between assisting both executives, helping with the

branding meetings, and now having to attend to the company's new publicist, Judith had a long, busy week ahead of her and that left no time to wallow away on worries or regrets.

****

Carlos sat back in his seat and rubbed his gritty eyes.

He'd been staring at the dual monitors on his desk all last night and had resumed again that morning. Most of his night had been spent in front of the computer. After he'd met with the executives, he had sifted through the surveillance videos on their floor. They had agreed to keep last nights' incident quiet, which left him to do the task alone. But the longer he looked at the footage, the more he didn't see anything out of the ordinary.

To his great annoyance, they had found that the other cameras in the central part of that floor had been disabled, which didn't leave him much to peruse.

Whoever they were dealing with was clearly a professional.

Just thinking about last night and what they'd discovered still left him puzzled, which irritated the hell out of him. Why had the person been downloading information from the company's servers? What exactly were they looking for?

Those were just some of the questions plaguing Carlos since he'd met with the two co-founders last night. He suspected the men didn't fully trust him yet and he could understand their reservations. It hadn't been that long ago since their last security chief had gotten them and the casino resort tied to one of the biggest money-laundering cases the city had seen in some time. The executives had been put under heavy scrutiny and Carlos couldn't fault them for their wariness.

However, he wouldn't allow them to challenge his competence.

The meeting last night with the two executives had been tense. They'd been full of suspicion, unspoken blame, and a bit of condescension. Not that Carlos had that problem with David, but the other one was proving to be just a bit more jaded. Carlos wouldn't have let the other co-founder's attitude bother him if the man wasn't so damn arrogant with his distrust. Carlos' only excuse for the other man's hard attitude was that, unlike David, he didn't really know him.

Not that David knew much about him either. It had been through a mutual friend that Carlos had landed the position at Royal Courts, and he prided himself on the fact that he'd come to the casino resort with an extensive amount of his own experience. Carlos had worked under the best in the field in several popular casinos after he'd completed his active duty in the Marines. He'd learned fast and it hadn't been long before he was managing a security unit of his own.

Coming to Royal Courts had been yet another great opportunity, and a step up as far as his responsibilities, but Carlos was also good at his job and was starting to resent having to prove to the other co-founder that he was nothing like their last security chief, Jeffrey Bates.

But it was evident he would need to show them, and the quickest way to do that was to find this bastard who'd slipped right under their nose.

Both executives had their theories about who it

could have possibly been, but Carlos would let the video lead him to the right direction. His gut told him the answer was here somewhere in these clips, he just needed to stay alert and watch for the sign.

Except the longer he looked at them, the less he was finding anything useful. All he'd seen so far were those who had been in the vicinity of the office and for everyone they managed to identify, no one came up as suspicious or not having a right to be there.

It was frustrating work, but Carlos wouldn't let up.

He returned his attention to the footage on the screen. He'd studied each piece of recording for hours now and still couldn't find anything that would help them get any closer to figuring out who'd managed to slip in and leave the flash drive. It didn't help either that they only had a few video footages to work with.

The angle also wasn't the best and there wasn't much traffic, but he kept his focus on the monitor. He caught a glimpse of a familiar red skirt and couldn't help but smile. He remembered that skirt—and what had been underneath it.

He also remembered their dinner date tonight and couldn't contain his anticipation. This was another step in breaking down her walls, though last night had confirmed for him that the attraction definitely wasn't one sided. Now, he would get a chance to be with her outside the office, and convince her that he wasn't some big, bad wolf who only wanted to eat her up…again.

Carlos grinned ruefully at the thought.

He glanced over at the small plastic bag containing the flash drive. He planned to drop it off with his cousin later. Tristan was an ex-cop and he was hoping his connections could help them get the small device checked for prints and possibly give them something more concrete to work with.

In the meantime, Carlos would continue reviewing all video clips from yesterday.

He pulled up another clip and began studying the next video footage. There was obviously a major flaw in their system, one that he had overlooked, that allowed whoever this person was to not only gain access into the building but also disable their cameras. Unless the person they were dealing with had gotten help from someone internally.

If that was the case, they had a serious problem.

He hated to think they could be dealing with that kind of shit again, but it was becoming a possibility he could no longer ignore.

****

"I'll type these up and send them over to you," Judith said, coming to her feet. "Is there anything else you need before I leave tonight?"

She waited as David rounded his desk to his seat, glad that the day had finally come to an end. It had truly been a whirlwind, one made worse by her colossal screw-up that had led to a firm talking to with her boss.

"Did you get the invoices over to finance?"

Judith nodded stiffly. "I did," she said, glancing down at the notes in her hands, still embarrassed by her failure to complete the simple but time-sensitive task. "Sorry again about this morning."

She had only needed to get two more signatures on

the invoices he'd handed her that morning, and one of them included his business partner's. The idea of going back to that office filled her with so much anxiety that she forced it out of her mind just to get through her other tasks. But then she'd completely forgotten about it and missed the noon deadline.

David hadn't been happy about it, reprimanding her in a way that made her feel useless and small. And when he'd confronted her about her obvious growing tension, she blurted the first lie that had come to mind—one that she had regretted after.

Lying about a sick relative was bad karma, she knew that, but a part of her knew that she already had no one. If she had, she would have never uttered those words just to excuse her incompetence and cover her growing anxiety.

"Don't worry about it, Judith," he said. His face now softened from the grim, disapproving expression that had been there earlier. "Everyone's entitled to have a bad day. If you need some personal time off to take care of your grandmother, just let us know."

She nodded again. "Thank you," she murmured hollowly. Over the years, she had gotten good at hiding her emotions, but it hadn't come in handy earlier, when she needed to keep him from seeing the guilt that was plaguing her. So she'd lied.

She was getting good at lying—and she was really starting to hate this person she was becoming.

"Now go home," David said, though his light tone took the bite out of the command. "You don't need to stay late working on that." He motioned to the now longer list of gala invitees in her hand. "I'll see you in the morning."

She'd planned to stay late and work on typing and organizing the list, to make up for her blunder that morning, but was grateful for his gentle yet firm dismissal. She needed to go home and sort herself out. She wished him a good night and made her way to the door just as a hard knock came.

"Yeah?" David called out.

She couldn't help the small tingle that crawled over her stomach when Carlos opened the door. Their eyes locked before he glanced over at David. Heat rushed to her face from the look in his dark, sensual gaze.

She hadn't seen him all day, but he hadn't been far from her mind and she'd been both relieved and disappointed when he hadn't made the effort to see her. Though, she should have been grateful, a part of her had missed his seductive smile and corny jokes. Seeing him now, a small bubble of joy swelled up inside her.

"Have a second?" Carlos asked.

David motioned him in the office and Judith rushed toward the door. Carlos, however, did not move from his stance there. Last night in the supply room was never far from her mind. Now, under the glaring office light, she tried to restrain the memories from flooding to her. Keeping her eyes carefully averted, she continued out of the office.

"Good night, Judith," Carlos said as she rushed past.

Her steps faltered. He rarely said her name, mainly when others were around, but it still held that special note in it. The kind that said she was...his. She paused briefly, trying to find her voice.

"Good night, Mr. Moreno."

She could literally feel the charged air passing between them as she slipped out of the office. She didn't release her pent up breath until she was safely at her desk. She wondered when she would get use to her reaction to him. It wasn't normal. She had never felt this way with anyone. Not even with Ken.

At the thought of her ex-fiancé, her stomach knotted and she shoved the crippling feelings back into the small, dark part of her where it belonged and instead glanced at David Carrone's closed office door. What were they meeting about? Were they discussing last night?

The stress of it all was driving her crazy. She kept waiting for security to haul her away from her desk. Or would they confront her in her boss' office? Would Carlos be there? Would he hate her after he found out about this? She didn't think she could bare it if he hated her.

The longer she sat there, pretending as if nothing had happened, the greater her anxiety grew.

While she could have been halfway to her apartment by now, Judith decided to stay and type the new list of names. It hadn't been much anyway, though she secretly knew it was just an excuse she was giving herself to linger so she could see Carlos again.

But she completed the task in no time and yet still, he hadn't emerged. It wasn't until she was preparing to leave that he finally walked up to her.

Without a word, he came around the desk and grabbed her hand.

She frowned. "What...?"

But he held a finger to his lips and pulled her into a nearby conference room. He shut the door then pushed her back against it. She held her breath, as he leaned forward. She waited for the heady sensation of his lips to touch hers, but to her surprise and disappointment, he placed a light kiss on her cheek, a fraction of an inch away from her lips. The coarse hair of his thin beard grazed a warm path down her face. She shivered and released a breath.

"What are you doing?" she asked fiercely, keeping her voice low.

"Nothing yet."

His hands were on either side of her, keeping her trapped between him and the cool door behind her. He was close, heat radiated from him, but they were barely touching. Though, the way he looked down at her was like its own sensual caress.

"We shouldn't be in here. Someone could come in and see us."

His dark brows furrowed slightly. "I'm getting tired of people butting in between us."

She tilted her head to the side, confused. But he shook his head, outlining the edge of her jaw with the pads of his thumb.

"It's nothing," he said. "I just hate the thought of someone coming between us, messing this up for us, when things are still so new."

She took a deep breath, his words secretly filling her with a heady pleasure and anticipation for something more. Her gaze travelled to his lips and she couldn't look away. He caught the telltale action and smiled.

"Did you miss me, *muñeca?*"

She had. Very much. But he would probably just gloat over it so there was no need for her to inflate his ego.

"I know you missed me," he continued when she remained quiet. "Don't pretend that you didn't."

"I've been busy," she retorted.

His gaze was penetrating, intense. She had to look away.

"I've been busy too, but I still missed you," he said.

Her eyes swung back up to his, and she swallowed hard. His words were like a warm, soothing balm over her rigid body. He was always so confident and open with his feelings. For a moment, she envied him for that, wondering what would it be like to share her feelings freely, to let herself be vulnerable again.

His gaze drifted down to her lips and he shifted closer to her. She placed her hand hesitantly on his abdomen to stop his advancement. It was hard to the touch and flexed under her fingers.

"Would you please stop looking at me like that?"

He grabbed her hand and drew it away from his midsection. When she tried to tug free, he held it firmly in his. "Like what?" he asked, his tone low and deep.

Like you want to eat me. She glanced down at his chest, her face heating up at the thought. She didn't dare say that.

"Seriously, Mr. Moreno, we—"

He groaned. "Don't start with that, *muñeca*. You don't have to be formal with me. It's just us in here." His eyes gleamed devilishly. "And I like how you say my name. Especially when you're hot for me."

She wouldn't have been surprised if her face had turned crimson through her brown skin in that moment. The memories that his words evoked were not something she wanted to have right now under the harsh fluorescent lighting of the small conference room. She would reserve them for when she was in the privacy of her bed and she could let the memory roam free.

Carlos released her hand then reached out and brushed her hair back. She sucked in a sharp breath when his knuckles lightly grazed the skin that was exposed from her dark, high collared blouse.

He tugged down the collar and frowned slightly, his gazed trained on her neck.

The make-up must have worn off.

"Did I do that?" he asked quietly. "Does it hurt?"

She stiffly shook her head, her gaze never leaving his face.

He dropped his hand. "I'll be more careful next time."

She shook her head again. "What happened last night was not…professional," she began. "It should have never happened."

"You're right," he said with a heavy sigh. "But can you blame me? You're beautiful and sexy and I wanted you."

Her stomach fluttered at his words. He took her hand again and brought it up to his lips. He kissed her palm and her hand tingled from the warm touch.

His dark eyes took on a glint and he gave her a crooked grin. "You know, if you were print on a page,

I'd call you *fine* print."

Her eyes widened in surprise by the sudden change in topic. A small smile tugged at her lips and she shook her head in exasperation. "You're so corny."

His eyes flashed brilliantly. "I'm corny for you, baby."

Laughter burst out of her and she clasped her hand over her mouth at the spontaneous action. His grin widened.

"Speaking of *fine*, you must be a parking ticket because—"

"Oh God, stop!" she interrupted, still laughing.

"Heard that one already, huh?"

She nodded.

He brought his hand under her chin, rubbing his thumb slowly along her jawline. Though a teasing smile curved along his lips, there was a possessiveness in his gaze that he didn't hide. "Well, if any other guy tries to drop you lines, tell them your man's got you covered."

Goose bumps lightly crawled up her arm and she wasn't sure if it was from fear or excitement—or both. However, she didn't have time to dwell on it. His next question had her completely flustered.

"What time do you want me to pick you up tonight?"

For a brief second, she was confused, then the realization that she had agreed to have dinner with him tonight made her stomach knot in that familiar way when she was with him. With all the stress today, it had completely slipped her mind.

"You forgot?"

Her brows pulled together apologetically and he sighed.

"I'm sorry," she said. "Today has just been crazy and tonight just seems... How about tomorrow night?"

He was shaking his head before she finished her sentence. "You promised me tonight, *muñeca*," he said with finality. "Don't go breaking my heart."

She scoffed. He was a great looking, self-assured guy who could have any woman he wanted. She doubted anyone could break his heart. Least of all her.

"Well, I thought you would be busy tonight," she began carefully. "I, uh, heard about last night and thought you would be stuck here again tonight."

He frowned and she held her breath, immediately regretting bringing it up.

"We were trying to keep that quiet," Carlos muttered. "What exactly did you hear?"

Judith shrugged, forcing nonchalance into her voice. *Pretend, remember...*

"Only that there was someone trying to hack into the company's system," she replied.

He relaxed and his expression softened. "Well, it's all being taken cared of," he said. "So I just need to finish my last rounds here and then I'm all yours tonight, dollface."

She smiled softly at the expectant look in his dark eyes. A part of her was giddy at the prospect of going out with him, while another voice screamed for her to run the other way.

She silenced that second voice.

"Okay," she said, hoping she wouldn't regret this decision later. "What time?"

****

Carlos was impatient to get his final rounds done.

But after the break-in last night, he wouldn't rush it. It was something he did, not because it was required, but because it gave him some piece of mind to check on things before he left for the night. For him, it was simply like checking all the lights and appliances were off before leaving the house.

The sooner he was done with all that, the sooner he could head over to pick up Judith. He'd found it endearing when she'd written her phone number and address down for him before she had left. But then, she couldn't know the ease in which he could have pulled that information, which he had. His obsession with her had led him to some digging on her, though he didn't consider it stalking.

He was just an impatient man trying to get more info about the quiet woman with the devastating smile that he couldn't stop thinking about.

He scoffed at himself. In other words, *stalking*.

But besides the general stuff, he hadn't been able to find anything that hadn't already been on her job application. It wasn't a big surprise that her records and background were clean, like someone who had spent most of their lives secluding themselves from the rest of the world. But he wouldn't let her seclude herself from him.

Carlos' final stop was the private floor of the resort, where only notable guests were roomed. He stepped out of the elevators just as an attractive and scantily clad black woman barreled into him.

He grabbed her arm, steadying her, and used his

other arm to keep the elevator doors open.

"Excuse me," she muttered.

"Can I help you, miss?" he asked, watching her closely. There was a vague familiarity about her that he couldn't pinpoint.

The woman studied him for a moment before pulling away from his grasp. "Uh, no, I'm just heading to my room." she explained.

"This is a private floor," he said.

Carlos didn't understand how she'd wandered this far up to the resort's VIP room on the thirty-fourth floor—unless she'd been entertainment for one of their guests. From the look of her short, tight black dress and thigh-high boots, it was a possibility. But, last he checked, there weren't any other guests staying on this floor besides the executives. There was a possibility that someone could have recently checked in but he couldn't take the chance of just dismissing the woman so easily.

But she produced a keycard to her room on the fourteenth floor. After a quick reminder of what floor she needed to get off at, he let her go, not at all taken by the flirtatious smile she flashed him. The elevator doors slid shut and still the uneasy feeling wouldn't leave him.

He finished his rounds, making a mental note to have the hotel manager take down the empty luggage cart parked at the end of the hall. As he made his way back to his office to lock up, the woman in the elevator and her striking features stayed with him. There was something about her...

It wasn't until his gaze landed on the dual monitors

on his desk that it hit him.

Son-of-a-bitch.

It was her.

She was the same woman from last night. The one on the video footage they'd managed to pull from the few working cameras. He'd studied those clips for hours, over and over again, until he almost had the faces and movements engraved in his mind.

But before he would call it in, he needed to confirm it.

Carlos headed to the special surveillance room and went directly to Samantha Hobbs, the Lab's most reliable computer geek. She wasn't the only computer tech working the night shift but she was the quickest.

"Hey chief, what's up?" she asked, peering at him through wide, dark-rimmed glasses.

"I need you to run an image scan for me."

He had her pull the footage of the woman right before she entered the elevators. With a screen shot of her face, Sam ran a system scan to find if there was facial recognition anywhere else at the resort. It would have taken forever to run a full scan so he narrowed it down to cameras on the thirty-fourth floor and the executive floor.

There was a match.

To his surprise, there was also a clip of the same woman wearing a cleaners' uniform, pushing a cleaning cart, then another clip with her dressed as a bellhop, pushing an empty luggage cart. It was only a *probable* match since the cart obstructed her face slightly, but Carlos had no doubt it was her.

He bit back a curse. This whole time, he'd never

guessed it was a woman he was searching for. Though they still didn't have proof that she'd actually been the one that had left the flash drive behind, her obscure presence dressed as a cleaning attendant, then a bellhop was setting off his mental alarm bells.

Clenching his jaw in frustration, Carlos pulled out his cell. He wouldn't make a move without letting David know what he'd just discovered. But he couldn't ignore the frustration that was rising in him. This woman had just ruined his night. There was no way he could make it out in time to take Judith to dinner.

For a moment, he thought about calling her and explaining his lateness. But then, she would either tell him not to bother coming or just ignore his call. Or would she even care? He winced at that thought.

He'd pushed for this date and now that he got his chance, he was already blowing it. Carlos, however, wasn't one to give up easily. He would see her tonight.

But first, he had an intruder to catch.

For the second time this week, he dialed David's cell.

chapter 5

A hard knock on her door startled Judith from the puzzle she'd been blindly staring at. She'd thought the game would help her relax—or at least tire her enough to get some sleep. Unfortunately, it hadn't.

Years of experience had taught Judith how to quietly approach the door. She peered through the peephole and sucked in a sharp breath when she saw who it was.

Carlos.

She stood there frozen for a moment. He should have been here over an hour ago. When he hadn't shown up or called, she had figured he had changed his mind. The overwhelming hurt and disappointment had surprised her, but then she only had herself to blame for getting her hopes up in the first place.

He knocked again.

Judith pushed away from the door and quickly surveyed her apartment. It was a mess. She rushed to the sofa and grabbed the empty chocolate foil wrappers from the table and floor and dumped them into the small wastebasket.

Another knock.

"Who is it?" She winced at her light, sing-song voice as she piled Prince's toys in a corner. She knew exactly who it was but she needed more time.

"It's me, *muñeca*."

Judith grabbed a lint roller and quickly passed it across her loose shirt.

"Coming!"

She got up as much of the cat hair off her shirt as she could. The roll of the large tube made her painstakingly aware that she didn't have on a bra. Maybe he wouldn't be able to tell.

Prince stood on the couch, fully alert, and released a loud meow.

"Oh, hush you," Judith muttered.

He let out a low grumble of a sound then fell back onto his belly. She could have sworn he was frowning.

"So you're saying I shouldn't answer?"

He blinked but otherwise ignored her. She took that as *"do what you want"* and rushed to the door.

Passing the hanging mirror, she came to a sharp stop. Yanking off the colorful hair scarf, she shook her head until her hair fell into place. She thought about removing the dark-rimmed eyeglasses, but straining to see him through her already tired right eye was where she had to draw the line.

Schooling her expression into calm indifference, Judith slowly pulled open the door. But cool aloofness was hard to maintain. Standing at her door, he looked more imposing and irresistible than ever. Without her heels, he was taller than she realized. His black, lightweight jacket even made his shoulders appear broader.

"Carlos, it's late." She tried to make her voice firm but instead, it came out low and breathy.

"I know, baby. I'm sorry." He began rubbing the back of his neck. "But I was hoping it wasn't *too* late."

"For dinner?" she asked, incredulous. "Yeah, I think it is. I already ate." Though the cold sandwich and chocolates hadn't been all that filling.

His lips tightened with regret. "I really wanted tonight to happen, but since I blew that, I was hoping it wasn't too late to come see you."

Her hand tightened around the door knob, loving and hating the way his words made her feel. "Yeah, it's too late for that too."

He grimaced. "Sorry if I disappointed you, *muñeca*. Something urgent came up at the job and I couldn't leave. I promise I'll make it up to you. How about Friday instead?"

She wanted to say yes, but now that she had time to think and let reality settle in, it was best she stopped whatever this was between them before it got to a point of no return.

You're already at a point of no return, a small voice rebuked. Memories of last night in the supply room flooded her and her face warmed.

"I'll have to check my schedule," she finally said.

He sighed, looking genuinely contrite. She believed he hadn't meant to be a jerk and blow her off, but still...

"You should've called," she blurted.

He stared down at her, silent for a moment. "I

know I should have. But I didn't want you to tell me to go to hell over the phone."

She probably wouldn't have said those exact words, but she'd certainly been hurt and disappointed by the lack of a simple phone call. His obvious tension and remorse, however, weakened her reserve.

"Can I come in?" At her hesitation, he quickly added, "You don't have to." He glanced back into her apartment then returned his piercing gaze on her. "I know you already had dinner, but I was going to grab a quick bite and was hoping you'd keep me company."

Now would have been a good time to resist any more temptations from him and end whatever it was he was trying to start between them. Once she said no, maybe then he would understand how serious she was about not continuing anything further with him. It would be a clean and complete break to their whirlwind attraction.

But she didn't want that.

"I'll have to change."

He smiled. "I can wait."

She stepped back to let him into her small apartment. It suddenly appeared cramped with him inside and she realized that this was the first time she'd let a man into her apartment in years. The building super didn't count. He was practically half of Carlos' size and probably twice his age.

It was all surreal to her, having her one, living, breathing temptation inside her private space. Thoughts of last night filled her mind and she was glaringly aware that her bedroom was not too far from where they stood. It would be so easy to just take his hand and...

Prince pulled her out of her thoughts as he brushed against her leg and cautiously made his way towards Carlos. They both stared as her curious cat began sniffing around his boot.

"I hope you're not allergic," she said to him, though he didn't look like the type to be allergic to anything.

"Nah," he said, getting down on his haunches and holding out his hand.

She was surprised and impressed by that. Not many people knew that easy tip when it came to greeting cats. But Carlos waited for Prince to smell his outstretched hand and familiarize with his scent, before he scratched behind his ears. She was equally surprised to see how fast Prince accepted him. The first time her super had come to her apartment to repair a leaky faucet, Prince had cornered him and stood hissing at the poor old Asian man. Her small, two-story apartment building was family-owned and she was grateful her landlord, who happened to be the super's brother, hadn't demanded she get rid of her feisty cat.

Prince purred loudly then butted his head against Carlos' hand until he rubbed it over his furry head and down his back. She couldn't help but smile as Carlos handled her normally skittish cat with care—just like he had done with her last night. She flushed at the memory.

"What's its name?"

"Prince Charlie. Well, it's actually Charlie. At least that's the name on his adoption papers but I just call him Prince."

Why am I rambling?

She watched as Prince continued to seek out Carlos' touch, remembering how he had won her over with the same action. She hadn't intended to keep him, not wanting to underscore her occasional bouts of loneliness by getting a cat, but when he'd turned those pale gold eyes on her and rubbed against her hand, she'd fallen.

Carlos eventually stood to his full height and Prince strolled over to his favorite sleeping area on the couch and plopped down.

"Cute cat," Carlos said, turning his intense gaze on her.

"Thanks." She suddenly felt awkward and self-conscious in her old cotton shorts and faded t-shirt. "Um, let me go change," she muttered before fleeing into her bedroom.

****

"Are you sure you don't want anything?" Carlos asked.

Judith looked down at the laminated menu. She'd thought about declining, but the aroma in the small neighborhood restaurant called to her stomach. The only problem was that everything was in Spanish and the only words she knew were *pollo*, *picante*, and *taco* so she went by the pictures.

"What about this?" She pointed to a picture of something that looked something like a taco salad.

He followed the path to where she pointed on the menu then spoke to the older woman behind the counter in rapid Spanish. Hanging on the wall behind the woman was the name of the restaurant. *Rosa's Taquería*. Just below it were the words "Dine-in/Take-out," with what she assumed were a translated version right above it.

Judith glanced around the small restaurant. There was an older man in the corner, enjoying a hearty meal alone and another couple at the other end of the restaurant. On the drive there, Carlos had told her that *Rosa's Taquería* was the best taco restaurant around and had once belonged to his aunt who had sold it a few years ago. But since the small restaurant was a neighborhood favorite, the new owners had kept everything pretty much the same, even the name.

"What do you want to drink, *muñeca?*"

Judith ignored the older woman's knowing look and stared at the two large perspiring jars behind her.

"What are those?" she asked, pointing at the large containers. One was filled with a pale red liquid and the other held a pale yellow drink that was more than half empty.

He explained they were fresh juices and delicious. "One's watermelon, the other's passion fruit," he added.

She chose the watermelon flavor and after they placed their order, Carlos led her to a small table by the window.

"Sorry, I keep telling them they should make the menus bilingual," he muttered.

"It's fine," she said with a small smile. She liked the authenticity of the tiny Mexican restaurant, which added to its charm. "I need to work on my Spanish anyway."

"I'll be happy to tutor you," he offered with a wink, taking the seat across from her. "Maybe even throw in some Portuguese in there."

"You speak Portuguese?"

"A little bit. My uncle's Brazilian and he taught us when we were kids, but I have to admit it could use some work."

She stared at him intrigued. If she had the patience, she would have loved to learn another language. She wanted to ask him more about his multilingual family, but found it hard to concentrate. He'd fallen silent and just sat back in his seat, studying her.

His gaze was unnerving and she glanced away, unconsciously pushing the glasses up her face. She may not have been on a date in years, but she never remembered being this self-aware around a guy.

"What?" she finally asked when he continued his silent staring.

He smiled crookedly. "I didn't know you wore glasses. I think you just gave me another fetish."

Judith vaguely wondered what other fetish she had given him but didn't dare ask. She didn't particularly care for her wide glasses, and preferred to wear the contacts when her eyes weren't tired. Since she only needed the glasses to see through her right eye, they felt cumbersome on her face. After the accident, no amount of surgery had been able to restore her vision in that eye, but she was just grateful she hadn't completely lost her sight.

"So what was the situation you had to stay late for at the office?" she asked, hoping to change the subject.

His expression turned weary. "You've heard about what happened last night, right?"

She clasped her hands tightly on her lap and

nodded. *Just pretend...* she reminded herself.

"The person we believe responsible was at the resort again tonight," he continued. "I needed to confirm her identity before I got Carrone involved, which held me up."

Judith stared at him, her heart thudding in her chest. *Her?* She realized she sat stiffly in her seat and forced herself to relax. But it was hard to do when she was eager to know more. Like, who was this woman they suspected? And what did they plan to do with her?

"What happened?" Judith asked casually, her heart still thumping in her chest.

He shrugged. "Carrone is taking care of it. I'll find out more tomorrow."

Judith fell silent. Right now would be a good time to come clean, to end the anxious churning in her belly.

But then what? Would he understand why she had done it? Would he even care? Things between them would change. He would hate her for what she'd done, and she didn't want that.

She wouldn't dwell on it. She just wanted to be normal again. To enjoy having a guy she liked take her out because he wanted to know more about her.

The woman behind the counter appeared at their table and silently placed down their drinks. Judith reached for the cold, tall glass, which only stiffened her already rigid hands, but she welcomed the icy distraction.

Carlos tilted the short, round bottle to his lips before asking, "So, besides looking so fine, what do you do for fun?"

His teasing helped draw her out of her anxious gloom and she thought about his question. Her Fridays after work consisted of movie nights with Prince, curled at her side, or Sundays working on a new puzzle. Saturdays she did all her chores and ran her errands. The rest of the week, she spent at work.

She took a sip of the sweet, rosy pink drink then rested her elbow on the small table and propped her chin on her hand. What could she say that wouldn't make her sound like a recluse or lonely cat lady? There was no getting around it so he might as well know.

"I'm actually a very boring person," she confessed. "I don't really get out much."

He raised a brow. "Really? I would ask about the guys who must ask you out all the time, but I don't think I want to know."

She smiled, though she was glad he didn't ask either since there wasn't much to tell. From the few guys who did approach her, and those she managed to dissuade, none of them were as persistent as Carlos.

"But you must have something you enjoy doing," he added. Then his dark eyes gleamed with amusement. "Other than drive me crazy."

She shrugged again. "I like putting together puzzles," she murmured. His eyebrows rose and her face heated up with embarrassment.

"I wondered about those puzzle pieces in your living room," he said, his tone filled with amusement. "Did I interrupt a session?"

Her face heated some more. "I know, I know. I'm a nerd."

"Hey, I'm the one filled with a lifetime supply of

bad pickup lines so I guess that makes me a corny nerd." He winked. "See, we're perfect for each other."

An older, petite woman from the back of the kitchen came over to their table and brought their meal to them. Judith was surprised by the mountain of food that was set in front of her. She waited until the older woman left them before she said anything.

"I thought I ordered a taco salad," Judith said, still staring down at the pile of lettuce, meat, beans, cheese, and tomatoes inside a large bowl of a tortilla. It could easily feed two or three people.

"That is the taco salad," Carlos said, digging into his meal. Judith glanced over at his plate, which contained three simple tacos. She should have stuck with that.

"Why didn't you tell me it would be this much?"

He shrugged. "I didn't even think about it. Besides, I don't mind feeding my woman."

She rolled her eyes. "That's good to know, but you're going to have to help me finish this."

"Yes, ma'am." Then he grinned. "I think I like you bossy."

They fell silent as they concentrated on their meals. She glanced over at him to find he had already wolfed down one taco and was already starting on the next. An apt word for him, too. Like everything else about him, even his appetite was voracious.

With his help, she managed to finish a little more than half of her meal. She laid her fork down and sat back, full and satisfied.

"You were right, that was great. Thank you."

He looked up at her, his eyes holding a glint of mischief. "But you haven't had me yet."

She shook her head, a smile tugging at her lips. "So, besides being a big, corny flirt," she teased, "what do *you* like to do for fun?"

He shrugged. "A lot of random stuff. Whatever I'm feeling up to that day. I'm usually hanging out with my cousin, though. He gets me into enough trouble, but he's cool."

Though she couldn't complain about her childhood, there had been times when she'd wished she had siblings of her own. Even a few cousins would have been nice.

"You two must be close."

He nodded. "We are. I grew up with my aunt and uncle, and three cousins. We were all like siblings, but Tristan and I are about the same age so we were always like each other's shadow."

"Where were your parents?" As soon as the question left her lips, she regretted it. It intrigued her to learn that he hadn't mentioned his parents. Since she herself was adopted, she wondered about his life growing up without them. But asking questions like that would only give him the permission to ask the same of her. And the last thing she wanted to talk about was her past.

"Last I heard, my father was still living somewhere in Columbia," Carlos said with a shrug. "And my mother passed away when I was about three or so. My aunt brought me over from Mexico soon after but I don't really remember much about my mother. Everyone says she looked like my aunt so I guess I have that to go on."

Judith's brows pulled together in sympathy for him.

Like herself, he was made an orphan at a young age, though in her case, she knew nothing about her parents. Still, they had more in common than she'd thought.

"I'm sorry to hear that."

"Thanks, baby, but don't be. My aunt and uncle have been great substitute parents. And they would love to meet you."

"Oh?" was all Judith could say.

He smiled, though he looked a bit chagrined. "Yeah, they know about you," he confessed. "I told my cousin who went and spilled it to the rest of my family. Now they all want to meet the girl who's managed to resist my charm for so long."

Judith was still getting over the shock. He had told his family about her? She was flattered and a bit unnerved by that. Then the reality of his words began to sink in and dread filled her. She could only imagine what kind of picture he had painted of her to his family. He believed her to be this sweet, innocent good girl when he didn't really even know her. His contempt for her would be justifiable when he realized she wasn't the girl he thought she was.

Her heart sank at the thought.

He finished the last bit of the taco salad before he asked her the same dreaded question. "So what about your parents? Do you have any brothers or sisters?"

She should have just kept it simple and lied. But she was tired of lying and she couldn't bear to lie in his face again.

"I don't really know my birth parents," she began hesitantly, "but my adoptive mom was great. She never had kids of her own and got me late in her life."

Her adoptive mother had been approaching fifty when she'd finally decided to start a family. Except her mother had never gotten married. It wasn't until Judith got older and had witnessed the closeness between her mom and her mom's "best friend" that Judith understood why. Her mother had not been completely comfortable or open with who she was and had never come out as a lesbian. It broke Judith's heart to think that for all those years her mom had felt forced to hide who she was to her friends and family.

"Did you ever ask your adoptive mom about your birth parents?" he asked, watching her closely.

Judith nodded. "When I was in high school, my mom even tried to help me find them, but nothing came out of it." She shrugged. "It didn't matter though. It was just me and her and I was happy."

"I didn't know single parent adoptions were allowed," he said, looking thoughtful.

She shrugged again. "I guess California is one of the more progressive states because now it's pretty common."

"California? I didn't peg you for a Valley girl."

She laughed at his exaggerated shock. "Because I'm not, I'm a San Francisco girl."

"Ah, San Fran."

She cringed. "Ugh, no. We don't like that. Or Frisco. It's just San *Francisco*."

He laughed and sat back in his seat. "Okay, Ms. San Francisco, what brought you here to Vegas?"

That caught her off guard and it took her a moment to answer. "Um, work," she said, which wasn't a complete lie. After she'd completed her physical therapy, the Agency had moved her out of Los Angeles and it had taken another year before she had felt normal enough to begin working.

"I thought you'd only started working at Royal Courts three months ago?"

She frowned slightly. "How do you know that?"

He cocked his head to the side. "You didn't tell me?"

She shook her head and almost laughed at the way he glanced away from her.

"Okay, maybe I did a little digging around," he said with a small shrug. "I just wanted to know more about you. You're not mad, are you?"

She shook her head hesitantly, but her heart was pounding. What else had he found out about her? *Nothing.* She didn't know where the small, quiet voice had come from but she forced herself to relax. He couldn't possibly have found out any more about her than what the Agency had arranged.

"No, I'm not mad," she said quietly. "But next time, just ask."

He inclined his head. "Fair enough."

"Before Royal Courts, I worked a few temp jobs and waited tables at an Italian restaurant just outside the city. Thankfully, I only did that for a few months." Working at Mia Bella's had been brief but back breaking. She'd never met the owners, but the managers there had been slave drivers. Luckily, Mary had put her in contact with the staffing agency that had gotten her out of there.

"So what does your mom think about you living

here alone in this great City of Sin?"

She shook her head, her throat tightening. It had been a little over eight years, yet the pain of losing her mother was fresh. Carlos sat forward, a frown marring his handsome features and she glanced down at the table. Didn't he know how unnerving his intense gaze was?

"What happened?"

Judith released her breath, her gaze still on their now empty dishes. "She passed away about eight years ago. During my first year in college." She didn't elaborate and hoped he wouldn't ask for more. There wasn't more for her to give, anyway. Her mother had gone in for gallbladder removal surgery and had never come out, passing away right in the surgery room from complications and Judith had been left with no one.

Until Ken. It wasn't long after her adoptive mother's passing that she had started seriously dating the handsome college basketball star who would forever change her life.

"Do you have any other family?" Carlos asked, his dark eyes probing. "People you spend the holidays with?"

She shook her head but smiled to cover the overwhelming emotion that was washing over her, thinking about her holidays with her mom. "No. It's just me and Prince."

"Hey, don't forget about me," he teased, his expression softening with a tenderness that left her warm all over.

I could never forget about you.

"Do you have any pets," she asked, trying to take

the focus of the conversation away from her.

He shook his head. "My cousins and I had a dog growing up, but none now. I don't really have the time."

The old woman appeared at their table again and took away their empty plates. She smiled down at her but said something to Carlos in Spanish.

"No, *gracias señora*," he said to the woman then turned to her. "Do you want anything else? More *agua fresca?*"

Judith shook her head. "No, I'm fine, thanks."

The woman cleared their table and they were once again alone.

"Your aunt. Her name's Rosa?" Judith asked, wanting to fill the awkward silence that had fallen between them and keep the conversation away from her. He nodded. "Why did she sell the restaurant?"

"A few years ago, she became sick and running the restaurant was too much. My uncle, Gil, tried to help out, but he has the gym and also wanted to be there for my aunt."

She wondered if his aunt was okay now. She'd never seen Carlos become this guarded before and could tell the subject was still very sensitive for him. "I hope your aunt's doing better," was all she could think to say.

His lips quirked. "Yeah, she's still ruling us with an iron fist. But she's so gentle about it, we never see it coming." He paused before adding, "I would love for you to meet her. She would love you. My whole family would. Though, my cousin Tristan tends to try too hard around beautiful women. He's the ugly one in the family."

She saw the affectionate teasing in his eyes and smiled.

"I hope it's not with corny pickup lines."

He laughed. "Where do you think I get it from?"

Judith shared in his humor. It was clear he loved his family and her heart skipped at the thought of meeting them. Carlos was a great guy and such a catch. She would have loved to meet his family, but didn't see that happening. She truly didn't understand what it was he saw in her—a socially awkward girl with intimacy issues. And it wasn't like she had been encouraging to him or his early advances.

He continued nursing his beer and she realized he was trying to linger. She hid a smile.

"How is that?" she asked, nodding toward the dark bottle.

"This? It's good. Why? You drink beer?"

She shrugged. His tone held a note of shocked disbelief, which for some reason annoyed her.

"Sometimes," she offered, though she really never had anything stronger than hard cider.

His eyes widened a bit more, but he shook his head. "I don't think you would like this, *muñeca*. It's strong stuff."

She read the challenge in his words and to both their surprise, reached for his bottle. She brought the nozzle to her lips, faintly tasting him on the cool glass. But the cold fizz went down harsher then she expected and she immediately began to sputter and cough.

He shook his head and grabbed the bottle from her hand. "Silly woman. That's what you get for trying to show off."

Judith didn't know if she should laugh or gasp in outraged by his unsympathetic comment. She could do neither. Her throat was still constricted.

"I'm choking to death and that's all you can say!"

He smiled. "If you were choking to death, you wouldn't be able to tell me you're choking to death."

She glared at him and he simply threw her a wink. She laughed, despite herself.

"You good?" he eventually asked.

She rolled her eyes, dabbing at the moisture that had gathered in the corner. "Perfect."

He grunted. "Yes, you are. But not everyone can handle this stuff," he said, finishing the contents in the dark bottle. "I told you it was strong. It's the kind of stuff that puts hair on a man's chest."

She snorted. "I'm sure you don't need any more. You do just fine fitting in with your wolf pack," she mumbled.

He looked at her, confused. "What?"

She blushed. She didn't want to explain to him how he reminded her like one of those wild, feral animals on the prowl.

"Never mind," she muttered.

"Oh no, *muñeca*, you're gonna have to explain that one to me."

She shrugged, her face still warm. "Sometimes you remind me of…a wolf."

He was silent for a moment, then threw his head back and laughed. "A *what?*"

Despite her embarrassment, she couldn't help but join in his amusement. "You heard me."

He laughed again. "Like the big, bad wolf in *Caperucita Roja?*"

"In what?"

"Little Red Riding Hood," he explained.

She nodded. "Yeah, but without the big eyes or teeth. I think it's all the facial hair." *And the eyes.* They were dark and calm, yet fierce and penetrating. Like a predator waiting patiently for its prey.

Right now, however, they were filled with amused incredulity.

"So you're saying I look like the big, bad wolf?"

"Well, I didn't say *bad*."

"Good, because you know they got that story all wrong, right? The wolf wasn't the bad guy. He actually was the hero in the story."

Her interest was piqued. "Oh, really? Sounds like something a wolf would say," she teased.

He shook his head. "It's a known fact that it's the Huntsman who turns out to be an ax murderer. The wolf just got caught in the middle."

She burst out laughing at his outrageous claim. "Well, the version everyone else has heard is that the wolf eats Grandma and almost eats Little Red Riding Hood before the Lumberjack comes and saves the day."

Carlos leaned forward in his seat. "Then everyone believes a lie. Let me tell you the true story of *Caperucita Roja* and Wenzel the Wolf."

Laughter burst out of her again. "Wenzel? Really?"

"Yeah, he had a name, you know," Carlos said, incensed, though his dark eyes lit up with mirth. "Wenzel also had feelings and he especially had a soft spot for little *Roja*. When he found out the Huntsman was in town, he followed her everywhere to make sure the ax murderer didn't get to her."

Judith listened, intrigued. His deep voice drew her into his every word as he continued his outrageous tale.

"One day, Wenzel decides to stop little *Roja* in the woods but couldn't convince her to turn and go back home. So, he raced to Grandma's house to stop the Huntsman." Carlos lowered his voice for dramatic effect and Judith found herself tense, waiting for what came next.

"But it was too late," Carlos continued. "The Huntsman had chopped Grandma into tiny pieces. Wenzel, not wanting little *Roja* to see her grandmother in such a state, eats the pieces."

Judith grimaced. "Oh God." She vaguely started to wonder where he'd heard this macabre version of the fairy tale, but was too enthralled to stop him and ask.

"When little *Roja* got to the house, Wenzel explained what the Huntsman had done. Together they set a trap for the real murderer and little *Roja* goes back to the village, begging for help."

"But no one offered?" Judith blurted.

Carlos shook his head. "No. But, just as little *Roja* and Wenzel anticipated, only *el Cazador* offered to help."

"*El Cazador?*"

"The Huntsman," he translated. "Little *Roja* heads back with the Huntsman to her *abuela's* house and that is when Wenzel gets him."

Judith waited for him to continue, but realized he had finished his tale. "But then what happened?" she prompted.

His smile was wicked. "As soon as they go into the house, little *Roja* screamed *'El Cazador está aquí'*."

Her Spanish was on the poor side but she knew what *aquí* meant—and now *el Cazador*.

The Huntsman is here.

"Suddenly, Wenzel bursts through the door." She jumped as Carlos grabbed her knee from beneath the table. "He began advancing toward the Huntsman, slowly, steadily." Carlos mimicked the same movements, gradually leaning toward her over the small table.

She held her breath.

"The wolf gets so close, he could almost smell his fear," Carlos continued in a low voice. "Suddenly, he leaped toward the Huntsman and eats him."

Carlos took a mocking bite of the air, his teeth connecting together with a sharp snap. She flinched back, laughing nervously. His dark eyes gleamed and his lips curved into a captivating smile.

She shook her head, amazed at his imagination. "Is this real?"

He winked. "You can't make this stuff up. The moral of the story? Don't judge a wolf by the size of his teeth."

Her gaze lingered on his mouth. "Even if they're big and scary?" Not that he had to worry about that, she thought. His sensuous lips were the gatekeepers to white, straight teeth and a generous mouth. A mouth that had been places she had only imagined in her dreams.

A daring glint flashed in his eyes. "Well, the bigger

the mouth, the better it is to——"

She leaned over the small table and quickly placed her hands over his mouth. "Don't say it!" she said fiercely, her eyes wide with horror. She frantically glanced around the small restaurant to see if the man who was still lounging in the corner had heard. He hadn't, but her face still burned with embarrassment.

Carlos kissed her palm and it tingled. He removed her hand from his mouth and held it. "I was just going to say *kiss* you," he said, his eyes lowering to her lips, still gleaming mischievously.

Her eyes narrowed. "Yeah, right," she muttered.

But all teasing was temporarily suspended as the familiar charge between them ignited and began to spread. They stared at each other for what seemed like an eternity.

The harsh sound of a fallen tray in the back kitchen finally broke their sensual trance.

She glanced down at her hand still clasp in his then pulled it away, her face heating up. This time it had nothing to do with embarrassment and everything to do with the irrefutable fact that she wanted him.

"It's getting late," he said, his eyes lingering on her lips. "I should take you home."

"Okay," she said, trying not to think too much about what would happen when they got there.

chapter 6

The drive back to her apartment was tense. Neither of them knew what to say or do to break the awkward silence that had taken over.

He walked her to her door and still few words passed between them. She agonized over the right words to say to invite him in. Tonight could be her one and only chance to know what it was like to have all of him.

When they stood outside her apartment, he finally broke the heavy silence.

"Tonight doesn't count, you know. I still owe you a proper dinner."

She smiled, though she didn't want to commit herself to anything. It wasn't far from her mind that he was investigating the person who had broken into their offices last night and that meant she would need to leave Royal Courts soon. But this could be her last opportunity and she couldn't let him leave here without ever knowing…

"Dinner tomorrow night?"

She glanced down at his chest. "Why don't we take it one day at a time?"

"Whatever you want, *muñeca*." And without warning, he cupped her chin and kissed her. A soft, gentle kiss. The kind that was meant to be savored.

She brought her hand up to his chest and leaned into his embrace. It soon turned hot and heavy and she lost herself to the desperate needs of her body.

But with a low growl, he tore his lips away. "I should go."

She licked her lips, trying to keep her disappointment from showing. "Okay."

"But I don't want to," he said, brushing her lower lip with his thumb.

She stared up at him, unable to look away from the hypnotic pull of his dark gaze. "Then don't."

His head jerked in surprise.

"You...you could come in...for coffee." She groaned inwardly at the clumsy words. At that moment, she wished more than anything that she had the courage to just tell him what she really wanted.

Him.

"Sure," he said, watching her closely.

They walked into her apartment to find Prince still on the sofa, his furry head rested on his paws. He opened his eyes just enough to verify that it was her coming to the apartment.

Now that she had Carlos inside, she racked her mind for what to say or do next. She was more lost and unsure of herself than before. She turned to find him staring at her, his expression unreadable. It was both unsettling and arousing at the same time.

"Um, can I get you something to drink?" she asked, needing to give herself something to do. "I actually don't keep coffee around, but I have tea and water or maybe—"

Her next words died on her lips as he strode toward her in quick, short steps. Without hesitation, he pulled her to him and kissed her—kissed her like it was their first and last time together, like he was afraid to let go.

With a soft sigh, Judith instinctively brought her hands up to his shoulders then moved them up to the sides of his neck, feeling the strength and restrained desire there.

He kissed her deeply, not leaving room for doubt of how much he wanted her. The sounds of their heavy breathing filled her small living room as his tongue dipped slowly between her lips, then made a slow retreat in the most erotic imitation of what her body ultimately craved.

And the quivering throb between her legs demanded more of his attention.

His hand slid down the curve of her spine and trailed past the small of her back until he came to the hem of her skirt. Slowly, he glided his hand over her thigh and she trembled from the gentle caress of his rough palm against her warm skin. She gasped when his fingers curved around her butt and gripped her tightly. He drew her up against his hard frame and she arched her back, desperately seeking out more of his touch.

He pulled away and stared at her with such stark need, it stole her breath.

"If you don't want this, *muñeca*," he said thickly, his

face hard and flushed with desire, "now would be a good time to kick me out."

He looked as if he was holding on to every ounce of his self-control. Her heart thudded in her chest. Just the thought of taking all that passion inside her made her body clench. Tonight, she would set aside all her inhibitions, all her doubts, and let herself get lost in the magnetic desire that tugged between them.

"I want this."

Need burned brightly in his eyes and he pulled away from her. Before she could register what was happening, he removed his jacket and shirt in record time. A black tattoo of a vicious bulldog was printed boldly on the left side of his broad chest with the words *Semper Fidelis* beneath it.

She was mesmerized by his muscular frame and the strength exuding from him. But, he was gentle with her when he pulled her to him for another long, searing kiss and her body began to ease and open for him.

He tugged off her thin sweater as he moved his lips down the side of her neck. She closed her eyes as shivers coursed through her from the light touch. It took a moment for her to process that he was now pulling up her skirt.

Judith quickly placed a hand over his, stopping him. He looked at her questioningly with passion-filled eyes, but she didn't want him to see her body. Not under the bright yellow glow of the lamplight.

Instead, she took his hand and quietly led him into her bedroom. There, in the darkness, she stripped out of her clothes. The dim glow of light coming from the window was enough for her to see his thick erection jutting toward her as he shed the rest of his clothes. The dimness helped ease her embarrassment as she stood before him naked. Before she completely lost her nerve, she went to him and slowly looped her arms around his neck and pressed fully against the hot, hard length of him.

He shuddered as a ragged groan rumbled in the back of his throat. Knowing she had that kind of effect on him, excited her. And increased her confidence.

Reaching between their bodies, she began to stroke his hard length, enjoying the steely heat in her palm. He closed his eyes and threw his head back, the muscles in his neck working as a low, harsh groan rumbled from him. She enjoyed watching him like this, completely open and consumed with pleasure. His erection pulsed and grew harder under her caress. She tightened her hold around him and he jerked out of her hand, releasing a muffled curse.

She froze. "Carlos?"

He let out a strained laugh and pulled her into his arms. "I'm sorry, baby," he said huskily, placing a damp kiss on her neck. "I'm just losing it too fast." He kissed her on her chin then the underside of her jaw. "I'm not even inside you and I'm ready to come."

She wrapped her arms around his neck, warmed by his admission. "It's okay."

He laughed again, though it sounded a little more like a groan. Grabbing her bottom, he lifted her against him and moved them until her back touched the cool bed sheets. He removed her glasses and placed them on the nightstand, then lowered his head toward hers.

He trailed light kisses down her neck and over the tops of her breast before pulling away and reaching for the lamp beside the bed.

She looped her arms around him and drew him back down to her. "Leave it," she whispered, kissing his neck, his jaw.

"I want to see all of you, baby," he said gruffly.

But she grabbed his head and brought his lips to hers for another mind-numbing kiss. He instantly took over, kissing and caressing her everywhere, and bringing her to a state of frenzy. He pulled her taut nipple into his warm mouth, sucking vigorously as he slid a finger into her. The slickness of her body eased him in and she gasped sharply, lifting her hips to get more of his teasing strokes. She clutched at his shoulders as tiny prickles of pleasure coursed through her core. The intense sensations from last night in the supply room returned, and her body quivered and tightened around his thrusting finger.

"That's right, baby. Come for me."

He continued his slow, deep strokes in and out of her as the familiar clenching in her belly drew near. With a shaky moan, she convulsed around him. He held her as the tremors continued to course through her body. But he didn't wait for her quivering to stop before he moved over her and guided his hard shaft into her. She inhaled sharply at the sensation of her body stretching around him. He pushed into the deepest part of her and they both released a trembling breath.

He kissed her and again she was lost in the heady pleasure of his lips.

"Hmm, baby, you were made for me." He plunged deeply into her then slowly withdrew before he drove heavily into her again. "How does it feel for you?"

She gave a jerky nod, smoothing her hands over the bunched muscles of his shoulders. There was a fire building between their connected bodies and she was unable to speak from the intense pleasure coursing through her.

"Talk to me, baby," he said hoarsely. "Tell me how it feels."

She gasped then moaned at another powerful thrust. "It…it feels g-good." Her voice quivered and she tightened her arms around him.

"Good," he said hoarsely then kissed her again. Deeply. Until she had no breath left to give.

Bracing an arm above her, he brought his other hand beneath her, raising her up into his surging hips. Her inner muscles quivered around his hard, retreating length and they both shook from the sensation.

"Jesus," he rasped. *"Me encanta la forma en que sientes, muñeca."*

She shivered at his low, passionate words and arched her hips to meet with each of his heavy thrusts. He buried his face in the crook of her neck, his harsh breathing arousing her own cries of pleasure. She dug her fingernails into his shoulders as another orgasm loomed near.

With a deep groan, he plunged into her again and again. She squeezed her eyes shut, overwhelmed by the intense pleasure taking hold of her body.

"Eres mía," he murmured thickly on another deep thrust.

She released a gasping moan as the bed shuddered from the force.

"*¿Es esta mía?*"

Judith bit her lip, trying to contain the harsh gasps that were being wrenched from her throat.

"Say yes, *muñeca*," he demanded huskily.

She didn't know what he was saying, but his rough command made her tingle all over and she gave him what he wanted.

"*Yes*," she gasped. On a heavy thrust, her body clamped down fiercely around him, it almost bordered on pain. A pleasant sort of pain.

With a low grunt, he gripped her hips tightly, holding her to him as he pumped into her.

Her whole world shook then shattered.

With a sharp gasp, she convulsed around him, her orgasm ripping through her almost violently. Her nails dug into his sweaty back as harsh whimpers of pleasure trembled from her throat.

A few more strokes and his strong body tensed over her. With a long, harsh groan, Carlos too descended into the dark void, joining her where nothing but pleasure and fulfillment awaited.

****

He wanted her again.

He was spent, his heart hadn't stopped racing, and his breathing was still shallow and rough. Yet, he wanted her again. From the delicious way her thighs still trembled around him, he knew she was still feeling the effects of their lovemaking.

That was too weak a word to describe what they just shared.

Carlos had never felt this way about a woman—never felt *this* with a woman. Broken yet whole, powerful but weak.

He brushed his lips across her shoulders and up to her neck until he fitted his lips against hers for a long, all-consuming kiss.

He knew, at that moment, he loved her. Loved her with everything he had. She had fought him long enough, but after tonight, she couldn't deny that there was something stronger than just lust between them. What they'd shared was far more Earth shattering.

Carlos pulled away and stared down at her soft, sated expression. Her eyes were closed as she lazily rubbed his back and shoulders. He stared down at their bodies, hypnotized by their merging, which were still joined together. He rubbed his palm over her soft, smooth thighs. He wished there was more light coming into the bedroom so he could see all of her clearly, see what shade of brown her nipples were.

"No puedo creer que eres toda mía." He brought his hand up to her soft breasts and placed a soft kiss on her jaw. "And no one else can have you."

She grew rigid beneath him and the sudden change in her startled him.

One moment she was stroking his back with tender abandon, the next she was shoving wildly at his shoulders.

Carlos rolled away from her and she scrambled out of the bed, pulling the sheets with her.

"Judith, what—"

"You have to go." Her eyes were wide as she frantically wrapped the single sheet around her.

He stared at her, stunned. "What? Why?"

She shook her head. "*I need you to go,*" she shrieked. "You can't spend the night. I don't want you to spend the night!"

"Why not?" he asked again, holding on to his patience. "Tell me what's wrong. What did I do?"

"Nothing's wrong," she said in a detached voice. She was looking at him but even her gaze was distant. "This was just a one night thing. That's all. Now, I need you to leave. *Please.*"

Anger and irritation flared up in him, but Carlos reined it in. Why did she continue to fight her feelings for him? She'd been climbing and falling right along with him, sharing in the most intense kind of intimacy—one he'd never experienced with any other woman—and yet she was making it seem as if it had meant nothing.

She was trying to reduce them to some cheap one-night stand, but he'd be damned if he'd let her lessen them to that.

He inched off the bed and she backed away from him. That only heightened his anger.

"Fine," he said tersely, jumping from the bed. "I'll leave."

But before she could move, he grabbed the sheet and hauled her to him, wrapping his arms firmly around her. He managed to trap her arms at her side as he pulled her onto his lap.

She offered no struggle. Instead, she sat rigid and silent against him.

"Why are you acting like this?" he asked gruffly. "What is this about?"

She simply shook her head. "I don't... W-we had a good time, Carlos. Nothing more."

Carlos didn't want to hear that. And it didn't sound like the woman who had burned with raw passion under his touch not too long ago.

"Who's talking right now?" he growled. "It's definitely not the woman who hugged around me so tightly, I almost came just entering you." He pulled her closer to him. "You were on fire beneath me, *muñeca*. We were magic together. What changed?"

She was clearly trying to remain unmoved by their lovemaking, as if she was accustomed to having one-night stands. But the way she had squeezed around him, so snug, he knew she hadn't been with a lot of men. Yet, she tried to put on this facade and send him off. He wasn't going anywhere without answers.

She remained silent, not acknowledging or denying his claim or giving him any indication that this meant something—that *he* meant something—to her. Carlos replayed the last moments before she had reacted this way. He couldn't think of what he had done to bring this on and she obviously wasn't going to tell him. Not freely anyway.

From the rigidity still locking her body, and the stark, wide-eyed stare she had given him, he wondered...

"Are you afraid of me?"

She stiffened further and to his surprise and disappointment, she nodded.

"Why?" he asked, easing his hold on her. Though he was grateful for her honesty, he was still floored by her response. "If you're afraid of me, why did you let me make love to you?"

Still, she said nothing.

He brought his hand under her chin and turned her face to his. He was shocked by the unshed tears gathered in her eyes. The sadness in her eyes tugged at him and he realized her pain came from somewhere deeper.

"*Muñeca*, tell me what's wrong," he demanded gruffly. He didn't mean to sound so harsh, but her distress had caused his heart to squeeze. "Who hurt you?" Someone had. Nothing else could have brought on this level of pain and fear. "Tell me," he urged.

"I-I'm just scared of what might happen if...," she began hesitantly. "If I let this go too far."

He maintained his reaction, not wanting to frighten her further by showing his fury at the bastard who had instilled this pain in her, who forced her into this shell where she was afraid to let herself love and be loved.

"What do you think will happen between us?" he asked gently, keeping his voice low.

She paused for a heartbeat. "That one of us will hurt the other," she finally confessed. "Intentionally or unintentionally, it doesn't matter. One of us will end up devastated and heartbroken."

Carlos processed her words before he responded. Had she recently left a messy relationship? Her behavior told him she had. She may even still have feelings for the bastard who'd broken her heart. That thought didn't sit well with him. He didn't like the idea that she may still be in love with another man. But right now, he couldn't think of that and he wouldn't probe her about that failed relationship. His main objective now was repairing whatever damage the one before him had done, so they could concentrate on building a relationship together.

"I would never hurt you, Judith. That's not who I am. All I ever want is to make you happy, to see you smile." He stroked her cheek. "You trusted me with your body," he continued. "You can trust me with your heart too."

She stared at him searchingly. "And what if I hurt *you?*" she asked in an anxious whisper.

He squeezed her reassuringly, wanting to ease her worry. Someone who was concerned about hurting others could never harm anyone. "You won't. You don't have it in you to hurt anyone."

She relaxed slightly against him and he leaned over and gently kissed her.

"Just promise me one thing," he said.

She stared at him curiously. "Yes?"

"I know that trust comes with time and is not always easy to hand over," he began. "We can take this as slow as you want or as fast as you want. But promise me you will never compare me to that bastard who hurt you. Okay?"

Tears welled in her eyes. "Okay."

Leaning over her, he kissed her again. She was no longer tense, but she didn't ease into him either.

"Do you still want me to go?" he asked.

She hesitated for a heartbeat then placed her hand on the side of his neck. "No."

He nodded, pleased. "Good, because I don't want to leave," he said, falling back into the bed and gathering her close. Her acknowledgment confirmed that tonight wasn't just a one night thing as she'd tried to profess, and for now that was a start.

He placed his hand over her abdomen and she tensed, but he continued to gently massage her. It was crazy of him, but he couldn't help the deep pleasure and possessiveness that came over him at the thought of her having his baby. Picturing her growing round with their child was a satisfying and arousing image.

"I'm sorry, baby. I didn't have any rubbers with me." And he'd been too hungry for her to stop.

She stiffened against him. "I won't get pregnant."

"Are you on the pill?" he asked, surprised by the slight disappointment he felt.

After a brief pause, she nodded stiffly.

He sighed. It was for the best. As much as he loved the idea of creating a baby with her, it was too soon. She still needed to learn to trust him and he fully intended to make her his wife before she had his baby.

For now, he would let her set the pace of how far and fast they took their relationship.

Whatever she wanted…

****

Judith woke with her back pressed against Carlos' warm, hard chest and his hand running lightly down her hip.

He continued the soft caress before moving his hand down her thigh then lifting her leg over his. Pressing his lips against the back of her neck, he pulled her hips back toward his probing erection and slid slowly into her slick folds.

She gasped from the incredible sensation of being filled by him again. She reached back and gripped his thigh as he pushed into her again then slowly withdrew. His grunt of pleasure filled her ears as he cupped her breasts with his free hand, holding her firmly against him. She rocked her hips back and arched against him, gasping and moaning, trying to take all of him. Her hand moved to cover his around her breast, and she held on tightly, straining against the pleasure of his pumping hips.

He kissed the side of her neck, her jaw and she turned to capture his lips. The rhythmic gliding of his tongue between her lips matched the slow thrusts of his shaft and she trembled from the erotic sensation.

He murmured words to her in Spanish, words she didn't understand but could still feel the heat in them.

"Turn around, baby," he rasped in her ear. "I want to go deeper."

But he didn't wait for her to move. Instead, he pulled out of her and rolled her onto her stomach. He came up behind her and in one fluid motion, pulled her to her knees and entered her again. He buried himself to the hilt, filling her completely.

A full body shudder racked through her at the incredible pleasure of his deep penetration. With her face pressed to the sheets, Judith clutched at the soft material as moan after sharp moan escaped her. She bit her lower lip to contain the harsh cries, but with every hard thrust, another was ripped from her.

He braced himself over her with one arm on the bed and the other wrapped tightly around her waist and pounded into her with such ferocity, she came with the same intensity. With a deep quiver, her body squeezed around his hard, plunging shaft, pulling and holding him tight inside her.

A harsh groan tore from him and he fell over her as the heat of his orgasm flooded her. He laced his fingers with hers and placed soft, delicate kisses along her shoulders and the back of her neck.

They collapsed on their side with him still behind her, though he shifted so he would not put his full weight on her.

"I can't seem to get enough of you," he whispered. Placing a light kiss on the back of her ear, he pulled her close.

She loved the heat of his large body cocooning her. In his arms, she felt cherished. And when he was inside her, she seemed to forget all her troubles. Everything just ceased to be important except him and the pleasure he gave her.

"Everything okay, *muñeca?*"

Judith nodded as she relaxed against him. "Yes."

He pressed his lips lightly on her shoulder and she listened to his deep breathing as he drifted off to sleep.

She'd wanted to have this night to remember him, but instead this had only opened the floodgates to a whole set of emotions she wasn't equipped to deal with. His passion and desire was unrestrained. And like everything else about him, he was an intense and demanding lover, not letting her hold any of herself back.

He wouldn't let her hide away from him so all she could hope for was that her body and heart were truly safe with him.

She was still a little embarrassed about her panic attack earlier. She knew in her heart of hearts, Carlos was nothing like Ken. But for a frightening moment, when he'd whispered those words to her, the memory of that fateful night had resurfaced and the pleasure they'd just shared had been stripped away, replaced by the cold, detached words Ken had shouted at her.

"If I can't have you…"

A small tremor passed through her and she tried to tuck the memory back in its box where it couldn't unravel the woman she was now. But the memory of the girl she'd once been in college stayed with her, keeping her far from sleep…

The young freshman cheerleader, who had let the charming college basketball player sweep her off her feet, had been much too innocent and trusting for her own good. Even after all these years, Judith cringed, thinking of how easily she had fallen for him. But then, Kenneth Tate had been popular and charismatic and she had been flattered by his attention. She had only joined the cheerleading squad to supplement her dance courses, not thinking she would catch the attention of the third-year ball player.

Eventually, after nearly two years of dating, and still heavily grieving the loss of her mother, she'd allowed him to convince her that they should get married. So she accepted his proposal.

And that's when everything had changed.

It was still unclear to her if Ken had changed into the monster that had taken pleasure in hurting her or if he had simply unleashed the monster that had always been within.

Not long after their engagement, she had given him her virginity, but sex with Ken had almost never been fulfilling. And that's when she believed he had become the man she would no longer recognize.

She had hoped the more they did it, the sooner she would eventually come to enjoy it. But she hadn't. The more stress she felt in trying to enjoy sex with him, to please him, the more her body shut down. Eventually, sex became something they did because he wanted to do it, even faking her orgasms just so he would stop asking her afterwards if she had come.

Eventually, he had sensed the disconnect between them and that was when the violent jealousy and angry outbursts had truly begun. What had started off as insults swiftly turned physical. She remembered every slap, every punch, every kick. There had been times when he was choking her that she wondered if his angry face would be the last thing she saw before she died.

But then, he would turn back into the charming guy she had first met and it all became a vicious cycle with them. A slap to the face, an apology, maybe an expensive gift, then forced make-up sex. And it would start all over again until she had found the courage to end it.

The engagement was as far as they had gotten and she shook with relief at that.

Carlos murmured something in his sleep, his arm around her waist, pulling her closer to him. She burrowed into his heat and eventually managed to drift off into a deep sleep.

The next time she woke, it was to find Carlos hovering over her, fully dressed.

"Good morning, *muñeca*," he said, brushing her hair

from her eyes. "I hate to leave you like this, but I have to take care of something before I head into the office this morning."

Judith noticed the pale glow of dawn peeking through the windows. In a few hours, they would both have to be at work.

"Okay." Her voice still throaty from sleep.

But he made no move to leave.

"Are you okay?" he finally asked, staring down at her closely.

Her cheeks warmed, but she gave him a quick nod, though not sure if he was referring to his lovemaking that left her a little sore deep inside or her meltdown last night that still left her embarrassed.

But he continued staring down at her with those intense, dark eyes of his. Even after last night, she wasn't used to it, especially not in the soft light of morning.

"God, I miss you already."

She smiled. "You'll see me in a few hours."

"Too long," he grumbled then leaned down and kissed her sweetly. He placed his hand lightly over her lower abdomen and her nipples hardened from the pressure. For a moment, she regretted having the sheet over her, regretted not being able to feel his warm palm on her skin. But the sheet did more than just keep her skin covered. It concealed other secrets as well.

With a long groan, he pulled away from her. "I have to go."

"I know," she said sympathetically, rubbing the hand that still rested over her navel.

"I don't want to."

She smiled, remembering a similar discussion from last night. "Then don't," she teased.

The corner of his lips tugged slightly and his hand flexed beneath hers. "I want to see you again tonight." His eyes suddenly lit up with amusement. "Maybe take you to a steakhouse and tell you the story about Wenzel and *Los Tres Cerditos*." At her confused look, he added, "The Three Little Pigs."

She laughed and his smile widened.

"I'm serious," he continued. "Not a lot people knew this, but Wenzel had really bad allergies and one summer…"

She laughed louder, but they were both startled when Prince jumped on the bed. Her fat, orange cat sat on his hind legs at the foot of the bed and stared at them with his wide gold eyes.

"I almost forgot about him," Carlos muttered then frowned. "I hope he wasn't watching us last night."

Judith glanced at Prince in horror then surprised herself with a mortified giggle. "God, I hope not either!"

To share in their sentiments, Prince let out a loud meow. They both laughed. Carlos kissed her on the forehead before he rose from the bed.

"Come lock up after me."

Disheveled and wrapped in the bed sheet, Judith walked him out of her apartment then rushed to the bathroom, nearly missing the raised toilet seat before she sat down. She shook her head and flipped it down, dazed at how much things had changed in her simple, quiet life.

Carlos wanted to see her again tonight and that

probably meant they would make love again. Her thighs tightened in anticipation.

But last night she had lied to him again.

She hadn't wanted to do it, but there was no way for her to tell him that an accident nearly five years ago had left her unable to have children. He would have asked more questions and she was unprepared to let him know about that dark part of her life. It was easier to just let him believe she was taking birth control.

But a deep, hidden part of her, relished the thought of having a baby—Carlos' baby. Though a baby with him should have scared her, it didn't. It was a dangerous fantasy to indulge in, but deep down she longed for the possibility of giving birth to her own child. And if she could give one to Carlos, she would.

Before she could entertain such fantasies, she needed to think of the huge wedge that would soon come between them once he found out about what she'd done.

She made her way back into the bedroom and stared at the rumpled bed. She crawled back into it, lying in the spot he'd slept on last night and inhaling his lingering scent.

After dinner tonight, she would come clean with him. He would be upset, of course, but maybe once she told him that she'd been forced into doing it, he would understand.

Then she would need to figure out how much to tell him about the monster who literally made her sick with terror.

chapter 7

"You'd better have a good-God-damn reason for waking me up this early."

Carlos shouldered past his sleepy-eyed cousin and went into the apartment. From the look of his half-dressed state, it was clear he'd just gotten out of bed.

"Sorry to disturb your beauty sleep, Pretty Boy," Carlos said, "but I need a favor."

Tristan followed him into the living room, rubbing a hand over his tired but still-too-handsome face. Growing up, Carlos had found it amusing how his cousin had managed to attract women of all ages. He'd even been a little envious of him. But now, it was something his family would tease him mercilessly about.

"Carlos, man, it's too early for this shit."

"It's eight in the morning," Carlos reminded him as he took a seat in the corner of the long sofa. "Did you plan to sleep the day away?"

Tristan fell into the single chair, his dark brows pulled together fiercely over his light brown eyes.

"When I get to keep cushy office hours like you then I won't complain."

Carlos grunted in sympathy. Tristan was an ex-cop turned bounty hunter, though he liked to refer to himself as a *Fugitive Recovery Agent*, and sometimes Carlos forgot that meant keeping late hours.

"When did you get in last night?"

Tristan leaned back in his seat with a heavy sigh. "Daylight was just coming up when I got into bed."

"Sorry man," Carlos said with genuine regret. He could just imagine what his cousin's night had been like, while he'd spent the most remarkable night with the woman of his dreams. Even now, it was hard to not think about her. It had been hard leaving her this morning. Carlos wanted nothing more than to spend the rest of the day in bed. He smiled at the thought. Maybe he could convince her to go away with him this weekend to his uncle's ranch house in the desert.

Tristan sighed again. "Don't be sorry. Just tell me what's so important you couldn't call first."

Carlos pulled out the small bag containing the flash drive and placed it on the center table. "I need a favor."

Tristan looked at the small bag and back at him. "Of course you need a favor. Do I even want to know what's on there?"

Carlos shook his head. "Doesn't matter, it's been stripped. I need your help finding out who this came from." He quickly filled his cousin in on Monday night's incident with the intruder. All he wanted was a name and he was hoping his cousin could use whatever connections he had left to get that for him. "And it would be nice if you could put a rush on it," Carlos concluded. "We'd really like to figure who this was."

"I may have to give out a few favors to get this done," Tristan mumbled, picking up the small bag.

"I'm sure if you used some of your *charm*, you won't have any problems getting this to me in no time," Carlos said, not at all concerned with his cousin's protest. Tristan had been using his looks to get what he wanted for as long as Carlos could remember. This wouldn't be anything new.

"How many people have handled this?"

"At the job? Just me." Carlos leaned back in his seat and stared at his cousin. He was going to hate to hear this but Carlos said it anyway. "I need another favor."

Tristan cursed.

"But this one is personal," Carlos rushed. "And there's no rush on this."

After a long pause, Tristan let out a heavy sigh. "What is it?"

Carlos relayed his request and when Tristan realized it was within his line of work, he was a bit more amiable about helping him.

"You must really be sprung on this girl," Tristan said in amazement.

Carlos shrugged. "She's special."

"I can see that," Tristan muttered, studying him closely. "There's something different about you. You're all smiles and shit."

"Man, shut up."

Tristan chuckled, but Carlos ignored him because he did feel different. Lighter, somehow, and fulfilled in a way that went beyond physical.

"Anyway, how did you know she was adopted?"

"We had dinner last night."

Tristan raised a brow. "Now it's all starting to make sense. Just don't get how you get—all intense and shit when you really want something—and scare her away."

Carlos lips quirked at his cousin's advice—advice he'd given himself yet found it hard to follow. Maybe he was a little obsessed with Judith, but he wouldn't admit it to his cousin. He would never hear the end of it. He had never felt this way about any woman before. He couldn't even remember the last girl he'd actually brought over to meet his family. He and Judith weren't even technically dating yet he hadn't been able not to talk about her when his cousin had wondered about his self-imposed celibacy these last several weeks. Carlos was selective with the women he dated and at first his cousin had been shocked, then highly amused, at his "office crush," as Tristan liked to call her.

But she was more than that, and after last night, Carlos was convinced that she was made for him.

After more unsolicited advice from his cousin, he rose to his feet.

"As much as I would love to sit here and listen to more love tips from a professional bachelor, I've got to get to work."

It was a little after nine when Carlos walked into Royal Courts.

And right into a shit show.

It started at the casino with a drunken guest who had apparently spent all night drinking and gambling. Carlos was annoyed that the pit manager at the time hadn't followed protocol and gotten the drunken man removed from the floor and put in a room.

Once Carlos got that commotion settled, he headed to his office. He read through the night's report left for him by Pete and found that it had otherwise been a quiet, ordinary night.

Now he needed to call David and get an update from him about the woman last night, to see if he had gotten anything useful from her. Carlos could have called his boss' directly, but he wanted to hear her voice. Just as he began to dial Judith's desk, he noticed the blinking red light. He rarely got voice messages. Everyone knew he spent little time in his office so the best way to reach him was through the handheld radio or his cell. Hell, even email was quicker.

Annoyed, Carlos pushed the button and the voicemail began to play. There was only one and it was from David.

"Moreno, turns out Judith Bell was in Gabe's office Monday night. I have someone who can ID her. Call me when you get in. I've arranged for Judith's computer to be taken and the Lab will be going through all her recent activity. Security will be alerted when she gets in." There was a brief pause, then he added, *"Call me when you have her. This could be nothing but I don't want her to leave this building until I've had a chance to talk to her."*

Carlos sat rigid in his seat. *Bullshit*, he thought viciously. There was no way Judith was involved in that mess. He replayed the message one more time. He didn't know who this *witness* was but Carlos would be damned if he'd let any of them treat Judith like some criminal.

His Judith was no thief. She was sweet, shy, and an all-around good girl.

Though his heart believed one thing, his mind began to piece together the possibility. He replayed that night in his head, from the moment he ran into her in the hall. There had been a jumpiness in her, and a sort of guilt in her large, brown eyes, that he had attributed to their moment in the supply closet. But then there had also been a sort of regret before…

His jaw clenched tightly, but he balked at the thought. A range of emotions raced through his head, and his blood pulsed at his temples.

Carlos pulled up the security video and replayed the footage. He paused when the red skirt came into view then replayed the entire sequence. She came into view twice, before and after the cleaning woman—the woman he believed to be the one behind this.

He needed to talk to her. None of this made sense.

He grabbed his phone and called her desk but wasn't surprised when the call went unanswered. He would have been alerted by now if she had come in and the fact that he hadn't only increased the heavy lump forming in the pit of his stomach.

Carlos carefully hung up the phone and tried her cell. It rang until the automated voice system picked up. He tried again and once again it went to voice mail. On the third try, he slammed the phone down.

The muscles in his gut tightened, but he still couldn't believe she was involved in this.

He refused to believe it.

****

Something solid pressed down on her chest and

Judith grunted. Soft whiskers brushed across her cheek as a small furry head nudged under her chin.

"Ugh, Prince, you're heavy," she wheezed as his heavy paws began kneading her the tops of her chest. She shifted him away and stretched out under the cool sheets. Turning to the clock beside the bed, she blinked. Then blinked again.

She was late.

Judith sprinted out of the bed and ran into the bathroom. She jumped in the shower, nearly slipping in the tub in her haste. She must have fallen back asleep after she'd walked Carlos out. Now she was going to be late for the first time in three months. And it was all Carlos Moreno's fault.

The thought, however, only made her smile. If she had to be late because of last night, so be it. She didn't regret it.

She showered in record time then grabbed the first outfit from her closet. As she dressed, she noticed the small red marks on her shoulders and breast. She paused for a moment in front of the mirror and ran her fingertips over the new love marks that stained her brown skin.

Judith shook her head, a small, bewildered smile forming on her lips. There was indeed a feral animal behind those dark eyes and sensual lips. Carlos certainly had a habit of marking her like one. She hadn't even noticed which probably made her just as wild.

She finished her dressing, popped in her contact lens, then rushed to pour breakfast for a vocally annoyed Prince. With his attention focused on his food bowl, Judith rushed to slip on her shoes. She paused at the muffled sounds of her phone ringing.

She located it buried in her purse and prayed it wasn't her boss demanding to know where she was.

But when she stared down at the number, she didn't recognize it. Not at first. Then the southern California area code jogged her memory and she knew who it was.

The Agency.

Judith frowned. They almost never called. If she needed anything, she was the one who called them.

Unless there was trouble.

She quickly answered it, her voice whisper soft as she braced herself for whatever news were to come.

"Judith?" A familiar voice came through the line. "It's Mary Cross."

She closed her eyes briefly at the memories that calm, light voice seemed to resurface. In that moment, she was brought back to that hospital bed, where she'd been lying in pain, confused as to how she had gotten there. Mary Cross, a young woman with kind eyes, who had identified herself as a counselor, had stood beside her bed, talking to her about her organization. The woman had apparently read about her case, found out about her protective order against Ken, and had come to the conclusion herself that what had brought her to that hospital had not been just a simple tragic car accident. She understood Judith's fears and had offered to help—as her organization had helped many women before her.

Judith cleared her throat before responding. She was no longer helpless and confined to a hospital bed.

She needed to get a grip and stop worrying herself about a discussion that could turn out to be nothing.

But deep down, something told her it couldn't be good.

"Mary, is something wrong?" Judith surprised herself with the direct question. She had meant to be pleasant, ask the woman how she was doing, since it had been a while since they last spoke. But it seemed her mind and her emotions weren't in the mood to put off the inevitable.

The woman was silent for a moment before she spoke again. "Well, we've been trying to get ahold of you for some time now but didn't have your current contact information on file."

It occurred to her that she had never updated her phone number with them after she'd started at Royal Courts. It was a habit of hers now to change her phone number every six months. For some reason, it just made her feel better to do it.

"I'm sorry. I forgot," she said.

"No, no," Mary rushed out. "I'm not calling about that. I just wanted to let you know that we would have contacted you sooner had we been able to."

Judith grip on the phone tightened. "Contact me about what?"

Mary sighed. "Kenneth Tate," she said. "He's been granted parole."

The bottom of Judith's stomach dropped. "When?" Her voice was barely above a whisper that she was surprised the other woman had heard.

"Sometime last week," Mary said. "I don't have the exact date, but it was fairly recent. "You were put on the list for his parole hearing, but you didn't show up. But I don't think you have anything to worry about. We've managed to keep everything about your new name and location concealed, but we just wanted to inform you of his release just in case."

He'd been released *last* week? A cold sensation began to crawl up the back of Judith's neck and lock around her throat. For a minute, she couldn't breathe. She had expected to receive a letter from the courts or even the Agency about his appeal for parole and his subsequent approval. Not that she would have gone to his hearing. Judith wanted nothing to do with him and nothing could have forced her into the same room with him. But it would have left her feeling less panicked to know before today that he'd been free since *last* week.

"You know," Mary added, "if you suspect your new identity has been compromised, let us know as soon as possible. But in the meantime, it's best that you take certain precautions that could…"

Mary continued speaking, but her voice became a distant hum as the buzzing in Judith's head grew louder. In the back of her mind, Judith had known this was coming—that the monster in her closet would one day be released and allowed to roam free—she had just not expected it this soon.

What should have been an attempted murder conviction, that put him away forever, had been litigated down to reckless endangerment and violation of a protective order. Unfortunately, Judith had been in the hospital fighting for her life when Ken had pled guilty to the lesser charge. She had never gotten the chance to tell her side of what had really happened that night she'd been trapped in his car.

The suffocating panic that threatened to engulf her was too much for Judith to handle. Her new name and new life gave her little assurance that he couldn't find her if he wanted to.

Someone already had.

Judith thought of the strange woman who'd sent her the package, who had blackmailed her into breaking the law, and who had lied about helping her. If Ken had been released last week, there was no way the woman could have done anything to stop it.

She had risked everything, and had lost a part of her integrity, all for nothing. Not peace of mind or a semblance of safety. None of it had ever been in her reach.

The knowledge of her stupid gullibility made her sick.

Judith fell into her sofa and rested her head on her hand, the pounding in her head made it feel heavy.

"Mary," Judith said, interrupting the woman. "Someone knows about me."

"What? Who?" There was a sharpness now in her tone that oddly made Judith feel better. Her usual soft, placating tone would have done little to soothe her right now.

"I don't know," Judith admitted. "I just got a letter. It was sent to my job and they knew all about me. The woman even told me that Ken was being paroled next week. I guess that was a lie," she added vaguely.

"Wait, you *spoke* to them?"

Judith stifled a groan. *Yes,* like an idiot, she had. If she could do it all again, she would have called the

Agency first or brought the letter and flash drive to Carlos. She should have done so many things differently...

But there was no time to dwell on that.

"What else did she say to you?" Mary asked next. "Did they threaten you in any way?"

Judith was selective in her response. If she said too much, she could risk losing any more support from the Agency. Mary had explained the "rules" to her from the start. The Agency was there to help her whenever she needed it, but any arrests would end all of that. It was important that she keep her big lapse of judgment away from the Agency.

"No," Judith said. "She was actually pretty polite. She just...wanted to tell me about Ken's upcoming release."

From the silence over the phone, Judith knew the other woman was trying to make sense of that. But sense or not, Mary understood the potential risk she was now in and Judith wasn't surprised by her next words.

"We're going to have to start over."

Judith sighed in resignation, though tears brimmed around her eyes at the thought of ending the life she'd made for herself and virtually disappearing again.

It was the only logical move and yet Judith's heart squeezed at the thought of never seeing Carlos again. He was the only good thing that had come into her life in a long time. Second to Prince, she thought ruefully. But while she'd spent most of her time making sure Prince was happy and comfortable, Carlos went out of his way to put a smile on her face and make her laugh.

Then again, maybe it was for the best. Carlos deserved someone who could love him freely, unconditionally. Someone who wasn't so…damaged.

And, unfortunately, she wasn't fixed yet.

Maybe she would ever be.

Taking a shuddering breath, she did her best to ignore the pain encasing her heart and instead filled it with resolve.

"Okay, Mary," Judith said into the phone. "What do you need me to do?"

chapter 8

Carlos could barely contain his rage. He wanted to break something, to drive his fist through the textured wall of David Carrone's office.

Instead, he kept his arms crossed over his chest and stood by the door. He was ready to leave the suffocating office, to drive to Judith's apartment and shake answers out of her.

He'd been an idiot, letting his feelings for her cloud his judgment and he'd failed in doing his job. And the woman sitting across David's large desk was testament that he'd failed at his job twice.

"Is that her?" David asked the woman, holding up Judith's employee photo.

Carlos studied the woman as she peered intently at it. Though the woman was dressed more sensibly today, he still recognized her from last night and from the video footage. Apparently, she and David had history and last night just been a misunderstanding.

Misunderstanding or not, Carlos was not prepared to trust the woman that he'd been suspicious of not too long ago. He would have much preferred to wait for the fingerprints to come in before he believed what she had claimed to see the other night.

Except Carlos didn't need to hear the woman's testimony or see the fingerprint results to finally accept what he'd been adamant against not too long ago.

Judith had done it.

She'd lied to him, betrayed him, and he'd let her.

The thought only heightened his rage and Carlos gritted his teeth, his jaw throbbing from the tight clenching. It had all finally clicked for him the moment David told him why Judith hadn't come into work today—and why she wouldn't be in for the rest of the week.

"Yeah, that's her," the woman said matter-of-factly. "She's the one I saw sitting behind the desk when I walked in."

David nodded at her then swung his gaze up to his. Carlos tried to reign in his temper, to keep his expression neutral, but it was impossible for him to do so. His stupidity was too glaring for him to ignore. Part of his anger was directed at himself, for letting his attraction to her cloud his judgment. But the biggest strike to his ego, his pride, was the way he'd made a fool of himself, for wanting her to want him, and talking himself into believing that he knew her when she was just a beautiful, manipulative liar.

"We'll have to wait until Judith gets back in the office to question her," David said to him. "Until we have something more concrete, let's treat this with caution."

Carlos gave him a curt nod, still too angry to speak.

David Carrone didn't know this yet, but Judith was playing one of them. Hell, maybe both of them. She still hadn't answered any of his phone calls and hadn't shown up to work. According to David, Judith had put in a request just that morning for some personal time off. Carlos had held out hope that he had been right about her, that it had all been a misunderstanding, until David had informed him that she was allegedly on her way to care for her sick grandmother.

A "grandmother" she had neglected to tell him about last night.

"I want the Lab to continue their sweep of her computer and have her access to the resort restricted," David continued.

Carlos gave him another brisk nod. If he was going to fix this mess, he needed to push his anger aside and focus. Telling David what he knew about Judith was not a smart move. Everything she had told him last night could have been a lie. What he needed to do was sift through what was real and what had just been bullshit. And the quickest way to do that was to get it straight from the source.

"Shouldn't we also verify that she is on her way to California to see her grandmother?" Carlos managed to ask without snarling. David sat back in his seat and looked thoughtful for a moment. "I can take the lead on that," Carlos added.

"Okay," David conceded, "but we need to start questioning all those that were here the other night and also start taking a closer look at the security systems so we don't have another week like this again."

Carlos clenched his jaw again. "We'll get started

first tomorrow morning," he said tightly then turned to leave the office. But not before he heard the woman's whispered comment.

"He's pissed."

No, Carlos was more than pissed. He'd been fooled by a pretty face and innocent smile and that was a harsh reality that he had to face. Like a fool, he'd fallen in love and she'd only been playing them—playing *him*.

Carlos made it into his office and carefully shut the door. He needed time alone, to think. Verifying whether she was on her way to California to care for her sick grandmother was not on his list of priorities because he already knew the answer to that. Nor was questioning those in the video footage. What he needed were answers.

Why had she done it? For money?

He paced his office like a caged animal before he fell into his seat. With a vicious curse, he slammed his fist on top of the desk as he replayed the security video over and over in his head. The image of that red skirt coming into the camera's view then later again—minutes after the cleaning woman.

She knew Kristensen's schedule, knew the best time to go into his office. She must have waited until the office had been completely quiet.

But she hadn't anticipated running into him. Carlos remembered her large, anxiety-stricken eyes when he'd stopped her in the hall that night. At the time, he'd believed it had been the stress of the job, but now he realized she must have been going back for the flash drive.

Had she left it behind on purpose or had that been a

mistake? Had she let him kiss her in the supply room in the hopes of distracting him? It had certainly worked.

And last night...

What had last night been? Had it just another way to get him to fall completely under her spell? He didn't want to think it was. He couldn't believe that last night hadn't meant anything to her, that she was capable of faking that kind of response whenever their bodies came together.

Yet, he didn't know her as much as he'd tried to convince himself he did.

And now she was gone.

The heaviness in his gut spread until he thought he would suffocate from it. She was not answering her phone and he had no way of getting in touch with her and he knew she was running—that after today, he would never see her again.

Carlos closed his eyes briefly, but it did nothing to soothe his burning rage. It coiled around him until he finally erupted.

"*Fuck!*"

He swiped at the phone on his desk, sending it crashing to the ground along with a flurry of papers.

He ran his hands over his face and through his hair and steeled his rage behind a hard, blank mask. The burst of anger gave him little relief, if only for a moment. What he needed to do now was clear his head so he could think and not screw this up more than he already had. This morning, she hadn't acted like a woman who was planning to go on the run. Maybe something had spooked her—maybe it had been something he'd said.

Carlos pushed away from his desk and headed out of the office. It didn't matter. He needed to find her, needed to make her pay for her betrayal.

But a silent, desperate part of him wasn't ready to accept that she was out of his life for good.

****

Judith zipped up her last bag and dragged it to the front of her apartment. It was late afternoon when she had finally completed everything Mary had instructed, though with a few exceptions.

Mary had told her not to have any more contact with anyone outside the Agency, not even her job. She'd assured her that they would settle everything with her employers once they had her at a secure location, but Judith couldn't do that to her boss. This week was a crucial week for them and David Carrone had always been good to her so she'd called in for her personal time and arranged for another assistant to cover for her.

That had been the easy part.

The hard part had been ignoring all of Carlos' calls. He must have wondered why she hadn't come in to work today. She had fought with herself to let them go unanswered, but she had wanted nothing more than to speak to him one last time, to assure him she was fine. She hated that she had to leave him like this, that she wouldn't get to say goodbye, but he would only insist on coming over and possibly ask questions she wouldn't be able to answer. Ending it this way was for the best.

After last night, it would be next to impossible to forget him and she didn't want to leave knowing he would wonder about her abrupt departure, wonder if their night together had meant nothing to her because it had meant everything.

She was surprised by the tear that trailed down her cheek and quickly wiped it away.

"Okay, Judith, pull it together," she muttered to herself. But her heart was still heavy and nothing she could do would ease her desolation. All she wanted at that moment was to be with Carlos.

She sighed, accepting that it was no longer a possibility. And it was for the best. Though, she would never be able to forget him, maybe this was a chance for him to find someone more deserving.

She paused for a moment and surveyed her once small, neat living room. It was now crowded with her things. Everything she had once owned was in bags and whatever large containers she had managed to find around her small apartment. Her things would come to her once she was settled in her new place. That had been another thing Mary had assured her.

For now, she would be leaving here with what clothes she'd managed to pack in the large suitcase. The Agency had arranged for her to stay in a motel just outside the city until they were ready to relocate her. Her only dilemma now was Prince.

With everything so uncertain, it was best that she brought him to a shelter where he could find a more stable home. Looking at the orange, long-haired Siberian lying stretched out on the small couch, however, she couldn't bear to part with him too. He was the only constant she would probably ever have in her life.

She grabbed the large tote bag and his head lifted when he saw her approaching. Past experience, and the faded scratch marks on her arms, had taught her to feed him calming treats before she attempted to put him in any carrier. Since the traditional cat carriers sent him into a fit, the tote bag was the best alternative.

Evidently, her cat still disagreed. He jumped off of the couch and dashed into the bedroom.

Judith sighed and followed behind him. "Come on, Prince. It's time to go."

As soon as the words were out of her mouth, a hard knock came to her door. Judith froze for a moment, a million dark thoughts and possibilities swarming in her head. *Did he find me?*

But she quickly dismissed the thought. Mary had informed her that part of Ken's parole required that he remain in California in a Halfway House. Besides, Ken had been released for about a week now and she hadn't received anything from him. No phone calls, no letters. Maybe he was rehabilitated from his sick obsession with her.

She very much hoped so.

The knock came again, this time louder, and she took ginger steps toward the door.

"W-who is it?" She could have looked through the peephole but years of caution kept her feet planted a few steps away, keeping distance between her and the other person on the other side.

"Judith, open up."

Carlos.

For a moment, a wave of relief and joy so great

rolled through her it almost made her lightheaded. It was immediately followed by uneasiness and she bit her lower lip. *Why is he here?* She couldn't face him now. She didn't want to continue lying to him.

"*Now*, Judith."

Her uneasiness transformed to fear at the hard edge in his voice and a tremor passed through her. She'd never heard it from him before, but she recognized the sharp bite of a man's anger. Then the cold realization hit her.

He knows.

She thought against opening the door, but nothing good would come out of ignoring him. And he was clearly a man who didn't take kindly to being ignored.

With hesitant fingers, Judith opened the door and sucked in her breath. The man who stood before her wasn't the same man who had spent two months wooing her with humorously absurd pickup lines—or who had spent hours last night loving her with spine-tingling passion and tenderness.

His face was hard mask of fury and loathing. He stepped into her apartment and she moved back, giving him a wide berth. She shut the door and slowly turned to face him again. Whatever memories they had created, was now as vague and bleak as his cold, dark eyes.

Unable to take his harsh glare any longer, Judith glanced away. Perhaps if she tried to placate him, make him understand, then he would leave her be. She hadn't meant to hurt anyone, least of all him. But he wasn't hurt. He was furious. And she didn't know how to handle him when he was this angry.

How was she possibly going to convince him of anything when he was staring down at her like...like he couldn't stand the sight of her.

But no matter how angry he was, she needed to remember that he would never hurt her. Carlos Moreno was nothing like Kenneth Tate.

Yet with the hard set of his jaw and his deeply furrowed brows, the distinction was harder to make.

Judith took a deep, unsteady breath. She needed to apologize, needed to try and convince him to let her disappear then...

Then what?

****

Carlos held himself still as he stared down at her. Even now, after everything he knew about her, after all her lies, he still wanted her.

The way her jeans molded around her hips and thighs were distracting. Memories of those thighs cradling him sent a sharp need surging through him. But it was the look in her eyes that forced him back into the reality of their situation. Her hair was clipped back and her face was bare of any make-up, like it had been last night. She had an innocent, vulnerable look about her. One that made him want to fold her into his arms and keep her safe.

But he wouldn't be swayed by her solemn, wide doe-eyes. Not anymore. Yet, he couldn't stop the low, gruff words that burst out of him.

"Damn it, baby, *why?*"

She winced slightly but still refused to look at him and for a brief moment, he hated her. Hated this weakness he had for her.

Carlos took a step toward her and she backed away. That annoyed him to no end. Then he noticed the large suitcase by the door as well as the bags and packed containers around the small apartment. She was really going to just leave.

"That didn't take long," he said harshly. "Did you wait until you had the door locked behind me to start packing?"

He felt like a fool. He'd spent the last two months chasing after her like some lovesick puppy when she'd plainly had her own agenda. And the shit he'd said last night and this morning—asking her to meet his family, wanting to see her again tonight when she clearly had no intentions of sticking around.

Running his hand through his hair, he shook his head, frustration and anger making it hard for him to even look at her.

"Where are you going, Judith? And don't tell me it's to see your sick grandmother," he snapped. "Unless you lied to me about that too."

She stared at him with wide, haunted eyes, saying nothing. He wanted her to say something, to help him make sense of what the hell was going on—and what last night had been all about. While he'd been staggering from the intense pleasure of being with her, she had been planning to disappear on him?

"Why'd you spread your legs for me last night?" he asked gruffly. "If you wanted to steal from the company, you didn't need to sleep with me to do it. You already had me wrapped around your damn finger."

You still do.

That thought only amplified his anger. He clenched his teeth against the unfamiliar tightness in his chest. If this was what a broken heart felt like, he resented the feeling—resented letting himself get duped and allowing her to make him feel this way.

Still, she remained quiet and her silence grated at him. She simply stared at him and he could see her withdrawing from him. Not physically, but it was plain in the hollow distance of her eyes. She may be accustomed to hiding behind that shell he'd tried for months to break down, but he wouldn't allow her to hide behind it now.

"Oh no, you don't," he barked, coming to stand in front of her. "You don't get to do that. You don't get to pull away and avoid this. You owe me answers. Now, God damn it, *talk to me!*"

She shook her head, the movement slow and jerky as her eyes eclipsed her face. She obviously didn't trust him enough to tell him or she was too guilty to be honest with him. Either way, his anger reached its tipping point.

She tried to take another step away from him, but he grabbed her arm and pulled her back to him. To his surprise, she yanked her arm from his grasp.

"Let go of me," she shrieked then shoved at his chest with all her strength. The action forced her back, but she was trembling with anger. And fear? Her dark amber brown eyes were stark with it.

Carlos stared down at her, stunned.

"Judith, what...?" He reached out to her, but she jerked back, glancing down at his hands, her body tense and braced. For what? For him to hit her? He was almost too shaken for words. "Do you think I'm going to hit you?" he asked incredulously.

She flinched slightly at the harshness in his tone, but he couldn't keep the furious hurt at bay. Did she think he was that big a bastard to deliberately hurt her like that? Based on her silence and the wariness in her eyes, she did. It was clear to him then that she didn't trust him. For some reason, that upset him the most. Everything he'd done to win her over, the time they'd spent in each other's arms last night, he knew now meant little to nothing to her. If she thought he was capable of that kind of violence toward her, she clearly thought less of him.

Carlos backed away from her. "I'm done with this," he muttered, his tone void of any emotion. "You don't want to talk to me then let's go."

She shook her head. "I don't have to go anywhere with you," she whispered.

He glared down at her. "I don't have time for your bullshit. It's me or the cops. Your choice."

She tensed. He made the threat, but he had no intentions of going through with it. Whether she deserved it or not, he couldn't bear to see her arrested and treated like some criminal, but damn if she wasn't making it hard for him.

He reached in his pocket for his cell phone, but before he could flip it open, she rushed toward him.

"Carlos, wait." She grabbed his hand and lowered it. "Please don't. I made a mistake and I'm sorry. I-I didn't take anything, I promise. I just made a really big mistake, but I'll leave and never come back. I promise. Just please don't do this. *Please*."

He frowned down at her. Her hand was now clutching on his forearm. She was scared but something told him it wasn't just of him or the idea of being arrested. He'd actually planned to enlist his cousin's help with getting her to talk. Tristan may not be a cop anymore, but he had all the gear to intimidate her into talking. And maybe it was best he brought someone else in. He clearly couldn't separate himself enough to do his job.

"Tell me what's going on, Judith."

"I...I can't," she said, staring at his chest. "I'm sorry."

She took a closer step toward him, until her breasts lightly brushed against him. His nostrils flared as he caught a light hint of her scent, which brought up memories of her beneath him, clasped tightly around him. She moved her hand slowly up his arm and over his chest. He couldn't stop his body from reacting to her touch and his cock jerked when she moved her hand down to his abdomen. Now that he'd tasted and touched every inch of her, he only wanted more. She moved even closer, pressing her body firmly against him and his thread of control snapped.

With a low growl, he hauled her to him and brought his lips down on hers. The kiss was hot, hard and fierce. He wanted nothing more than to lay her down and go in deep, but knew it would never be enough. He would always want her, always crave her, but not like this. Not with so much anger and bitterness and distrust between them.

Not when it was plain she was trying to use sex as a way to get around this.

He pushed her away from him, his breathing labored. Her attempt at seduction didn't fool him for a minute. He grabbed her chin and stared down at her. "Sex is not the only thing I want from you, Judith," he growled.

She hadn't been unaffected by their kiss either. She clutched fistfuls of his shirt as soft tremors coursed through her.

"What...what is it that you want?" she asked quietly, keeping her gaze on his chin.

Your heart. He wanted her to love him, to trust him.

But he'd been the stupid one to fall in love with her. He now needed to accept that she would never feel for him what he did for her.

He released her and took a step back, needing to put distance between them. If she refused to trust him, then there was nothing he could do to change that. But he had a job to do and he couldn't continue to let his *lust* cloud his judgment.

"What I want is for you to be straight with me," he said carefully. "Fucking me is not going to change anything."

She sucked in her breath. "I didn't mean to—"

"Yeah, you did," he bit out, infuriated that she would try to deny it. "But it's a waste of time. Your pussy is not gonna get you out of this so don't try it. You're only going to piss me off."

Her eyes widened then slid away from his. He knew he was being crude but didn't care. It was reflexive, a way to let out some of his bitterness and hurt and maintain his resolve. Yet, it did little of both.

"Okay, I-I'm sorry," she stammered. "I shouldn't

have—"

"No, you shouldn't have," he snapped. "Don't do it again." He couldn't stand to see the despair on her face, but he steeled himself against it. "Now tell me what the hell's going on with you. Why did you do this?"

She hesitated for a moment then told him a disjointed tale of an envelope and an anonymous phone number.

"The woman said she just wanted to copy a file and all I had to do was stick the flash drive into a computer. I hadn't planned to use Mr. Kristensen's computer, but I was already there and…" She shrugged. "It just all happened so fast."

He studied her, trying to gauge if what she was telling him was the truth. "What was this mystery woman looking for?"

"I don't know. She said it was just a file from the server. But whatever it was, I don't think she got it."

"How do you know?"

She told him about the "cleaning woman," who'd walked in on her, and about her panic, which had led her to disconnect the call and ultimately terminate the transfer before it could be completed.

Carlos frowned, not quite sure what to make of her bizarre story. "Why you?" he asked after a while. "Of all people at the company, why would this person want to target you? And why would you be stupid enough to go along with this?"

Did she secretly have ties to this person that she wasn't telling him about? Did she think he would never find out? With his foolish infatuation, he thought with disgust, maybe he wouldn't have.

She shook her head, her apprehension and fear once again clouding her eyes. "You wouldn't understand."

He bit back a curse. "Maybe not," he snapped. "But believe it or not, I'm trying to help you."

Again, she stared up at him with those large, stark eyes before she responded. "She...she promised to help me with...a problem I have. Thinking back on it now, I should have never believed her, but I...I was too scared not to."

Carlos frown deepened. "Is it money?" He would hate for her involvement in all this to boil down to that, but in his experience, people did a lot of stupid things for money. Then again, he couldn't think of a valid excuse that would make what she did okay.

"No, it wasn't anything like that. It's something that...no one can help me with. Not really. I just need to leave here." Her eyes were earnest now. "Please Carlos, just let me go and I promise I'll stay gone."

Her plea only added to his irritation. Was it that easy for her to walk away?

"You should have come to me." Those words weren't planned but he couldn't take them back. The protectiveness he felt for her had not lessened. If anything, it had grown stronger. He wanted to pull her into his arms and comfort her, tell her without words that he would keep her safe.

But would she believe him? She'd already proved that she didn't trust him.

"What would you have done?" she asked hesitantly.

"I could have at least set a trap for this woman," he said curtly. "Maybe even find out who, or where, she was."

She fell silent for a moment as she thought about that then sighed. "You're right. But all I know is that I couldn't let... I couldn't take the chance. Maybe if I had more time to process it all, I would have come to you. But I—"

"No, you wouldn't have," he interrupted. "You clearly don't trust me enough to come to me for help." And that ate at him the most. She was the one who'd betrayed him, didn't trust him, yet he still wanted to protect her. He ran his hand through his hair, frustrated with himself and her.

She wrapped her arms around herself, her shoulders slumping in defeat. "It's not you, Carlos," she murmured. "I just have a problem with trusting all the wrong people."

He wasn't particularly happy to hear her infuriating admission, but at least she was being honest.

"Do you still have the phone number for this woman?"

She went to her large purse and pulled out a small note. "I tried calling it again, but it doesn't work anymore."

When she handed it to him, their fingers briefly touched and she swiftly drew her hand away, balling it at her side. But it couldn't be ignored because he'd felt it too. The electric spark from just a simple touch.

He quickly read the short note. "Is this it?"

She crossed her arms under her breasts then turned away from him. "There was also the flash drive," she said over her shoulder. "But you already have that."

He folded the note and slipped it into his pocket. It

wasn't much but at least now they had something to start with. And something to verify whether she was telling him the truth.

"Okay," he said. "Grab your bag and let's go."

She whipped around to face him. "What? Where?"

"You said you couldn't stay here, right? Well, until we can find this woman and find out what she was looking for, I'm not going to just let you disappear."

She stiffened. "Carlos, I'm telling you the truth."

"Then you won't mind me keeping you close." The uncertainty in her eyes irked him. "Trust me or don't trust me, either way I'm not letting you leave," he said bluntly. Then he sighed. "I'm only trying to help you, *muñeca*."

Her brows furrowed slightly. "Why?"

Because I love you, damn it. But he couldn't tell her that. She didn't trust him, and the last thing he wanted was to have her question what he felt for her.

"You wouldn't understand," he muttered bitterly. "And right now, you don't have many more options. Now let's go."

chapter 9

Carlos pulled into the driveway of a wide, brown and creamy beige single story home and shut off the engine.

"I'm only going to be a second," he said, pulling the key from the ignition. "Stay in the car."

Judith nodded, staring straight ahead. The ride to Carlos' uncle's house had been strained and she wondered how she was going to endure the hour long ride to his family's ranch home just outside of Moapa. She held Prince on her lap. Surprisingly, he rested quietly in the large tote bag she carried him in.

She watched as Carlos went to the front of the house. She didn't know why she'd agreed to this but then, as he'd said, she really had no other option. She either accepted his help and stayed where he put her, which appeared to be deep in the desert, or risked him getting the police involved. Being arrested would void any assistance from the agency and she couldn't jeopardize her only chance at starting over.

She'd seen the way Carlos looked at her when she'd told him what happened. Even to her ears, it sounded ridiculous—something out of a bad mystery novel—but it had been as much of the truth as he needed to know. Her past and Ken's recent parole was her problem and her problem alone.

Even if she wanted to confide in him, there would be no point to it. He didn't want her anymore. He had pulled away from her when she had stupidly touched him, thinking he had wanted her as much as she had him at that moment. She had only wanted a moment to forget everything, to lose herself in him again. But he'd mistaken her desire for him as just an act and now resentment and regret were wedged solidly between them.

She could only hope that Carlos would find the woman who'd blackmailed her into this—and soon. He would see that she had been telling him the truth, and maybe then he would consider letting her go. Then she would be free to start the new life the Agency was creating for her.

There was a commotion coming from the front of the house that pulled Judith out of her thoughts. Carlos was walking toward the car, a fierce frown on his attractive face. This one worse than the one he'd had before he'd left the car.

Following close behind him was an older Latina woman, who Judith assumed was his aunt. An older man, with graying dark brown hair came outside the house to stand next to the beaming woman.

Carlos walked up to her side of the car and opened the door. She had no choice but to look at him as he leaned into the car.

"My aunt and uncle want to meet you," he said

briskly. "You're just going to say 'hi' and then we leave."

She glanced at the petite woman standing in front of the dark gray sedan in her pink floral housedress not at all feeling up to carrying on whatever pretense Carlos expected her to.

He must have sensed her apprehension, because he grasped her chin and forced her back to face him. "Don't you dare do anything to upset them."

With a small frown, she stared at him searchingly. "Carlos, why would you even say that? I would never do anything to upset your family." She would never intentionally hurt anyone and, from their brief time together, she would think he'd at least know that much.

Apparently he didn't.

"Well, I can't say that I really know *you*, now can I," he snapped releasing his firm grip around her jaw.

She stiffened at the truth in his words. No, he didn't know her. And based on the cold man standing before her, she couldn't say she really knew him either.

He strengthened and pushed the car door wider. "Come on."

She stared down pointedly at the bundle on her lap. "Is it okay if I bring Prince?"

He nodded curtly.

She stepped out of the car, the July heat not at all sympathetic to her sweaty palms or racing heart. But she contained her anxiety as the older woman came toward her, curiosity and delight in her kind, dark eyes. Eyes that was vaguely similar to Carlos'. Judith returned her friendly smile. She was a small woman with streaks of gray in her dark, wavy hair. Even at her age, she was an attractive woman.

"So this is your Judith, Carlito?" the woman said with a smooth yet thickly accented voice.

"*Tia*, this is Judith. Judith, this is my aunt Rosa," Carlos said, neither confirming nor denying whether she was *his*.

The woman walked up to her and kissed her on the cheek and they exchanged greetings. Her welcome was warm and genuine and Judith found herself losing some of her nervousness.

"*Muy bonita*," Rosa said, patting her cheek then grabbed her arm and pulled her toward the house. "Come meet with my husband, Guillermo."

Carlos took the tote bag carrying Prince as Rosa dragged her to the stocky, older man standing near the house. "Please, just call me Gil," he said, greeting her with the same warm friendliness. He kissed her cheek as well, which tickled from his gray-peppered beard.

His English was laced with an underlying accent that was barely noticeable. However, it was the contrast of his beautiful greenish-brown eyes against his swarthy skin that she found to be the most striking. There was also an astuteness in his eyes that was eased by his welcoming smile.

The couple ushered her into their large, beautiful home, which was spacious and cozy. Gil glanced over at Carlos, who stood by the door, staring intently at her. She purposely kept her gaze averted and concentrated on the two older people doting over her. It was unnerving but nice to have their warmhearted attention. She had lost that with Carlos and didn't realize how much she missed having someone treat her with such affection.

"Carlos, whoever you stole this beautiful *dama* from must be weeping right now."

Everyone shared a laugh except Carlos.

"*Tío*, we can't stay long," Carlos said. Judith glanced at him, but his gaze was on his uncle.

Gil waved at him dismissively. "I'll get you the keys," he said, the corner of his eyes wrinkling. "But after we eat."

"*Tío*—"

"You will have plenty of time with her, Carlito," his aunt interjected. "Let me feed her first, at least."

Judith could feel her face getting warm at his aunt's words. "I'm fine, really, *Señora* Rosa. But thank you."

Rosa threw a frown toward Carlos then patted her hand. "Don't let Carlito pressure you. We will eat, okay?"

Judith nodded. When Carlos brought his gaze to her, she glanced away. He was done with her, he made that clear. But his family thought they would be spending time together at their family ranch home. It was a thought she hadn't even considered. Carlos had made no mention of staying with her. But then, if he did, maybe she could prove to him that she wasn't some devious woman who had set out to conspire against him, that was she felt for him was unusual but real.

And maybe then, he would start looking at her with a little less contempt.

****

Carlos watched the way Judith charmed her way

into his family's heart.

With every laugh and smile, her pretty dimples would appear, captivating his aunt and uncle until even he found himself drawn to the sound and sight of her.

He hadn't wanted them to stay, to have his family fall for her as he had, but it was clearly too late. A burst of laughter came from the kitchen where his aunt had whisked Judith away, and a whirl of mixed emotions flooded him. This pretense was hard to keep up, especially when he wavered between wanting to kiss her and shake her.

Carlos pulled open the sliding glass door and stepped outside to the back patio. Leaning against the wall, he stared out into the distance, needing to be in his own thoughts for a moment, away from the pull of her sweet voice and easy laughter.

It wasn't supposed to be like this. What had once been a moment he anticipated was now something he couldn't wait to end. It would only add to his embarrassment when he had to later tell his family that the woman he'd been infatuated with had turned out to be nothing but a beautiful little liar.

For now, he would continue to pretend that the woman in the kitchen helping his aunt with their dinner was the same woman he had told them about.

Carlos turned when the glass door slid open and his uncle stepped out. From the look on his uncle's face, he knew there was a lecture brewing on those stern lips.

"Judith is a sweet girl," Gil began.

Carlos returned his gaze to the low mountaintops in the distant horizon, not responding.

"It's a good thing that you're taking her to the ranch house," he continued. "It's quiet enough for the two of you to spend some quality time together. Maybe then you two can work out whatever problems you seem to be having."

"*Tío*—"

Gil raised his hand. "Hey, I know it's none of my business, but I see the way you two look at each other. Or at least when you think the other isn't looking." He scoffed and shook his head. "When she looks at you, you look away. When you look at her, she looks away. It's foolishness. But I know how it is. I was young once. Just don't let it get out of control. You have a good girl there. Whatever it is that's bothering you two, either talk about it or let it go. You're only wasting precious time being angry when you could be using most of that energy making love."

Carlos cocked a brow.

Gil laughed and slapped his shoulder firmly. "This is coming from years of experience, *mijo*. And some very hard nights."

Carlos stared at his uncle, appalled and baffled all at once. Then he shook his head, a small smile curving his lips. "TMI, *tío*," he muttered.

Guillermo Delgado tended to be a blunt, straightforward man, which Carlos believed came from his time as a detective. But the older his uncle got, the more uncensored he became.

His uncle made a sound in the back of his throat. "You're a grown man now. You know what I'm talking about. Now you need to start acting like one and start settling down with a good woman who will give you some beautiful children."

"Why don't we focus on getting through dinner first?"

A few months ago, Carlos would have just ignored his uncle's words or brushed them off with a joke. A few hours ago, he couldn't have thought of anything better than raising a family and he'd had one woman in mind to start that. But that woman was a liar, a fraud, who didn't even trust him. A future between them was as nonexistent as her feelings for him.

"Just don't wait too long, Carlos. I've been ready to buy you and Tristan cufflinks for some time now."

Carlos shook his head. Wedding cufflinks for the groom was a tradition his uncle was trying to start but had only been able to buy them for his first son and only son-in-law. Unfortunately, his uncle would have to wait before Carlos would be ready for them.

"Ignore me if you want," his uncle continued. "But I'm telling you, you waste time and another man will take that beautiful girl right from under you."

A sudden burst of excitement came from inside the house and he and Gil reentered to see what had made his aunt cry out in delight.

"Oh," Rosa exclaimed as Tristan gathered her into a tight hug. "I'm so happy to have my boys with me tonight. You have to stay and eat with us," his aunt said in Spanish.

"Of course, *mama*," his cousin said, kissing her cheek. "You know I can't find anyone else who can cook like you."

Tristan came up to his father and shook his hand in greeting and Gil patted him on the back. Carlos didn't even flinch when Tristan punched his arm by way of greeting.

"So..." his cousin drawled, a gleam in his light brown eyes. "I hear you've finally brought your Judith over."

Carlos stifled a groan. He had wondered what had brought him by. The lack of surprise from his uncle at his son's unexpected visit said he was possibly the one who'd gone and spread the news. Though they were a close family unit, they didn't get together for family dinners often, something his aunt constantly complained about. Except for him and Tristan, his two other cousins were married and had their own families to tend to and it was especially rare for them to see each other in the middle of the week like this.

"Judith went to go feed the cat," his aunt said to them in Spanish. Then she turned to him as if she needed to explain. "She thought it was better to put him in the laundry room so it wouldn't get near the food."

Just then Judith came out from the back of the house and all eyes turned to her. He was surprised—and more than a little annoyed—by the small shift in his breathing at the sight of her. She stood there frozen for a second, clearly uncomfortable with the sudden attention. She glanced at him, and for a moment their gazes locked before she let hers slip away.

"You must be Judith," Tristan said, walking over to her.

Carlos noticed the transfixed expression on her face. It was the same look all women got when they met his cousin for the first time—or whenever they happened to look at him. Tristan always found it amusing, Carlos thought it ridiculous. But seeing Judith gaze up at Tristan the same way filled him with a fierce jealousy that burned in his gut. And apparently he wasn't the only one who noticed it.

"*El tiempo a nadie espera,*" Gil muttered.

Carlos spared his uncle a quick glance. *Time waits for no man,* indeed. But then again, he'd gotten them all wrong. She wasn't his future. She was nothing more than the woman who'd made him look like a fucking fool.

"It's nice to finally meet you," his cousin said. "I'm Tristan and I have to say, Carlos is a very lucky guy."

Judith smiled bashfully at his cousin and the fire in Carlos' gut intensified. His fists clenched at his sides when Tristan took her hand and placed a light kiss on the back of it.

"Thanks, Tristan. It's a pleasure to meet you."

"Oh no, angel," he replied, flashing one of his signature charm. "The pleasure's all mine."

Carlos gritted his teeth at his cousin's ridiculous flirtation. "Let go of her hand, Tristan," he snapped. "*Now.*"

Everyone turned to look at him, but he ignored their curious and amused gazes. He couldn't stop the possessiveness that was surging through him so he didn't bother. Not that he believed Tristan would try to take her from him, but Carlos didn't want to even think that Judith could possibly find his cousin attractive. Their relationship may be only a pretense at the moment, but right here, right now, she was still *his.*

Luckily, his cousin didn't try to test him. Tristan released her hand and took a step back. His aunt took that moment to pull Judith away.

"The food is almost ready," she called over her shoulders. "Don't you boys cause trouble before then."

They watched as the women disappeared into the kitchen. Knowing his aunt, she was probably not letting Judith lift a finger and just filling her with stories about him. If things had been different, he would have found it cute. But now he only wanted dinner to be done and over with so that he could tuck her away in the ranch house and away from him.

"Lovely lady," Tristan said absently, pulling him out of his thoughts.

Carlos didn't respond and thankfully his uncle steered the conversation to the renovations of his mixed-martial arts training gym.

"Tristan, since Carlos will be with Judith, it will just be you, me, and Jay tomorrow at the gym."

Tristan nodded. "I'll be there, Pop."

After his early retirement as a homicide detective, Gil had used the jiu-jitsu training he'd received growing up in Brazil to start his own MMA gym, which was now in desperate need of repairs. With money being tight, his uncle had enlisted their help with the project.

Carlos didn't like leaving his uncle in the lurch, but he didn't correct him about his assumption that he would be staying with Judith at the ranch house. Though he fully intended to bring her there, where it was safe and secluded, he had no intentions of staying. He would return to work and continue his investigation so he would have something concrete to share with David Carrone besides a bizarre tale and mystery notes. The thought of sharing Judith's story with David had crossed his mind, but before he made himself look like a gullible fool again, Carlos wanted something a bit more substantial to go on.

Gil turned to him and said sternly, "Just because I'm letting you off the hook with the gym Carlos, doesn't mean you get a pass from your *tía's* birthday party. I expect everyone to be there."

"Of course, *tío*. Where else would I be?" Carlos said.

Hopefully by then, Carlos would get this investigation wrapped up. His uncle had been planning his aunt's fifty-fifth birthday dinner for months now. She believed it was just a simple dinner with the family, but his uncle had actually rented a banquet hall and was setting up a surprise dinner with a large guest list.

Only the closest family knew this was more than just a birthday party. It was also a celebration of his aunt's fifth year as a breast cancer survivor. It wasn't something she wanted to make a big deal over so as far as she and everyone else knew, it was just a simple birthday dinner.

Eventually, his uncle took a call outside and left them alone. Tristan turned to him.

"Before you even ask, I got your request fast-tracked and should have the results of the fingerprinting by the end of the week."

Carlos shook his head. "It doesn't matter." At his cousin's confused frown, he quickly filled him in on their new discovery, including Judith's involvement. Only with Tristan could he be this open, even at the expense of his pride.

"Do you think she was really blackmailed into doing it?" Tristan eventually asked, his deep frown still in place.

Carlos shrugged. "I don't know. Hopefully, I'll know for sure once I find who it was that sent her this." He pulled out the small note and handed it to his cousin. Tristan quickly scanned it.

"What do they mean?" he asked, still staring at the cryptic note. "What were they helping her with?"

Carlos shook his head. "She wouldn't say. Only that she needs to disappear."

"Sounds like she's in some serious trouble."

Carlos grunted, not saying anything when Tristan tucked the note in his pocket. He'd already committed the number to memory and Carlos intended to pull a call log to verify what she'd told him. But with his cousin's help, he could expedite the process. "Well, she doesn't trust me enough to tell me so that I can help. And I can't force her."

Tristan was silent for a moment, then he let out a low whistle. "Just this morning, you were a man so in love, you were practically grinning from ear to ear. My, how so much can change in such little time."

"I never said I was in love," Carlos growled. But they both recognized the lie.

"Maybe she just needs some time," Tristan offered. "She looks like an innocent little lamb."

Carlos scoffed. Tristan's assessment would have been correct expect he knew better. She was just a criminal playing at being innocent.

A wolf in lamb's clothing.

Funny, how she had called *him* a wolf. It was almost a bad joke. Except he wasn't laughing.

"Seriously," Tristan continued. "There must be a good reason she got herself involved in all this."

Carlos contemplated his cousin's words then shrugged. "At this point, I don't think it really matters."

A lie was a lie and nothing could change that.

chapter 10

"Please *Señora* Rosa, let me help you." Judith followed the other woman into the kitchen, carrying a large bowl that had once been piled with yellow rice. The men in this family sure could eat.

"No, *mija*, I can do it," Rosa said, placing the dirty dishes in the sink. "You just go relax."

Judith nodded and stole away to the bathroom, once again taken by the large potted plants in almost every corner of the house. There was one thing that was indisputable about the older woman—she loved her family and she loved her plants.

Not wanting to return to where the men still sat at the table, Judith lingered in the small half-bath longer than she needed. Though Carlos' family was warm and welcoming, they were also a bit intrusive.

No, she shouldn't say that. They were just normal people asking normal questions of someone they wanted to get to know better. After her vague responses to their questions, dinner had almost turned awkward, but thankfully Tristan had filled in the silence since Carlos hadn't seemed inclined to.

Dinner had only ended a few minutes ago and soon she would be trapped in the car for another hour and half with him. Except for the occasional glare, Carlos had said nothing to her most of the evening. Thanks to his aunt, she had gotten to know a bit more about him—down to his favorite dish. But it was the sacrifice and care he'd done for his aunt during her breast cancer treatments that had really wrenched at Judith's heart, however. Apparently he had finished his enlistment in the Marine Corps when she'd been diagnosed to help the family. Judith could see the love and affection in the other woman's face whenever she spoke of him and his devotion to her.

Judith sighed. She had gotten to experience that tender side of him—a side she was already starting to miss. Against her will, she had occasionally found her gaze wandering to his, but each time she looked at him, he would fix her with a hard glare that had her turning away. It was a wonder she had managed to hold on to her resolve for this long when her insides were literally twisted in knots.

She left the sanctuary of the bathroom and headed back into the main dining room. She couldn't hide from Carlos forever.

But neither was she in any rush.

As Judith made her way down the long hallway that separated the living area and half-bathroom, she paused at the wall of family pictures. It was decorated with a variety of small and large photos, and she couldn't help but admire them. She stopped at one large family portrait hanging on the wall and smiled. It was an old one, perhaps twenty years old, but they were all wearing their Sunday finest and big smiles to go along with them. The Delgados looked like a happy, loving family. From her time with Rosa, she could see that they were as close as Carlos had mentioned.

Her eyes lingered on a young Carlos and she was amazed at the chubby young version of him with the thick, curly dark hair smiling back at her. He looked so sweet and innocent then—a complete departure from the fit and rugged man who oozed sensuality. Yet with his dark eyes and teasing smile, he managed to still resemble himself.

She continued down the wall of photos, pausing at each one. And in each one she sought out Carlos. She found one that she nominated as her favorite by far. This one only had a younger Carlos in the picture, who looked to be about six or seven years old. He was dressed in an all-white suit, with a sly smile on his young, round face. With his dark hair slicked back and one small hand in his pocket, he looked like an adorable little heartbreaker.

There were more photos of the family. Tristan's older brother and little sister were both married and raising their own families, but it was nice to put a face to the two other Delgados that had been mentioned occasionally during dinner. They were an attractive bunch, but not as attractive as their middle brother.

"We were twelve there," Tristan said, startling her out of her intense concentration.

Judith glanced up at Tristan, suddenly realizing she'd been standing there looking at a photo of him and Carlos in their preteens, clad in white karate uniforms with a green belt wrapped around them. The two young boys stood with serious expressions on their face while a proud looking Gil stood behind them, a hand on each boy's shoulder.

Tristan stood next to her, staring at the same photo. Even at his young age, he had promises of becoming a strikingly handsome man. But he'd certainly grown out of his adolescence and into a tall, well-built man. Unlike his siblings, Tristan shared his father's hazel eyes, which were framed by dark brows with a small, thin scar that ran across the left one. But despite the small imperfection he was probably the most handsome man she'd seen outside a cover magazine. She'd known Carlos had been teasing when he'd called Tristan ugly, but she hadn't realized by how much.

It didn't matter because it was Carlos who held her attention.

"You both look so serious," she said with a small grin, staring back at the picture.

Tristan laughed. "It was all for show. We were the youngest ones in our class to get our green belts and we thought we were bad asses."

She had never imagined Carlos practicing martial arts. From what she knew of the sport, which wasn't much, she couldn't picture him wearing a white robe or breaking wooden slates with his feet. "Do you guys still practice karate?"

"We spar from time to time in my dad's gym, but it's nothing like karate," Tristan said, humor in his voice. "We trained in Brazilian jiu-jitsu, which is just a different form of martial arts. My dad thought Carlos and I could use the same training since we spent most of our time after school fighting."

Judith glanced up at him with a small frown. "Each other?"

He laughed. "Well, I did have to kick his ass a few times, but we mostly fought a lot of assholes. Our junior high was about ninety percent Mexican-American and they were pretty damn prejudiced against any other Latino who wasn't, especially Colombians. When word got out that Carlos was half, he was always getting jumped. And of course, I couldn't just stand around and let my cousin get his ass kicked."

Judith frown deepened as she thought of Carlos getting bullied for something so petty. It made her angry enough to want to go back in time and beat some sense into those silly kids too.

"I'm glad your dad had you guys properly trained."

Tristan nodded. "Me too. He figured he couldn't stop them from coming after us so might as well prepare us. But since we spent most of our time at the center, it actually became less of a problem." He grinned. "And there was this one time Carlos went *loco* on this one dumbass who just wouldn't quit. He really messed up the guy's face and people finally stopped fucking with him then."

She couldn't imagine Carlos losing control and going *crazy* on anyone like that, but she wasn't sorry to hear that he'd given that bully his comeuppance.

Tristan lingered at the wall of photos with her, filling her in on the remaining few she hadn't gotten to. There was a bronze novelty frame with the Marines emblem engraved on with Carlos' military headshot held inside. Along the frame were the words that were also tattooed on his chest. *Semper Fidelis.*

Remembering his naked chest and the way it had repeatedly moved over her and against her last night made her body clench with desire.

Judith blew out a soft breath and tried to concentrate on what Tristan was telling her about a photo of a Gil standing beside a large man, wearing nothing but dark boxer shorts and a fierce frown. His size and long tattoo only added to his intimidating presence.

Though Tristan was polite and friendly in his "guided tour", she secretly got the sense he was really using this moment to feel her out. She, in turn, tried to remain open and relaxed despite the sudden tension invading her muscles.

They eventually made their way back to the sitting area and caught the tail end of an argument between Carlos and Rosa.

"We can get them on our way there, *tía,*" Carlos said with obvious frustration.

Rosa replied to him in Spanish so Judith didn't understand what she'd said but, from Carlos response, it was clear he was eager to leave soon.

"Okay, *tía,*" Carlos said with barely concealed exasperation. "But please be quick. I'd like to leave before dark."

The older woman muttered in Spanish as she headed to the kitchen. Judith felt Carlos' gaze on her and carefully averted her eyes.

"Judith, we're leaving in five minutes," he said. "You should go and get Prince ready."

She nodded, not bothering to tell him that Prince was already prepped to leave. Her poor cat had been so unnerved by the new surroundings that he'd barely bothered to eat his own meal. He kept himself huddled in the tote bag, waiting for her to take him away.

Without another word, Carlos left her and Tristan standing there. Her eyes followed him until he disappeared to the back of the room. To her embarrassment, she found Tristan watching her.

Thankfully, he didn't make any mention of it. Instead, he told her embarrassing stories about Carlos and she smiled and laughed where appropriate, wishing that she had come to meet his family without this strain between them, that things were like they had once been. That he was once again the fun-loving guy he'd been with her, the one his family seemed to adore.

"I wish I had some embarrassing high school pics to show you," Tristan said with a slow grin. "But that bastard knows how to take a picture."

Judith thought back on the photos she'd seen of him and had to agree. Even her favorite of him in the white suit, he'd been a little charmer.

With her, however, that guy was gone. She realized then she should have appreciated him when she'd had him and had been the center of his attention.

A heavy hand rested on her waist from behind, startling her. Carlos leaned close to her ear so only she could hear. "If you're done flirting with my cousin," he said tightly, "I'd like to go now."

She wanted to snap, *when was it a crime to be nice,* but she glanced over at Tristan, who was pretending not to notice their little exchange, and she let the words fizzle from her lips. Soon they wouldn't have to pretend anymore, so she would endure.

Judith pulled away from him and headed to the laundry room to get the one guy who didn't care about her past, who she had been or what she had done.

She carried the tote bag with Prince inside back to the front of the room and found Carlos carrying several large bags, the muscles on his arms flexing from the weight. The only assistance Tristan offered, was holding open the front door. Before she followed after Carlos, Judith said her goodbyes to her hosts.

"It was very nice meeting you, Judith," Rosa said, pulling her into a hug and planting a parting kiss on her cheek.

Judith echoed the same sentiments. "Thanks again for dinner," she added.

"My pleasure, *mija*."

Gil also pulled her into a warm embrace. "Don't make us wait too long to see you again, sweetie," he said. "Make sure Carlos brings you back for Rosa's birthday dinner."

With a strained smiled, Judith nodded, but her heart was in her throat. They were really so nice she felt terrible about misleading them into thinking she would come around again.

She made her way outside and found Carlos and Tristan standing by the car. The two men stopped speaking and turned to her.

She offered a friendly smile to Tristan, fully aware of Carlos and his hard glare on her. He could think what he wanted. She wasn't going to be rude just because he thought she'd set her "lecherous" eyes on his cousin.

"It was nice meeting you, Tristan."

He flashed her one of his dazzling smiles. "Don't be a stranger, angel."

With the heat of Carlos' gaze on them, she suddenly felt awkward in her parting with him. She knew it was customary in some cultures to kiss friends and family on the cheek as part of their greetings and farewells yet she tensed when Tristan reached for her hand. Whether he intended to kiss it again as he'd done earlier or pull her in for a hug, she would never know. Carlos grabbed her hand from his grasp and pulled her to his side. His hold was tight.

Tristan tried to contain a laugh. "Well, you two drive safely," he said then nodded in Carlos' direction. "I'll be in touch, man."

Judith pulled her hand out of his hard grip. "You didn't need to embarrass me like that. I was trying to be nice."

He looked down at her, clearly taken aback by her sharp retort. She was usually better at keeping her feelings to herself, but today had been long and tiring and everything, including his attitude, was trying her patience.

"Funny how you were never that nice to me when I was practically tripping myself over you," he bit out.

Judith sighed. Because it wasn't Tristan she wanted. She wanted the old Carlos back, the one who flirted outrageously with her and made her laugh. But that guy was gone and she only had herself to blame. He was obviously still angry at what she'd done and wasn't prepared to forgive her even though he was offering to help.

Her biggest mistake, however, had been in sleeping with him and creating a kaleidoscope of emotions that neither of them had been prepared for.

"How many times, Carlos?"

He frowned. "What are you talking about?"

She sighed again. "How many times do I have to say 'I'm sorry' before you stop being an asshole to me?"

His jaw clenched and he yanked the passenger door to his car open. "Get in."

They eventually got on the road and made the hour and a half long drive to his family's ranch home in silence. From what she'd gathered, it was a secluded house Gil had built as a desert getaway. It was past the Fire Valley and on the outskirts of Moapa, a place she had heard of but was only now realizing its magnificence.

The scenery that surrounded them during the drive was incredible. She had never ventured this far from the city, and the sight of the calm desert beauty was mesmerizing. Carlos had driven off the main roads and continued on to a narrower road, which seemed isolated from the rest of the world. High, rugged rocks loomed all around them, ranging from pale browns to burnt orange and rustic red.

The sun was quietly making its evening descent behind the far distant mountains, casting dusky silhouettes over the lovely landscape. It was like they were the only two people in this part of the world, driving on this long stretch of road. Except they weren't alone, not really.

In the distance, she caught sight of a large truck

parked up on one of the hills. She could vaguely make out a figure standing on the back bed of the black pickup truck. For a moment she envied the person's ability to freely bask in the evening sun and desert air and enjoy the peacefulness surrounding them.

They passed a few single-family homes along the way, each with enough distance between them to make calling them neighbors a stretch.

Judith glanced over at Carlos, who had slipped on dark shades and kept his gaze on the road. She wondered what he was thinking right now. He had been silent during their drive, not that she had expected him to draw her into conversation, but it was as if he wasn't aware of her sitting only inches away from him. He was distant, miles away from her, and for the first time she wondered if that was what others sensed from her when she withdrew into her protective shell.

The slight shifting in the tote bag brought her attention to the bundle on her lap. She widened the opening of the bag and Prince inched his head out, sniffing the air. She absently petted his head and he purred then let out a low meow.

She continued her slow petting until he nudged her hand with his furry paw. When he tried to climb further out of the bag, she held him firm.

"Oh no, you don't," she muttered.

Her stubborn cat fixed her with his wide, golden-eyed gaze and let out another meow that started out like a low growl before it ended in a loud mewl. She recognized that sound and shook her head.

"Don't even start," she said to him. "You should

have eaten when you had the chance."

"Didn't you feed him a little while ago?" Carlos asked.

Judith glanced over at him, startled, and half embarrassed that he'd caught her talking to her cat as if the animal understood her. Though there were times she believed Prince understood more than he let on.

"Yes, but he didn't eat," she replied. "He was too shy."

Carlos glanced down at her lap. "That chatterbox?"

She smiled at the unexpected amusement in his voice. "Yeah, Prince pretends like he's this cool cat, but he's really an introvert like me."

He briefly turned his gaze to her but said nothing, and she wondered if she had broken that lighthearted moment between them.

"How long have you had him?"

"Not long. A little under a year." Then she proceeded to tell him about the condition in which she had found him, which only angered her to think people could be so cruel.

"He's such a sweetie," she finished, rubbing his furry head. "I don't know why anyone would lock him in a cage and put him out like he was trash."

"People are capable of doing shitty things," Carlos said simply.

She stiffened at his words. Was he including her in that group of people? But his next words surprised her—and oddly, warmed her.

"He's lucky you found him."

She smiled down at her cat as he sat on her lap, his ears the only thing peeking out of the tote.

And I'm lucky you found me.

She glanced over at Carlos, knowing those words hadn't been meant for Prince. Carlos had come into her life and disrupted it beyond anything she had ever experienced. She had always valued her quiet, simple life, but now she found that she wanted the distractions, the unpredictability. She wanted him.

The question now was did he still want her.

He glanced over at her when she continued her staring. "What?"

Ignoring the butterflies fluttering in her stomach, she blurted out the first line he'd tried on her. "If sexy was a crime, you'd be guilty as charged."

A dark brow rose behind his shades, then he shook his head and to her small delight, chuckled. Though he didn't respond to her attempted flirtation, at least his stoic expression was now relaxed and he didn't seem so far away anymore.

That was a start…

They finally made it to their destination and she was surprised by how isolated it really was. She was also pleasantly amazed to find that there were trees and shrubs surrounding the single-story ranch home. It was like they were in their own little oasis and for the first time she looked forward to their time here. Maybe it would give them a chance to repair things between them.

Carlos pulled into the paved driveway of the long, wood-structured home, which had an old, rustic feel to it, yet the large windows gave it a bit of a modern look. It was certainly not what she had expected, but she liked it.

Except for the darkness.

The sun had completely left the sky, leaving behind a purplish glow as night moved in to take its place. There were no city lights or noise and the surrounding dusk gave the low, beautiful home an ominous feel.

"Wait here," Carlos said as he got out of the car. He went into the house and within a few minutes, light glowed through the windows. He came back to the car and opened her door. "It's not as stuffy in there as I expected," he said. "But it'll take a little time for the air conditioner to circulate."

Inside the house was more modernized than she'd expected. Furniture was sparse but comfortable and appeared solid. The kitchen was large and also well supplied with a variety of modern appliances. She realized she had expected something a bit more antiquated, maybe even with a lone tea kettle on the stove. But, to her relief, everything was contemporary and cozy.

She placed Prince and her luggage in one of the three spare bedrooms and went to the kitchen where Carlos was unpacking the bags he'd gotten from his aunt. She realized then it was a variety of food things and was grateful for the woman's consideration. She hadn't even thought about the place not being properly stocked.

Judith went over and helped Carlos unpack. He had removed his shades and when his dark gaze locked with hers, she smiled tentatively at him. His eyes took on that fierce glow that she sometimes found unnerving and she glanced away.

In silence, they unpacked the bags, moving stiffly

around each other, careful not to touch.

"I really like your family," she said, wanting to break the strained, awkward silence between them. If they were going to stay here together, she would force him to at least have a normal conversation with her.

"They like you too," he said vaguely.

They fell into awkward silence again. It wasn't long before they were done putting everything in their place and stood staring at each other. His dark gaze was intense but guarded. Yet with every second, the cold indifference on his face began to melt, replaced by a flicker of desire. She wanted to fan those flames, but uncertainty kept her from going to him. She couldn't be sure he wouldn't pull away from her as he'd done only hours ago in her apartment.

It was safer to just wait for him. And she desperately wanted him to come to her as he'd done before.

Carlos, I need you.

He must have heard her internal plea, or read the need in her eyes, because his nostrils flared and the muscles in his jaw flexed. She took an uncertain step toward him. "Carlos," was all she could manage.

And that was enough.

With a harsh sound, he closed the gap between them and hauled to her him. She wrapped her arms around his neck as his lips claimed hers. Her body fell against his in what felt like a reprieve. The kiss was hard and fierce, as if their lips had been starved for each other.

He gripped her bottom then lifted her high against him, without breaking contact. She felt the hard edge of the counter before he sat her down on it. Everything was moving fast, but she reveled in his fierceness, his passion. His hands slid down her waist then came up to mold over her breast. Her nipples beaded and pushed firmly against his palm and she leaned into him, seeking out his fervent caress. He growled low in his throat and brought his hands inside her shirt, pushing the cups of her bra aside and gently kneading her aching breasts. She moaned into his mouth, her body eager for his touch, his possession.

She clutched at his thick shoulders as he kissed her chin and jaw and down to the most sensitive part of her neck. His thin beard softly scraped her flushed skin and the pressure of his lips sent small shivers coursing through her.

"No puedo coger suficiente de ti, muñeca," he murmured against her neck, flicking his warm tongue against her skin. He rubbed his thumb across her budded nipple and she released a shuddering sigh.

Wanting to give him the same electric sensations he was giving her, she trailed her lips over his chin before kissing his jaw and down his throat. His low groan was deep and it fueled her own arousal. He captured her lips once again with and she lost her herself in the pleasure of his kiss, the flames of desire licking through her body.

But it was quickly doused when he began pulling up her shirt. The cool air lightly brushed against her heated body and she pushed away from him, yanking at the thin shirt. But he refused to release it. Instead, his grip tightened around it and for the briefest of moments, they wrestled over the delicate material.

Panicked, she tore her lips from his. "Carlos! *Stop!*"

He reacted as if she'd struck him and released the now twisted material as if he'd been burned. Their breathing was labored and he stared at her with a mixture of longing, anger, and regret. He carefully pushed away from her, his body rigid. Turning his back to her, he ran his hands through his hair and muttered a curse.

She slid down from the counter and quickly adjusted her clothes. Suddenly he turned to her and the haunted look on his face made her regret her sudden outburst. She started toward him and reached for his arm.

"Carlos…"

"Don't," he interrupted, effortlessly slipping his arm from her grasp. He took another step back. "Damn it, don't look at me like that," he snapped. "You don't want me to touch you so I won't."

She wrapped trembling arms around herself and shook her head. "It's not like that. It's just…"

"What?" he barked when she couldn't continue. "What is it with you? One minute you're hot for me, the next you're playing hard to get. Are you waiting for me to beg for it or do I need to pay to have you again? Which is it? 'Cause you're really not worth the trouble."

A rush of pain flooded her at his harsh words and for a moment she could only shake her head at herself for believing he was different. "If you're trying to hurt me, Carlos, you just did."

His dark eyes became as hard as flint. "Then I guess that makes us even."

She sucked in a sharp breath. How had she hurt him? She understood that he was angry with her, but how had she caused him pain?

He cursed again then grabbed his keys from the counter. "I need to get out of here," he muttered.

She frowned as he started toward the door. She followed him and he had the door open before she could say anything. He paused then turned back to her.

"Don't even think about leaving this house," he said tersely. "There's no one for miles and you're only going to get yourself hurt. I'll check up on you later."

Check up on her? "Wait. You're leaving me here?" she asked, incredulous.

"Isn't that what you wanted?" he said, studying her closely. "A place to hide?"

She drew up, her back stiffening. He made it sound as if that was what she had been doing all along.

Isn't it?

"But where are you going?" she asked quietly, ignoring the mocking words that echoed in her head. "When will you be back?"

His expression was unreadable when he bit out, "I'm going to do my job and fix your mess." With that, he firmly shut the door behind him.

Judith stood there, unmoving, for what seemed like forever.

But when will you be back?

chapter 11

"When Jay referred you to me, I didn't figure you for a quitter."

Carlos clenched his jaw. If David Carrone was trying to get a rise out of him, it was working.

"I'm not. But I'm man enough to admit when I'm in over my head."

Yet, it wasn't in his nature to admit defeat. Hell, Carlos couldn't remember ever giving up on anything. But how was he to take pride in his work when he was giving up so much of his integrity? He needed to accept the fact that he wasn't cut out to fulfill the responsibilities for this job.

The problem, however, was David's refusal to accept his resignation.

"Do you want to tell me what this is really all about?"

Carlos leaned forward in his seat, meeting his boss' intense scrutiny across the large desk. "It's nothing personal, Carrone," he said evenly. "I just don't think I'm cut out for this. I'm willing to stay through the end of the month until you find someone to replace me."

David released a heavy sigh and sat back in his seat. "Look, I know these past few days have been shit and we're no closer to finding this bastard, but no one is blaming you for any of it, if that's what you think. And I certainly don't want you to quit because of it."

Carlos glanced at the large windows behind David. Though it was late Friday afternoon, the sun still shone brightly, and dusk was still hours away. Carlos, didn't want to drag this out for the rest of the afternoon. He'd already made up his mind. The last couple of days since he'd left Judith at the ranch house had given him some time to think about everything—especially about the situation he currently found himself in. David Carrone was a decent guy and Royal Courts was a good company that had recently suffered under a corrupt security chief. The last thing Carlos wanted was to leave behind the same legacy.

What he was doing with Judith violated so many of their policies, but deep down, in a place where remnants of his feelings still lived for her, he couldn't possibly let anything happen to her, no matter what she'd done. She was a liar, and maybe even a thief, but that didn't mean he wanted to see her treated like some low-life criminal. Despite everything, he still cared about her and would do whatever he could to keep her safe. He had told her she wasn't worth the trouble and that had been a damn lie. She was worth everything.

And that realization made it impossible for him to continue working at Royal Courts.

"Tell you what," David continued. "Why don't you take some time to clear your head and think about it?"

Carlos shook his head. "I've already made up my mind."

"Then a few days off won't change it," he argued. "And if you're still determined to leave us in the lurch when you get back, then I won't stop you."

Carlos raised a brow, not at all swayed by his boss' attempt at a guilt-trip. Though Carlos was confident his team could manage without him for a few days, he didn't feel right leaving them while they were in the middle of implementing important security changes. Then again, there was the new Cyber Security Specialist starting next week that David had brought on to facilitate and monitor some of the new changes around the department. It was a point neither of them had bothered to openly address. His pride had stung from knowing that his boss had brought on someone else for him to "collaborate" with to improve the security around the casino resort.

But Carlos had ignored the inadvertent insult, and had continued with the pointless task of questioning those who had appeared in the footage. It was clear to Carlos now that *both* executives didn't fully trust him or his ability to do his job—and the irony was that they were right not to. Between Judith's mistrust and the executives' doubts, he wasn't sure why he even bothered.

Your heart is too big, Carlito.

His aunt's words echoed in his head. She would affectionately remind him of that on occasion and at times, he thought it was a compliment, something to be proud of. But now he realized it was probably his biggest flaw—he cared too damn much.

"All right," Carlos finally said. He wouldn't belabor this discussion any further. If David wanted him to take some time off, then he would. But when he got back, he fully intended to make his resignation official.

"I'll take a week to think about it," he continued. "But I'm telling you it won't change anything."

David sat back in his seat, his expression neutral. "Enjoy the time off," he said simply. "I'll see you when you get back."

Carlos inclined his head and got up and left the office, intending to make the most of his time off starting now. Neither he nor Tristan was any closer to finding out who it was that had sent Judith the note. The only thing they'd managed to find out was that the cell phone she had called had been a disposable one and had indeed been activated the day and time of the break-in.

But before he could commit himself fully these pass two days to finding this mystery woman, he had one woman he needed to check on. Enough time had passed for the guilt of his last, angry words to lessen.

Yet still, it felt as though no time had passed at all.

****

Three days.

Judith hated that she had been counting the days, but it was now Saturday afternoon and she was growing tired of having no one to talk to except Prince. Her cat was tired of her company as well, preferring to go off to his new favorite hiding place behind the couch facing the window, until he was hungry or wanted his head scratched.

Judith washed the few dishes in the sink, dried them

and placed them back into the cabinet. She had been meticulous with her use of things around the ranch house. She never let it slip her mind that she was a guest here and whatever she used, she either replaced or properly disposed of.

It was a lovely place with enough to keep a family of his size comfortable, and with the large whirlpool tub in the back of the house, there was plenty of opportunity to make the place a potential romantic getaway.

But for her, it was just a place to hide.

On her first night there, she had remembered to call Mary and let her know that she had found a safe place to wait until they got everything set for her new…move. The woman had told her to start thinking of a new name and Judith had drawn a blank. Who was she supposed to pretend to be now?

As she finished tidying around the kitchen, she couldn't help but think about the early morning phone call she'd had with Carlos. That had been the first time he'd called her since he'd left her here Wednesday night. Their exchange had been abrupt and his tone had been far from engaging.

"I'll be by later tonight to check in on you. Do you need anything?"

"Um, no. I don't think so."

"If you think of anything, let me know before five."

"Oh, wait."

Silence, then, *"Yeah."*

"Prince needs more cat food. He likes anything with salmon."

"Okay, I'll pick some up." More silence. *"Anything else?"*

"No. Thanks."

He'd ended the call after that, as distant and cold as he had been when she'd answered the call. Their exchange had literally taken two minutes and in that short time, she had finally come to the realization that he wanted nothing more to do with her beyond getting this mess settled. His only objective now where she was concerned was finding the woman who had put her up to the security breach so he could either validate her story or have her arrested.

The possibility that he might not find the woman, worried her, but it wasn't what kept her up at night. Knowing that Carlos now hated her—that she would never get back the man who had been passionate yet tender with her—was what led to her sleepless nights and made her heart ache. For the first time in years, she wanted more out of life, more *from* herself, than merely existing. And she embraced those desires.

But it had been Carlos who had sparked those cravings, and now she wouldn't be able to explore this new awareness of herself with him. He had given her a peek of what it was like to experience true joy and she wanted it again. But, with him, it was over.

The sound of a car coming up to the house pulled her out of her melancholy thoughts and she went to the wide window. Pushing aside the light curtains, she was surprised to see Tristan exiting the silver SUV. She opened the door for him as he walked up to the house. In his hand was a manila envelope.

"Hi Tristan," she began. "If you're looking for Carlos, he isn't here."

He flashed her one of his captivating smiles. "I

know. I actually came here to see you."

Frowning, Judith stepped back as he entered the house. They stood by the door, staring at each other and she was a bit uneasy as to what he wanted to see her for.

"Carlos doesn't know I'm here, and out of respect for my cousin, and for my own protection," he added amusingly, "I'm not going to touch you. But I hope you don't mind that I'm here."

She slowly shook her head, not sure if he was teasing her or not. Why would she be? This was his father's house after all.

They made their way to the living room and she offered him something to drink.

He grinned. "You're a sweetheart," he said, placing the envelope on the center table. "But I'm fine, thanks."

Judith sat down beside him, since it was the only sofa in the living area, and asked him the nagging question that had been swirling in her head since he'd walked through the door.

"What did you want to see me about?"

He stared at her, silent for a moment. "You know, when Carlos told us about you, we all knew you were *the one*," he began. "He's never talked about a girl the way he talked about you. Hell, I don't think he's ever told my parents about any girl he hadn't been dating for at least six months."

She continued staring at him, not sure where he was going with this. "Carlos is a great guy."

His lips quirked. "Yeah, he can be a charmer, especially with the ladies. But I also know he can be a real asshole when he needs to be."

For some reason, Judith wanted to jump to Carlos' defense, but having been the recipient of that side of him, she didn't disagree. She also didn't want to talk about him with his cousin. Not like this, anyway.

"What is this about Tristan?"

His expression grew serious. He picked up the envelope and looked at it. "You know, when Carlos brought you by the other day, I could see why he was taken with you. And when he told me about what you did, I understood why he was pissed off and hurt."

Judith froze for a moment. So he knew. *Of course he knew.* He and Carlos were close.

"I didn't mean to hurt him," she whispered. Before, she hadn't understood how she had managed to do that. But these past three days had left her with plenty of time to think about Carlos and what he must have thought after he'd come to her apartment to find her packing. Maybe if she had answered his calls that morning, maybe if she had assured him that their one night together had meant more to her than she could say, he wouldn't have felt so betrayed.

Tristan's solemn, direct gaze was unnerving but she stared back at him, unflinching.

"I believe you," he finally said. "Though looks can be deceiving, I can see you're not a bad person. And my parents are in love with you," he said with a small smile. "But my family is small and we're really close and that makes me very protective of them."

Judith swallowed. He'd mentioned before that he had been a police officer and a sinking feeling came over her as she glanced down at the envelope in his hands.

"So when someone comes into my family," he continued, "I want to know exactly who they're dealing with. And I want them to know too." He opened the envelope and pulled out the documents. "But they don't know who you really are, do they Abigail?"

Judith stiffened. Tense silence stretched between them. Tristan stared at her closely, his hazel eyes almost hawk-like as he watched her, and she slowly shook her head.

"Please don't call me that," she said hollowly. "My name's Judith."

He glanced down at the document. "Twenty-six years ago, you were adopted by Margaret Bellamy. You were barely a year old when she got you and you legally became Abigail Judith Bellamy."

Fear and anxiety kept her frozen in her seat.

"You spent most of your life in San Francisco before you went to UCLA. Your mother passed away shortly after but after four years, you graduated and got a job as a dance teacher at a local junior high. But then that's where it all stops." He fell silent as he glanced up from the document. "I don't know if Carlos told you what I do, but I make my living getting information and finding people," he said quietly. "Before Carlos found out about what you'd done, he had me run the prints on the flash drive. Now, imagine my surprise when the results came in and the names didn't match. At first I was going to call Carlos and let him in on this little mystery, but my cousin is in love with you and it would really piss me off to see him get hurt a second time by you. That's why I wanted to first find out what game you were playing."

Judith shook her head again, thoroughly humiliated by his frank words. "I-I'm not playing any games."

He sighed. "I know," he said. "I also know about Kenneth Tate and what happened five years ago." He studied her closely. If he was waiting for a reaction, he would be disappointed.

"I know about the protective order you had against him," he continued. "And I think I have a good idea as to why you changed your name and decided to go into hiding."

He didn't know. No one truly did.

Tristan paused before he continued. "What I don't understand is why you haven't told Carlos any of this."

"Because...Abigail Bellamy is dead," she whispered. "She died in a car accident five years ago."

Tristan's eyes softened and Judith glanced away. She didn't want his pity. His acceptance, perhaps. Maybe even his understanding, but not pity.

"You know, I became a cop to follow in my dad's footsteps," he began. "I was working my ass off trying to make detective, like him, but then I got this one case..." He fell silent, his gaze staring straight ahead, as if that moment was right now replaying itself. "I got called into a domestic disturbance of a man who had violated the rules of his custody and gone to see his wife and son without supervision. We were called in when he refused to leave the house." He released a heavy sigh. "Long story short, the man turned out to be more dangerous than the courts realized."

Judith's brows pulled together. Just like Ken. They

had given her the protective custody, but in the end, it had done nothing. He was more dangerous than even she had realized.

"What happened?" she asked softly when he didn't continue.

Tristan turned to her, his expression blank. "He murdered his wife and his son then turned the gun on himself. His son was two."

Judith sucked in her breath and tears sprang in her eyes. How could anyone kill their own child? She hadn't cried much these past few years, but this... this broke her heart.

"After that," Tristan continued, "nothing I did seemed important. What should have been a simple arrest had turned out to be vicious murder-suicide with a—" He shook his head, running his hand through his dark brown hair. "Anyway, that case stayed with me for a long time until I could think of nothing else. I wanted to forget that whole thing, but it was impossible, so I eventually left the force." He grabbed her hand and gave it a gentle squeeze. "I get it," he said simply. "Believe me, I get how you feel. That day, I wasn't inside that house, but the nightmare of hearing those gunshots...it stayed with me."

Judith let the single tear roll down her cheek. He squeezed her hand again.

"Other than Carlos, no one knows why I really quit the force. Not even my father, who'd seen enough shit to force him into early retirement. But with Carlos, I knew I could trust him to listen and understand how I was feeling. He didn't try to talk me out of leaving. He didn't try to rationalize how I was feeling. He just listened and helped me get through the worst year of my life." Tristan released her hand and handed her the file. She regarded it for a moment, then took the documents.

"I won't tell him about this," Tristan said. "I think it should all come from you."

Maybe he was right, but she wasn't ready yet.

"Thank you," she said quietly, relieved that he wouldn't take what he knew about her to Carlos.

"But," he added with emphasis, "if he asks me about the results of the prints, which he hasn't yet, I won't lie to my cousin."

Judith glanced back down at the files then nodded jerkily. "I understand. Just…give me some time?"

Tristan didn't offer his agreement, but neither did he push the subject.

"My cousin loves you. Talk to him. You'll be surprised how far he would go to protect you. He's already put his job on the line by bringing you here and he doesn't even know half of what I do."

Judith's hands tightened on the files. She hadn't thought about Carlos' obligations to Royal Courts. She would hate for him to jeopardize his career just because he'd offered to help her instead of bringing her in. But the way things were between them now, Tristan was wrong. Carlos could barely stand to look at her, much less be in the same room with her.

"H-he doesn't want me anymore," she whispered thickly. She had spent the past few days coming to terms with that, but it still hurt to acknowledge it.

Tristan shook his head, a small grin forming on his lips. "You'd be surprised at how bad he still wants you.

My cousin's a sensitive guy. Something I've tried to beat out of him, but he is who he is," he said with a shrug. "I just think you broke his heart a little."

Another tear slipped from her eye and she quickly dashed it away. "I didn't want to do that."

He gave her arm a gentle squeeze. "You can trust Carlos, Judith. Just talk to him. Then you can stop running."

chapter 12

Carlos pulled up to the ranch house, irritated by the sudden eagerness that welled up in him. It wasn't enough that he hadn't been able to stop thinking about her these past few days, now he was acting as if she would throw her arms around him the minute he walked through the door.

He shook his head and got out of the car. There was no way she missed him as much as he'd missed her and he needed to remember that.

Grabbing the shopping bags from the back seat, he headed toward the house. Though sunlight still streaked the now graying sky, it was still later than he'd intended to come over. But he'd gotten himself distracted at the store, getting more than she'd asked for. She'd simply asked for cat food but he'd come bearing three heavy bags of…stuff.

She must have heard him pull up because the door opened just as he began to bound up the short steps leading to the house. She stood at the opening, her curvaceous figure silhouetted by the light inside. He stopped directly in front of her and they simply stared at each other for what seemed like forever.

"Hi," she whispered.

One simple word and he wanted to drop the bags and haul her into his arms. Except, he wouldn't be satisfied with just holding her. He wanted to feel her soft, full lips again, wanted her naked beneath him, with his cock nestled deep inside her.

There was a look in her eyes that almost resembled longing, but her reaction the last time he'd touched her was still fresh in his mind. He had misread her response before, he wouldn't do it again. Seeing desire in her, where there was none, was just another of his shortcomings.

The weight of the bags pulled him back to reality and shifted them in his hands. "These are heavy."

"Oh, sorry." She took a step back and he walked past her into the house, vaguely aware of her light, sweet scent.

She followed him into the kitchen where he deposited the bags on the counter.

"Thanks for this," she said quietly.

He nodded then dug into one of the bags, emptying them onto the counter. She peeked into the other bag then slid him a quick glance. He'd bought things he'd thought she would like based on the items he'd noticed in her apartment. He figured she'd want more than the spicy foods and doughy snacks his aunt had packed.

Like a repeat from the other day, they began putting away the food stuff. In silence. There was one last bag and she pulled out the cans of cat food, which was the same stuff he'd seen her feed Prince the other day. In that same bag, there was a small puzzle box he'd also purchased.

She just stood there staring down at it and he suddenly felt awkward about the last minute purchase but he ignored it. If she thought it was stupid, he wouldn't care.

He didn't realize he was staring at her, waiting for her reaction, until she glanced up. Her eyes were wide and suspiciously bright, but he couldn't tell what she was thinking.

"This was sweet of you, Carlos," she finally said.

He shrugged. "It was on sale." But he was secretly pleased that she was pleased. "And I figured you'd want something to do to pass the time."

She smiled then. "Thanks. I think even Prince is getting bored of playing with me."

Without thinking, he returned her smile. Not because of what she'd said, but because of the way the small action lit up her face. Everything she did mesmerized him—and turned him on. He forced himself to look away as he put the last few items in the cabinets. "Where is the little guy anyway?"

"Probably sleeping in his second favorite hiding place. Under the bed."

The last word brought up images of both of them on top of that bed, rising and straining together. Almost everything she said or did reminded him of that night, reminding him that he hadn't gotten his fill of her. Agitation and frustration began to build in him and awkward silence fell between them.

He needed to leave soon. Either that or he wouldn't be able to stop himself from pulling her into his arms.

"If you need anything else, give me a call," he said,

reaching into his back pocket and pulling out his keys.

She frowned. "You're leaving?"

He nodded curtly and headed toward the door. She surprised him by stepping in front of him.

"But you just got here."

His brows pulled together and he stifled an exasperated sigh. "And now I'm leaving."

"But I was...I was hoping you would stay."

He crossed his arms over his chest. *What game was she trying to play?* She'd already made a fool of him once, he wasn't about to let it happen again.

"Why?"

She stared at him, her eyes wide and lost. "Because I don't... It gets lonely here at night."

He cocked a brow sardonically. "This is what you wanted, Judith," he said, not at all sympathetic to her sudden plight. "Besides, you have Prince."

She shook her head, not looking at him. "You know what I mean."

"Actually, I don't," he said, staring down at her. From her embarrassed hesitation, he had an idea but refused to interpret what she wanted from him. He was getting tired of guessing what it was she was thinking or feeling.

"What is it you really want, Judith?"

She kept her gaze on his chin. Then, without warning, she slowly walked up to him and placed her hand on his abdomen. He sucked in his breath and instinctively, the muscles there tightened. His arms fell to his side and he kept his gaze on her bent head as she moved her hands lower and began undoing the buckle of his belt. He stood completely still, his body reacting to her closeness and to the feel of her fingers brushing against him.

Part of him wanted to let her to continue but instead he cupped her chin and raised her face to his. "What are you doing?" he asked quietly.

Her eyes were wide as she looked up at him searchingly. "I want to...I want you to..." She let her words falter and he quickly grew impatient.

"To what?"

She paused for the smallest of seconds then leaned up and kissed him. It was a soft, tender kiss that invited him to take the lead.

And damn it, he was only a man.

The kiss soon turned hungry and fierce, her fingers clutching at the material of his shirt. She parted her soft lips for him and he swept his tongue inside, tasting the subtle sweetness there. But this wasn't enough. He wanted to feel her naked skin pressed along his. He wanted the soft warmth of her hands to touch his heated flesh.

But he had no clue what she wanted or why she was doing this. Clasping his hands around her hips, he tore his lips from hers and pushed her away from him. What air he could draw was labored and rough. He'd be damned if he let her use sex to control him.

"What the hell is this, Judith?" he growled, grasping her arms and giving her a small shake. "I don't need you to be my whore tonight."

Her sharp gasp was like thunder in his ear and the crushed look on her face almost stopped his heart. Her hurt gaze slipped away from his as silence settled heavily between them in the kitchen. She pushed away from him and he cursed.

"Judith, wait." He grabbed her arm but she tugged again at her arms. "I'm sorry," he said, pulling her back to him and holding her firm. "I'm sorry, okay?"

She stopped her short struggle and he pulled her closer to him, taking in her light scent, wishing things were different between them. That he wasn't filled with this crazy lust and bitterness whenever he came near her.

"No more games," he said. "Just tell me what you want?"

"I'm not trying to get anything from you, Carlos," she said, her eyes fixed on his chest. "I just wanted you to…"

He cupped her chin and lifted her gaze to his. His eyes bore down on hers. "Make love to you?"

She nodded jerkily.

"Then say it."

She took a deep breath and stared at him directly. "I…I want to be with you, Carlos. Please make love to me."

She didn't get out another word. If she wanted him, even just a little, he wasn't going to turn her away. He brought his mouth down to hers, slanting his lips over hers and taking in everything she had to give. The kiss was demanding and urgent, and he wanted more.

He pulled away from her and tugged his shirt over his head, never looking away from her. Desire flushed over her smooth brown face and her soft, full lips were parted slightly. In that moment she was breathtaking.

Before she could react, he grabbed her shirt and pulled it over her head. She wrapped her arms around her middle, but his eyes were drawn to the swells of her breasts peeking over the small trim of black lace in her bra. There was nothing more erotic than that tease of flesh.

He took a deep breath to steady his racing heart, but it did little to help. His hands itched to touch her while his cock strained to be inside her.

But there was an unnatural stillness in her. He could sense the rigidity in her as she stood there with her arms wrapped tightly around herself. She was already losing the fire that had just burned brightly within her moments ago. He cupped her chin and lifted her face to his, unclear of what was going on inside that head of hers. The last thing he ever wanted, was for her to feel obligated into sleeping with him.

He rubbed the pad of his thumb over her smooth jaw. "No, don't look at me like that. I still want you, but we don't have to do this," he murmured, though his body protested those words vehemently. "I'll still stay the night if you want me to."

Her eyes glistened and she moved her gaze to his chest. "I want this," she whispered. "I want *you*."

Her arms dropped to her side. With the surge of lust pumping through him from her words, it took him a moment to notice the dark, angry marks slashed across her stomach and sides. He frowned and glanced up at her. She kept her gaze on his chest. There were a few faded marks on her lower abdomen, which were deliberate and precise and he recognized them as surgical scars.

He reached out and lightly traced the largest of them that crossed just below her breast and down to the opposite end of her hips. Was this why she didn't want him to see her in the light? Why she had pulled away from him the other night—and was emotionally pulling away from him now?

"What did this?" he asked gently.

She placed a hand over his to still his movements. "It was…I was in a car accident a long time ago."

He stared down at her then hooked his fingers inside the band of her jeans and pulled her toward him. She looked up at him then, startled.

"You have nothing to be embarrassed about," he said, kissing her in a way that told her how much he wanted her. He moved his lips over her cheek, her jaw, until some of the stiffness melted away from her. "You're still very beautiful, Judith. And I still want to make love to you."

In response to that, she unsnapped the button of his jeans and lowered the zipper. His entire body tensed with anticipation as she moved her hands inside, slowly stroking him. He sucked in a sharp breath and he closed his eyes for a moment, letting the intense pleasure flow through him. He grew harder, pulsing against her soft palms. Her gentle strokes wrenched a deep groan from him and he knew he would lose it now if he didn't get her into bed.

He pulled away from her tormenting touch, and drew her to him for a fierce kiss. Without breaking the fevered embrace, he lifted her to him and her legs instinctively wrapped around his hips. He started toward the darkened bedroom, letting his instinct guide him. She kept her arms around his neck as he guided them to the bed.

He pulled away long enough to strip off his pants and removed the rest of her clothes. She tried to pull the sheet over her, and he knew it was to hide herself, her scars, from him.

"Don't," he murmured, grabbing the sheets and pulling them away. "Let me see you." He didn't want her hiding from him ever again.

Positioned between her legs, his cock straining painfully between them, he could make out her full breasts and round hips in the dark room. He ran his hands over the tops of her smooth thighs, enjoying the feel of her soft skin.

Moving his hand between her legs, he slid his finger into her and he gritted his teeth against the intense pleasure of her damp, snug heat clenching around his finger. She grabbed his biceps and bit down on her lower lip, cutting off a low moan as she lifted her hips toward this thrusting finger. He imagined the same, soft pulsations around him, and his cock jerked. He wanted to do more, but he'd waited too long to have her again.

With a harsh groan, he hooked his arms under her legs and pulled her to him. Guiding his hard shaft into her, he watched as it slowly disappeared inside her. Her inner muscles instantly clamped around him and he shuddered from the pleasure of it. He fell over her, bracing himself on his elbows as he thrust into her as deeply as he could get. Her soft moans rang in his ear and he held still above her.

"You feel so good, *muñeca*," he whispered hoarsely, placing light kisses on her brow, her cheek, down to the corner of her lips. Even the pressure of her breasts against his bare chest sent prickles down his back and to his tight balls.

He buried his face in the crook of her neck as he began to inch his way out of her slowly before pushing back in. His breathing was labored as he continued his leisurely thrusting. The intense pleasure of her tight body clasped around him almost bordered on pain and a harsh groan escaped him. He passed the tip of his tongue over the base of her neck, then made his way back to her lips. Her hands clutched his shoulders as he teased and tasted her with every lick and pull of her soft lips.

He tore his lips away and rested his forehead on hers. Her eyes were closed but the fire between their bodies blazed bright. With every thrust, she quivered and clenched around him, bringing him that much closer to sweet release.

Not yet, he told himself. *Not without her.*

"Baby," he said thickly on a deep thrust, "look at me."

Her lids fluttered open and it was there in her eyes that he saw it—her distance. Her detachment. He stilled his movements and hovered above her.

She may have been rising to meet his every thrust, her body clenching fiercely around him, but she was still keeping a part of herself hidden away. Out of his reach. She wasn't connecting or sharing or getting lost in sweet oblivion with him.

She may have been physically with him, but she wasn't truly *with* him.

And he wouldn't accept that.

With painful effort, he pulled out of her tight body

and fell to his back. He threw his arm over his eyes, trying to control his raging lust, but his damp shaft strained toward his navel with unspent need, begging for release.

"Carlos?"

He turned toward her low, confused voice. She sat up on the bed, the sheet once again clutched close to her. Her hair was tousled and her eyes were wide, different from the woman who had lain there while he'd been consumed by her, trying to get as deep in her as he could possibly get. But he'd been in that alone—getting lost in the pleasure of their union by himself.

With his jaw clenched, he turned away from her. He placed his arms behind his head and stared fixedly at the dark ceiling. "What do you want, Judith? From me? From *this*? Huh? Because I'm tired of guessing with you."

Silence followed and he wasn't all that surprised.

"Okay, fine, then I'll tell you what I *don't* want," he said harshly. "I don't want you to give me the use of your body, Judith. I don't want to *fuck* you. I want to *make love* with you. I need you to be with me when I'm inside you. I need us to be in it *together*. Can you understand that?"

She tensed beside him. He was still painfully erect and wanted nothing more than to slide back into her and find his release. But he kept his hands behind his head, fighting for control.

"When we first made love, we were... I don't even think there's a word to describe it," he continued quietly. "With every stroke I felt all of you. You were *with me* in that moment. That's what I want again."

He glanced over at her. Even in the dark room, he could see that her eyes were now closed. Again, locking her thoughts and feeling inside herself. Away from him. He gritted his teeth in frustration.

"I want you to open more than just your legs for me, Judith. I want it like it was before. I want us to *connect*. I want you to *want me* because I want *all of you*, damn it."

He turned away from her again, but not before he saw the single tear slip down her cheek. Though he wanted desperately to pull her into his arms, he didn't dare. She would have to be the one to come to him. He was done chasing after her.

He tensed in surprise when she tentatively placed a hand on his chest. The surge of desire that passed through him from the light touch was not unexpected.

"I *do* want you, Carlos," she murmured, then crawled over him and straddled him.

His cock jerked against her heated flesh, but he placed his hands on her thighs, not sure if she understood that he meant every word of what he'd just said.

"Judith..." he began then sucked in a sharp breath when she grabbed his rigid shaft and guided him into her. A loud hiss ripped through his teeth and it took every ounce of willpower he possessed not to come into her right then.

She rocked her hips downward until he was lodged deep inside her. She leaned forward for a slow, soft kiss and he brought his hands to her waist to hold her against him as he deepened it.

She pulled up and rode him slowly, her dark, shoulder-length hair curtaining the sides of her beautiful face. He stared up at her and brushed the strands aside. With each rise and fall of her hips, they both gasped and shuddered from the intense pleasure.

But they never broke eye contact, and together they experienced the bliss of being one. Just as he wanted it.

When it became too much, when he knew their pleasure would soon overtake them, he rolled her beneath him and held still, savoring that moment. She brought her hand up to his cheek and he turned his head toward her warm palm and kissed her hand.

"I love you, Judith."

He spoke the words in Spanish yet her expression softened with what looked like understanding and her eyes glistened. He slowly thrust into her again, lost in the dark pools of her misty gaze. They moved together, completely in sync, as they chased away all the hurt and pain between them…until there was nothing left but their hearts laid bare.

In the still of the night, with just their cries of pleasure, they found their release together. He held her close and didn't let go even as he felt the wetness of her tears against his neck.

****

Judith kept her arms wrapped tightly around his neck, waiting for the onslaught of emotions to pass. She didn't know how long they stayed like that, but she refused to let him go.

She never wanted him to pull away from her like that again.

It had felt like a core part of her had been severed when he'd pulled out of her. She realized now how important he was to her and how close she had come to driving him away.

When he eventually rolled to his side, she moved with him, keeping her face buried in the crook of his neck. He held her to him and they now lay on their sides, holding each other close, and she wanted them to stay like this forever. If only to remind herself that she still had him.

"Baby, why are you crying?" he asked quietly.

She hadn't noticed the tears until now. And they shocked her. She hadn't cried in a long time and now she couldn't seem to make them stop.

Confused by the overwhelming feelings pouring through her, she shook her head. "I don't know," she murmured huskily. "I just...I don't want to lose you." She tightened her arms around him. "I don't want you to leave me."

He smoothed his palm down her back to curve under her butt and he pulled her close. "I won't." He pressed his lips to her shoulder. "That won't happen."

She eased her tight hold around him and pulled back to look at him. Even in the darkness of the room, she could see the warmth and concern in his eyes.

In that moment, she realized that if she didn't let go of her fears, her insecurities, and learn to fully trust him, then she could very well lose him. He was a passionate man who was open about his feelings and he made it clear that he wanted the same thing from her. He wouldn't accept anything less.

And he didn't deserve any less.

She placed her hand on his cheek, lightly threading her fingers through the trim hairs on his jaw then kissed him.

He gave all of himself to her and in return, he demanded the same. If she wanted to be with him, to please him, she needed to learn to open herself completely to him—both in and out of bed. And she wanted him enough to give him that.

She just didn't know if she had it in her to give.

chapter 13

"Judith? What are you doing out here?"

Judith turned to find a bed-rumpled Carlos walking toward her where she sat huddled on the couch. His dark boxers were the only thing that covered his beautiful body and she found it hard to look away.

"Nothing," she said, as he fell into the seat beside her. "I just couldn't sleep." She didn't even know what time it was. Though the light from the hall offered a soft glow in the dark room, it was still dark outside and she suspected dawn was still far from the horizon.

He unfolded her legs from beneath her and draped them over his lap. "Everything okay?" he asked, gently running his warm palm over her bare thighs.

His shirt had been the only piece of clothing she had managed to find in the dark and after slipping it on, she had come out to the living room to sort through her thoughts. After so many years of keeping all her secrets and horrors inside, she was desperate to tell him everything.

Remembering her life with Ken was like rehashing a

nightmare, but she couldn't find the right words, and she didn't know where to start.

Carlos' slow movement stilled on her leg. "Judith, what's wrong? Is it about last night?"

She shook her head, her throat suddenly too tight to speak. She took his hand and laced her fingers through his, holding him tight. To stop the trembling.

"I need to tell you something," she whispered.

He gently squeezed her hand, waiting patiently for her to continue. She'd never spoken to anyone about the girl she had once been or the man who had turned her into the woman she was now. Despite her fear, she wanted Carlos to know all of her—and the girl she had buried a long time ago.

"Tell me," he prompted.

She took a shuddering breath and began. "There was this girl. Her name was Abigail Bellamy, but everyone, except her mother, called her Abby. Her mother loved her given name, and she would get so annoyed when people took it upon themselves to shorten it." Judith smiled softly at the memory, remembering the frowns her adoptive mother would throw the violators. "But Abby never really minded, though," Judith continued. "She was easy going like that. Her mother was always a bit overprotective, keeping Abby sheltered from a lot of things, except dance, but still Abby managed to make friends everywhere she went. She never really had a problem fitting in, not even when she went away to college and started dating the star athlete at her school."

Carlos gently squeezed her hand again when she stopped and she focused her gaze on him. His dark eyes were piercing as he silently encouraged her to continue. She glanced down at their hands as her mind pulled her back into her past.

"Kenneth Tate was the cutest, most charming guy Abby had ever met, and they began dating." She paused for a moment, emotion tightening her throat. "Abby had barely finished her first year in college when her mother passed away and she found herself alone...lonely...without her. But then Ken asked her to marry him and Abby agreed. Ken had also lost his parents when he was young and Abby felt as though he was the only one who understood what she was going through. With him, she didn't feel so alone anymore."

Judith shook her head. Ironic that the loneliest moments in her life had been during her engagement with Ken. And even after all these years, she couldn't move past him.

"It's okay, baby," Carlos urged. "You can tell me."

She took another deep breath and the words poured out of her. "The first year with Ken was great. He was sweet and courteous and by that time I thought I loved him. He had a trust fund and would help me pay for my classes. I moved in with him after we got engaged and...that was when we started to have sex. I hadn't really felt ready for it, but I figured he was right. He was going to be my husband soon and it wasn't like I was saving myself for marriage so I gave him my virginity."

Judith fell silent for a moment, vaguely aware of the tension that invaded Carlos' body. She wondered what was going through his mind but didn't dare lift her gaze to find out.

"After that, it was like he changed overnight. He became...almost like another person. He was jealous of anyone I spoke with or spent too much time with. He lost his temper at everything I did, and everything I said was taken the wrong way. He could make me feel like I was cheating on him when I didn't pick up his calls fast enough. It was...scary."

Ken's sudden dark side had kept her on edge for much of their relationship. His dual personalities were extreme and erratic and there were times she seriously believed he was mentally unstable. Except no one else ever saw that other side of him.

"Did you leave him?"

Carlos' harsh question jarred her from her thoughts. She glanced up at him and was taken aback by the fierce frown that marred his face. But she wasn't frightened. If anything she was comforted by his outrage for her.

"No," she said with a slight shake of her head. Absently, she stroked his arm, trying to ease some of his tension. "Not even when he started...hitting me. At the time, I didn't know what to do. It was just easier to let myself believe in his apology, believe every excuse he gave and promise that he would never do it again. But I was so stupid," she whispered. "I should have left him when I had the chance instead of letting him believe he could do whatever he wanted to me."

Carlos cursed, his body radiating with fierce rage. She continued to stroke his arm, taking comfort in the small touch and the closeness of their bodies.

"After two years of trying to figure out what I could

do to avoid setting him off, I realized that I couldn't live like that anymore. I tried to leave a few times only to have him beg or bully me into coming back. I guess, in a way too, I felt like I owed him. For all that he was doing to help me stay in school. But my last semester, I finally left him for good. I changed my phone number, got a new apartment, and tried to focus on getting to graduation."

But then the stalking began, and she told Carlos everything—about the phone calls, the love letters and emails, the random appearances until she had been forced to get a protection order against him. She shuddered, thinking of the one time she suspected he had come into her apartment when she hadn't been home. And the other time he had tried to come in while she'd been asleep. Luckily, a neighbor had scared him off, but that had pushed her into getting the protection order.

"I thought that would help him realize how serious I was," she continued. "Make him realize that we were over and he should finally move on and leave me alone." She shook her head, thinking how foolish she had been to think things would be so easy. "But he didn't. When he found out about the protective order, he was furious. He would call and leave me threats one day, then send flowers with an apology the next. That went on for weeks."

"Did you call the police?" Carlos asked roughly.

She nodded. "But he was smart about not doing anything that I could connect back to him. It was like no matter what I did, he would win every time. So I waited until the semester ended before I decided to move again. I was finally finished with school and had gotten a job teaching dance. The night before my move, I went out to get something. I can't remember what it was or why I needed to get it that night, but as I was heading back to my car, Ken was there."

She took a deep breath, waiting for the memories, the lingering terror and the helplessness of that night to stop overwhelming her. "I was so scared when I saw him standing there, I literally couldn't move. He could see how scared I was and yet he seemed surprised by it." She let out a hollow laugh and shook her head. "He was *actually* shocked that I was scared of him. As if he hadn't spent three years of my life terrorizing me. He said he just wanted to talk and I was too scared to do anything else, I let him drag me to his car. But there were so many things I could have done that night. That I *should* have done."

She gripped his arm, remembering every moment of that horrific night. "But instead I told him the truth. That I didn't love him like he claimed to love me. That I would never marry him." Unexpected tears blurred her vision. "He didn't like hearing that because the next I know, he's choking me right there in the car. And he's crying and kissing me, but still choking me and I couldn't breathe and *he wouldn't let go*."

She didn't realize she had her fingernails digging into Carlos' arm, until he pulled her to him and settled her on his lap. He placed his hand under her shirt and over her abdomen, the pressure and his warmth doing more to chase her rising anxiety than anything else.

"Did he do this to you?"

She placed her hand over his and stared into dark

eyes that were filled with part fury and part anguish. But the hand he rested over her was light and gentle.

She shook her head and the tears fell on the side of her face. "I must have passed out because the next thing I know, we were on the highway and he was driving really fast. I tried to get him to slow down, begging him to let me out, but he kept shouting that everyone he loved had left him and I wasn't going to leave him too. That he wasn't going to just *let* me leave."

Carlos closed his eyes and she couldn't be sure which of them was trembling.

"The more I begged and screamed for him to stop, the faster he drove," she continued. "The last thing he said to me before he drove the car over the rail was that if he couldn't have me—"

"*Jesus*," Carlos burst out.

She wrapped her arms around him, taking some of his strength and letting him borrow some of hers. A sense of calm seemed to settle over her now that she had finally told him and managed to get through the worst of it.

"I don't remember much of what happened after. I spent four months in the hospital and then two years in physical therapy. My right arm and leg had been crushed. My collarbone and pelvis had been broken. My right eye retina had been torn, and even after surgery, I needed glasses to see from that eye. The seat belt gave me the big scars. Some of the glass and the surgery to my pelvis gave me the smaller ones."

He was rigid against her as she ran through her list of injuries. She wasn't telling him this to gain his sympathy or pity, and certainly not to upset him. She needed him to know so that he understood what a broken mess she really was. So that he knew what he could and could not get from her.

"You deserve more than I can give you, Carlos," she said quietly, her voice trembling. "I can't give you children. I can't give you a family."

He remained silent. Still.

Tears flowed down her cheeks then. She wanted him more than anything, but it wasn't fair for her to expect him to want her after what she had just told him.

But then he leaned down and kissed her. It was sweet and gentle and undemanding. He pulled away and rubbed a thumb over her tear stained cheek. "If you think that's going to change how I feel about you, you don't understand how much I care about you and how much I want you." He paused then asked, "Was he the reason why you did what you did at Royal Courts?"

She nodded and told him everything—about the Agency, the compromise to her new identity, the promise to keep Ken in prison though he had already been paroled. When she was done, she stared down at her hands, the realization of her weakness only added to her despair.

"I'm sorry I lied to you. About everything. I always told myself that Abigail Bellamy died in that car that night." Her voice cracked. "But she didn't. She's still very much a part of me." She shook her head, her brows pulling together slightly. "I'm still that same stupid girl who is still afraid of the man who tried to kill me five years ago." She closed her eyes and released a shaky breath. "I know it makes me weak, but he still scares me to death."

He pulled her closer to him. "Being scared doesn't make you weak, Judith. It makes you human. There are different kinds of strong and I think you have a lot of inner strength. You literally went through hell and yet you still manage to smile. I don't know a lot of people who could have gone through everything you did and do that."

She stared at him for a long while, her throat tightening from a wave of emotion. "Why couldn't I have met you nine years ago?"

His expression remained solemn as he continued to rub her back. "You have nothing to be afraid of, *muñeca*," he said. "I promise, I won't let that bastard come near you again. *No one* will ever hurt you again."

Drained, she rested her head on his shoulders. Though his words comforted her, she knew nothing was ever promised. Not even tomorrow.

****

Carlos felt Judith's eyes on him as he flipped through photo after photo of the mangled car that she'd been trapped it. She'd handed him the folder that she'd received with the flash drive and looking through the materials now, he could understand her panic. These people had done their research.

Now it was his turn.

He tried to control his reaction as he stared down at a photo with her lying in the hospital bed, bloodied and bruised, and connected to so many machines. The images were permanently burned into his mind and his stomach twisted with anger and disgust.

But he only had the pictures. After surviving all that she had, Carlos couldn't imagine what memories Judith kept stored inside her head.

"I don't know how they found out about me, but when I saw those, I panicked." She sighed. "I never wanted to cause any trouble."

Carlos glanced over at her on the couch, purposely keeping her gaze from drifting down to the file. It was late morning now and she was still dressed in his shirt. It had been a rough night for them both and their emotions had been strung high. But when she'd finally managed to fall asleep, he'd simply held her, wanting to both shield her from any more hurt and kill the bastard who'd caused her such pain. A monster like that didn't deserve to live.

"Were you able to find out who sent this to me?" she asked, tucking her hair behind her ear.

Carlos shook his head. "Not yet. But we're working on it."

She tightened her hands on her lap, but nodded. He was expecting Tristan to return the message he'd left early that morning. Tristan wouldn't like it, but Carlos needed one more favor and he planned to take full advantage of his cousin's resources.

"Do you remember anything that she said that struck you as strange, anything that made you think she could have been an employee?"

Her brows pulled together as she thought about it, then she slowly shook her head. "No, not really. Her accent sounded familiar, but I can't remember where I heard it before. And I did think it was weird that she seemed to be a pretty nice person despite the fact that she was blackmailing me."

"Nice how?"

She shrugged. "Just the way she would say things and she kept calling me 'hon', like—*oh my God*." Judith stared at him with wide, dazed eyes, her mouth gaped open.

His muscles bunched with concern. "What?"

But her eyes were unfocused as she stared off, trapped in her thoughts. He closed the folder and tossed it on the table. Grabbing her hand, he pulled her to him, out of her thoughts and back to him.

"Judith, what is it?"

"I think I know her. I think it was Laurie. Laurie Fiori. She was a waitress at Mia Bella's, the restaurant I worked in before I came to Royal Courts. I think she was from New York or New Jersey and that's why I thought I recognized her accent. She would always call everyone 'hon' and was always nice to me."

"Do you still keep in touch with her?"

Judith shook her head. "I haven't seen or heard from her since I quit months ago. I wasn't really close to anyone there, but she was always so friendly and talkative, she was probably the only person I could say I had full conversations with that wasn't about the job. And I-I think I must have told her that I was coming to work at Royal Courts."

"How did she know about you?"

She flinched. "When I found Prince, it was outside the restaurant one night. I mentioned to Laurie that I would be adopting him and I think I let it slip that I was adopted."

He continued to rub her back, trying to ease the

tension in her. That bit of information wouldn't have gotten the woman much, but Carlos didn't tell her that. The probability that the woman wasn't working alone in this was high. There was someone with a lot more money and motive behind this.

"Anything else?" Carlos prompted. "Did she ever mention Royal Courts or seem desperate for money?"

"Actually no. If anything, she would always gush over the rich guy who she was dating. There were rumors that she was dating the owner of the restaurant, but she had never confirmed or denied them and she was always careful not to mention his name. Ever. I figured she was either making him up or she really was dating the owner. Either way, she never seemed to want for money."

Maybe money hadn't been a motivator but, for whatever reason, the woman had been looking for something. Carlos' mind raced as he thought of his next steps. Finally, they were getting somewhere.

"I'll have Tristan do some digging on this woman. And if you're certain she's the one who called you that day, then maybe we'll find something that'll connect it all back to her."

Judith nodded. "I'm certain it was her." She paused for a moment then said quietly, "I got a call from the Agency the other day. I told them I would be in touch with them as soon as I was ready to leave." She fell silent for a heartbeat. "They want me to start thinking of a new name."

Carlos' brows snapped together. "You're not going anywhere," he said strongly. The thought of her leaving filled him with a dark void. There was a hidden despair in her eyes that said she also didn't want that.

"You trust me, right? Then don't leave. I promise, I won't let Kenneth Tate get anywhere near you," he said. "Not while I'm around."

Though Carlos needed to find this woman who had targeted Judith and find out what it was she had been trying to steal from Royal Courts, he first wanted to make sure Kenneth Tate was where he was supposed to be and that he kept his distance.

"What do we do now?"

He rubbed his thumb across her cheek, enjoying the smooth feel. He wanted to wipe the anxious look in her eyes, to see her smile again.

"Well, we're both on leave, so why don't we make the most of it."

She frowned in confusion. "You took time off?"

"Let's just say, Carrone highly recommended it."

"So you're not leaving here?" she asked, a faint hopefulness in her guarded gaze. "You'll stay here with me?"

"Do you want me to?"

She glanced down at her hands. He hooked his finger under her chin and turned her back to face him.

"Do you?"

She nodded. "Yes, I'd like that."

"Good," he said, brushing his thumb across her cheek. "Because I plan to." He couldn't resist any longer. He leaned over and placed a kiss on her soft lips. "You know, it's okay to tell me what you want and how you feel. I want to know. Okay?"

She stared at him searchingly. "Okay."

He didn't need to tell her just yet that he planned to

resign. Right now, he was alone with her, away from the world and his responsibilities and he planned to enjoy every minute of it. And he would start by taking her mind off everything except him.

"I think they miss me."

"Who?"

"Your lips," he said with a slow smile, glancing down at her mouth. "It might be time for another reunion."

He didn't know if her coy smile was genuine or playful. It didn't matter. It was captivating.

"Again?"

He nodded. "Again," he murmured then gently pressed his lips against hers. Their lips moved slowly against each other—demanding nothing but exploration. Her fingers ran through the tapered ends at the back of his hair and he groaned low at the soft caress. He drew in her lower lip into his mouth and sucked at it leisurely. Just as he began to deepen the kiss, the shrill ringing of his cell phone punctured their cocoon of desire.

With a low groan, he pulled away from her and reached for it. It was Tristan.

"Answer it," Judith said, rising from the couch. "I have to feed Prince anyway then I'm jumping in the shower."

Carlos watched as she made her way to the kitchen. Prince suddenly appeared from behind the couch and began trailing after her. "Sure you don't want to wait for me to join you? Saving water saves the world, babe."

She laughed. "Maybe later," she said over her

shoulders, but he didn't mistake the stiffness in her tone as she headed to the bathroom.

He sighed and answered the phone. It was still apparent to him that she was still self-conscious about him seeing her body. He didn't know what he could do or say that would convince her that she didn't need to hide herself from him. He would just have to give her time.

"Where are you?" Tristan's annoyed tone cut through his thoughts.

"With Judith," Carlos said. "Why?"

She had told him about Tristan's little visit yesterday and Carlos wasn't too thrilled with his cousin coming to see her without him knowing. Even if it was to convince her to open up to him, as Judith had defended, Carlos could do without the secret meetings and the meddling.

Tristan was silent for a moment. "I just went by your place... so you spent the night there?"

Carlos rolled his eyes at his cousin's surprise. "Yeah."

"Did she tell you?"

"Everything. But next time—"

"Yeah, I know," Tristan broke in. "And I wanted to tell you, but she had to be the one to do it herself."

With that, Carlos agreed, despite his mild annoyance.

"Anyway, I got your message, but I've hit a brick wall with that phone number," Tristan said. "So unless—"

"I have a name," Carlos interjected "Laurie Fiori."

"How?"

"Judith remembered the woman's voice."

Carlos quickly filled his cousin in on what she'd remembered exactly. He could practically hear Tristan's brain churning.

"That's a start," Tristan finally said. "But that doesn't prove she was the one who sent Judith those things."

"I know, but it doesn't hurt to ask, right? Find out where she is and I'll set up a meeting. Either way, whether she agrees to meet or not, I'll have an answer."

"The whole thing just seems odd. What would a waitress need to steal from a casino?"

"I think you just answered your own question."

"Then let me clarify," Tristan said. "*Why* would she go to such lengths? What the hell was she looking for?"

"That's exactly what I want to know and this woman seems to be our best chance at getting some answers."

"Well, like you said, it certainly doesn't hurt to ask."

Carlos grunted. "Now, I need another favor."

Tristan cursed. "Seriously? You know, I have my *own* shit to get to."

"This is quick." Carlos paused to hear if the shower in the bathroom was still running before he continued. "Just find out where Kenneth Tate is."

"He's still in California, in a Halfway House," Tristan said smoothly. "I checked him out yesterday, before I came to see Judith. He's been keeping quiet and checking in with his PO regularly."

Though that should have eased some of Carlos'

tension, it didn't. Violent rage just at the thought of the bastard burned within him, and he wanted to know exactly where Kenneth Tate was. For his peace of mind, he told himself.

"Can you get me an address?"

A long pause filled the line before Tristan responded. "No."

"Why not?" Carlos barked.

"Because I don't need you to do anything stupid."

Carlos grip tightened around his cell phone. "I won't," he snapped. "I just want to be sure that son-of-a-bitch is as far from Judith as I can make happen." He hated that she was still afraid. Nothing had ever made him feel so helpless and the only thing he could do was to try and keep his promise and make sure the bastard stayed away from her.

"And he is," Tristan said then let out a heavy sigh. "Look, I know you love her and want to give the guy what's probably been a long time coming, but you're no good to any of us—to *her*—if you get your ass locked up."

But you didn't see what I saw.

Carlos kept the words unsaid. From what Judith had told him last night, no one knew that the bastard had tried to kill her. Carlos glanced at the folder and the hairs in the back of his neck still prickled at the thought of how close he had come to succeeding.

But it wasn't just her physical scars. His cousin hadn't seen the haunted look on her face or the fear that she tried to keep buried inside her, when she spoke about what had happened. Carlos had always noticed everything about her and that was something she couldn't keep hidden from him, despite her best efforts. He only wished he'd recognized the signs of someone who'd gone through such a traumatic experience sooner.

"Fine," Carlos finally said. "But I want you to let me know if *anything* changes with him."

"Sure. Just take care of your girl. She needs you right now."

chapter 14

"Are you finally going to tell me what you're cooking?" Carlos asked, coming into the kitchen.

It had been a big surprise all day, and his curiosity was getting the best of him. They were quickly eating through the packaged foods he'd brought that Saturday night and she'd insisted on making them a proper home-cooked meal.

Judith looked up from the baking dish she was oiling and smiled. "Your favorite. Chicken tamale casserole."

He returned her smile, but it was strained. "So that's why you wanted my aunt's number?"

She nodded. "She mentioned this was your favorite. I wanted to make it for you and she was nice enough to give me the recipe."

Carlos walked up to her and looked down at the assortment of familiar ingredients lining the counter and stifled a groan. Judith had asked to speak to his aunt that morning, then had him take her to a nearby grocery store, which had been more than a half hour drive, only to surprise him with the last thing he wanted to eat tonight.

To this day, he regretted the little white lie he'd told his aunt. Everyone in their family hated what she believed was her best dish, but he'd been young and eager to please and like an idiot, had gone on to praise it.

"Baby, you didn't have to go through the trouble."

Her smile widened. "I know, but I wanted to." She went back to preparing the baking dish. "But don't get used to it," she added with a small laugh. "I don't plan to spoil you like your aunt does."

Carlos lips curved. His aunt did tend to spoil him, but that was because he went out of his way to please her. Or at least he tried. She was the only woman who came close to being a mother to him. Growing up, she kept the spirit of his own mother alive by telling him as much as she could about her, and he loved her for that.

He just hated her chicken tamale casserole.

But every year, especially on his birthday, he had that to look forward to. All because he had wanted to spare his aunt's feelings. Watching Judith now, he knew he would also do the same.

He sighed. "Need any help?"

"Sure. Here," she said, handing him the glass dish. "Mix in the corn muffin mix with the rest of those."

They switched places and he began to throw in everything she had set aside on the counter into a large bowl—the cheese, milk, can of corn, and corn mix. Judith continued to shred the cooked chicken breast and mix in the spices and sauce in a separate bowl.

Carlos didn't do much cooking, not even for himself, but he followed direction well and proceeded to pour the corn mix in the glass dish Judith had pointed to. Just as he was about to place the dish in the oven, she stopped him.

"Wait. I think we're supposed to mix some of these in there."

Judith threw in the rest of her spices and some red and green peppers in the corn mix. For some reason, that didn't seem right to him, but then he'd never really watched his aunt make the casserole so he couldn't be sure. Carlos put the dish in the oven then leaned against the counter, content to just watch her.

He'd spent the past few days with her at the house and it had made up for the lost time he'd spent without her. It was nice, this moment alone. They got a chance to leave everything behind and get to know each other. But the week was fast coming to an end. He'd promised his uncle that he'd be at his aunt's party early to help set up and he wasn't going to bail on him. But then, neither did Carlos plan to leave Judith behind or let her out of his sight. The only option left was to take her with him.

"How would you like to go to a party?"

She glanced up at him curiously, still shredding and mixing the remaining ingredients in the bowl. "Tonight?"

He chuckled. "No. This Friday night. It's my aunt's birthday."

"Oh, right. Yes, that should be fun." Then her eyes widened. "Oh no, did I miss yours?"

He frowned. "No, mine's was two weeks ago, but how did—" He snapped his mouth shut, remembering the little lie he told her to get her to have dinner with him. That seemed like eons ago.

She was obviously remembering too, and her brow rose slightly, but she said nothing.

He groaned. "Okay, I know. I'm an ass. Just say it. I can take it."

"It's fine," she said a little too serenely. "Just glad to know I already missed it."

"Ouch," he said, grabbing his chest. "That hurts."

She laughed. "You said you could take it. Besides, I was thinking *manipulative* ass."

He smiled crookedly. "Manipulative? That sounds so demeaning. I would say I'm an *opportunistic* ass."

She shook her head and returned her attention to the bowl. "So how old are you now?"

"Thirty-three," he said, studying her closely. "Too old, according to my aunt, to still be unattached."

"Well," she began, "I'm sure when you're ready it won't be hard for you to find a woman to attach yourself to."

She kept her attention to the bowl and he couldn't read her expression. Her tone said she was teasing, but he couldn't be sure.

"It's actually proving harder than you think."

Her movements stilled briefly, but she said nothing. He knew she still had her doubts about how he felt for her. Though nothing she'd told him about her past changed how much he wanted her, he couldn't shake the irrational desolation he already felt at not being able to have children with her. It was silly of him, and maybe even a little selfish, but having children—his *own* children—had always been something he'd expected in his future and he was already missing them.

But if that's what he had to give up in order to have Judith in his life, then he would just have to cope with the premature sense of loss.

Eventually the corn muffins were ready and he bent over to pull them out of the oven. Her next words nearly caused him to drop the glass dish.

"You must be a baker, 'cause you've got a nice set of buns."

He let out a bark of laughter and placed the hot dish on the counter.

"I'm glad you noticed," he said still chuckling. Though he'd seen her playful side before, it surprised him, this sexual teasing without his prompting.

While he held the dish, she began pouring the chicken mixture over the baked bread.

"Hmm, smells good," he said. "Better than I remember."

And it was true. He couldn't remember the casserole smelling so savory while his aunt was preparing it.

She beamed at that. "Thanks."

He stared down at her bent head and couldn't help but add, "The food smells good too."

She shook her head, trying to contain her smile. When she finished, he slid the dish back into the oven then caught a glimpse of Prince ambling into the kitchen.

"There's the little prince," Carlos muttered. "Almost forgot about him."

The cat let out a loud meow before affectionately brushing himself against his leg. Carlos leaned down and patted his head. "Hello to you too."

As soon as Judith opened a can of cat food, Prince ambled from his side and began rubbing around her leg.

Carlos shook his head. "Opportunist," he muttered.

She snorted as she placed the dish in front of Prince and he dove right in. "It must be a guy thing."

It wasn't long before their dinner was ready and she pulled out the hot dish, covered with melted cheese. He stared down at the steaming casserole, impressed. He suddenly found himself starving.

"Wow. That looks great."

Her face lit up. "Doesn't it?"

He took down two plates and grabbed some silverware before following her to the small dining table. He picked up the wooden spoon and began cutting into the gooey casserole. He could practically smell the spices, which didn't bother him one bit. He loved his food spicy.

But it took one big bite, and a millisecond for it to settle on his tongue, for him to realize even he had his limits.

The stinging moved from his tongue to the walls of his mouth and down his throat. His eyes began to water and he cleared his throat to cover it.

Shit. He liked spice, but this was the kind of heat that burnt hairs off a man's chest.

She looked at him expectantly. "Well, how is it?"

He cleared his throat again. "It's got a little spice." He winced at the rasp in his voice and he fought not to dab at the corner of his eyes. *Damn it*. Now his least favorite food was calling into question his manhood.

But he would gouge his eyes out before he let a tear slip.

She frowned and picked up her fork. His tongue was fast becoming numb and he was slow to react when she took a bite. Then promptly spit it back on her plate.

"*Oh my God,*" she cried then started coughing into her napkin then fanning her mouth.

He wanted to laugh at the way she scrunched her face, but he couldn't make his mouth move. When she reached for the glass of water, he pulled it from her hand.

"No water," he slurred. "You'll make it worse."

He quickly grabbed the carton of milk from the fridge, took a long swallow then handed it to her. She also drank directly from the carton.

"Oh wow, I really messed that up, didn't I?" she said, wiping the corners of her mouth.

"Are you sure you used jalapenos and not Habanero peppers?" The residual stinging in his mouth told him it had to be the latter.

She lifted her shoulders and shook her head, looking so miserable he wavered between laughing and pulling her into his arms. He should have used this opportunity to come clean—to tell her that he hated chicken tamale casserole and that regardless of the heat, he was certain he would have hated hers too.

Turned out he wasn't an opportunist after all.

And he was undeniably in love with this woman.

"It's okay, *muñeca,*" he said, placing a quick kiss on her cheek. "You'll get it right the next time. Now come on. Let me make us a sandwich."

****

Judith was going to miss their little hideaway.

The past week had been perfect with just the two of them. Even Prince had given them room to just explore each other. To not have to think about anything—or anyone—and just laze about, making love or working on the three hundred piece puzzle he had bought her.

They hadn't talked about Ken or her accident again and she was grateful for that. Instead, Carlos told her more outrageous stories about Wenzel the Wolf, about his short time in the marines, and the time Gil had convinced him to temporarily work as a jiu-jitsu trainer at his gym.

She in turn told him about growing up in San Francisco and how her passion for dance started when she'd been five only because she had wanted to wear the pretty pink tutu everywhere. She was slowly opening up to him and Carlos was allowing her the time and space she needed to do that. She chose to trust that she was safe with him, and the more time she spent with him, the more she believed that both her body and her heart were safe with him.

Carlos came into the bathroom where she was tying her hair up for her nightly shower. Despite the thick, white towel wrapped around her, he stared at her as if she were already naked.

Wearing only his dark boxers, he leaned against the door frame and silently watched her. She caught his eye in the mirror and she found herself drawn to his warm gaze. He had a way of making her smile more than she ever had in a long time.

"What?"

"You're beautiful," he said simply.

She glanced down, annoyed by her sudden bashfulness but flattered by the unexpected compliment. She had on her glasses and her hair was pulled up in a messy bun. She didn't particularly feel beautiful, but he had a way of making her believe she was.

She tried to think of a clever response but the way he looked at her made her forget her thoughts. All she could muster was a quiet, "Thanks."

"It's our last night here," he added, "and we haven't put that bathtub in the back to any use."

He had been alluding to bathing together for some time now and though the idea intrigued her, she didn't think she could be comfortable enough to expose herself to him in bright light with nothing between them but water. She knew the scars didn't bother him, but they were still painfully noticeable to her.

"I can't get my hair wet," she protested, finding any excuse to forget the idea. "And I don't have my flat iron or anything."

"That's okay," he said, his eyes gleaming. "I like my women rough around the edges."

It took a moment for his words to sink in but when they did, she burst out laughing. "What do you know about rough edges?"

His grin widened. "I've dated a few black girls."

She glanced away. Of course he had, she thought, trying to ignore the stab of jealousy. He was a good-looking guy with the right amount of charm and rugged assertiveness.

"Don't be jealous, *muñeca*," he said with faint amusement, coming up behind her and pulling her into his arms. "You're the only woman this big, bad wolf wants." He playfully nibbled on her neck.

She rolled her eyes to mask her shiver of pleasure, but she couldn't quite contain the joy and desire that spread through her. In a way it was unnerving to have him know her every thought and feeling, but then again, she loved how in-tune he was with her. He tended to know when things were good or bad before she'd even say a word.

"So what do you say?" he murmured against her ear. "Will you conserve our planet's natural resources and take a bath with me?" He must have read the hesitation on her face because he grabbed her hand and led her out of the small bathroom. "Come on. You'll like it. I promise."

He led her to the large, master bath with the whirlpool tub at the back of the house and she gasped at the sight that greeted her.

One large candle glowed at each corner of the wide tub, giving the dimly lit bathroom a soft, romantic ambiance. It was perfect. Water filled the tub halfway with soap suds floating at the top. The soft glow of the candlelight and the water would help conceal her lingering insecurities.

She turned to him, still in awe. No one had ever done anything so touching or romantic for her. "This is beautiful, Carlos."

He shrugged sheepishly. "I wanted to add flowers and champagne, which looked nice in this magazine ad I saw once, but I didn't plan ahead. I couldn't find any more candles either."

She shook her head slowly. "This is perfect," she breathed.

Carlos removed his boxers and came up to her. Her hands tightened on her towel, but instead of pulling them away, he placed his hands on her arms and slowly rubbed them.

"You don't have to be shy with me, *muñeca*," he said. "And you don't have anything to be embarrassed about either."

He pulled off her glasses. If they hadn't been standing so close, he would have been a slightly blurred figure. But in the low light, she still saw all of him clearly.

Next, he tugged on the towel and she let it fall—along with all of her apprehension and insecurities. She kept her gaze locked with his as he brushed his thumb across her cheek.

"Of all the gorgeous curves on your beautiful body," he began slowly, his eyes filled with warmth, "your smile is my favorite."

The breath she hadn't realized she'd held suddenly escaped her and she felt herself melt for him just a bit more. "Okay, that was a good one."

"But it's true." He gave her a quick kiss then took her hand. "Ready?"

She nodded and they eased into the warm water. The tub wasn't as big as it looked and she ended up between his legs, her back pressed against his chest with the water coming up just above her breasts. She leaned fully against him as he ran his wet palm along her legs, over her thighs, and up her abdomen.

"I've thought about us doing this for a long time," he murmured, placing a kiss on her damp shoulder.

With a soft sigh, Judith closed her eyes, enjoying the feel of his hard frame cradling her. "This is nice."

He kissed her shoulder again. "I told you, you would like it. Next time, I'll remember to pick up some champagne."

"And chocolate."

He chuckled.

They sat in the water, lazily stroking each other, her foot leisurely rubbing along his leg. His lips trailed along the back of her neck and she couldn't help the shiver that raked through her body. She wished they could stay like this, in their little oasis, forever. Instead, tomorrow, they would be joining the rest of the world and she would have to once again face her actions and an uncertain future.

"Carlos?"

"Hmm," he murmured, his fingers trailing along the outside of her thigh.

"What happens after tomorrow?"

His movements stilled. "Do you mean about us or the investigation."

"Both, I guess." Her initial concern had been regarding the investigation and what would happen once they got back into the city, but then whatever ended up happening with that, didn't necessarily give her any insights into what would happen to her—or *them*. He would have to eventually return to Royal Courts and tell David Carrone everything he knew.

"Once I have more information on Laurie Fiori, you'll come back with me to Royal Courts and we'll explain exactly what happened."

Her stomach clenched at the thought of facing David Carrone after what she'd done, and her attempt to flee from it, but she couldn't continue running from the consequences of her actions.

"I'm sorry about all this," she said, the guilt of what she'd done weighing heavily on her. She took his hands in hers and squeezed it. "I know you could probably lose your job for helping me and I appreciate the risks you're taking. And I'll try to help however I can."

"You let me worry about my job," he said close to her ear. "Everything will work itself out, I promise. And when we're old and gray and trying to figure out how to send text messages through our brain chips, this will all be a distant memory."

She smiled at the thought of growing old with him. She may not know what tomorrow would bring but for now, she would relish the fantasy. Stroking his arm, she turned her head to face him and he gave her exactly what she wanted.

He kissed her long and deep, his fingers travelling between her thighs and into her slick folds. A soft gasp escaped her when he twirled his finger around her most sensitive area before slipping it inside her. She lifted her hips slightly to give him better access and she covered his slowly moving hand with hers as the familiar tightness in her belly began to spread to her core.

His free hand held her face turned to his as he continued moving his lips over hers. "*Eres mía, muñeca,*" he said against her mouth. "*Toda mía.*"

The slickness of herself and the lukewarm water

made his movements easy, bringing her to heights only he could. His lazy strokes between her thighs grew stronger and everything around them ceased to exist. Her body clenched fiercely around his pumping finger, but he never released her lips as he continued his gentle assault.

The tension grew unbearably tight and with a series of soft gasps and moans, she clutched his thigh and convulsed around his finger. Her head fell back against his shoulder, the water lapping smoothly around them as her thighs trembled from the aftermath and his erection pressed urgently behind her.

"Let's go to bed," he murmured thickly, his breathing heavy and fast against her ear.

There, he made love to her tenderly and slowly, whispering sexy words to her in Spanish, encouraging her and guiding her in what he liked. As always, it was fiery and intense yet filled with a sweet tenderness.

"Open your eyes, *muñeca*. Look at me."

She opened them and stared up at his intense, dark gaze. With every slow push, her breath caught.

"Every time you close your eyes, I want you to feel this, remember this." He braced himself on his arms as he leaned down and kissed her deeply. "I want you to dream of me, of us, each night," he said, trailing his warm lips down her neck. "I can't take away your nightmares, but I can try to erase them, try to replace them with happy memories of us."

And they did.

He loved her so gently, so tenderly, that there was no room for anything else. No room for darkness or pain. It was just them in that moment, still learning each other, loving each other—and making lasting memories.

After, she lay against him, running her palm over his rising and falling chest. He lifted her hand and brought it to his lips.

"*Eres el amor de mi vida, muñeca.*"

"What does that mean?"

He was silent for a moment. "That you are the love of my life," he whispered. He hugged her close. "I love you, Judith." He placed a soft kiss on her lips. "You don't have to say anything. Just know that I do."

Tears welled in her eyes. Until he had said those words, she didn't realize how much she needed to hear them. She knew that he cared about her, but his love fed something inside her that made her feel indestructible. Where she had once felt weak and broken, she now felt whole again.

She rested her head back on his shoulder, trying to make sense of the different emotions ricocheting inside her. He'd seen the worst of her—what she was willing to do when she let fear take a hold of her, the scars that marked her body—yet he loved her despite it all. Years of guarding her emotions made it harder for her to express herself in the same way without feeling the uncomfortable tightness in her throat. And neither was he pressuring her to. He was simply telling her how he felt—something she was still relearning to do. One thing was certain, though—she was completely enthralled by him.

Suddenly he jerked his leg and looked down at their feet. "*What the hell!*"

"What?" She rose on her elbow and followed his

gaze to find Prince perched at the foot of the bed. His mouth gaped open in a wide yawn.

"I think he just licked my toe," Carlos said wryly.

She giggled. "Aww, he's showing you affection."

Carlos rolled out of the bed and carried Prince out of the bedroom. Her spoiled cat released an indignant meow just as Carlos shut the door behind him and got back into bed.

Judith rolled into his arms, seeking out his warmth. "Why'd you put him out? He really likes you."

"I like him just fine, too," Carlos said with a wide yawn of his own. "But I'm not about to make this a threesome."

He hauled her back into his arms as she dissolved into laughter.

chapter 15

"What do you think of this?"

Carlos stared at the large, glowing plant-like ornament. They had made it back to the city late that morning and he'd dropped both her and Prince off at her place while he'd gone to his apartment to shower and change for his aunt's party tonight. It had been while he was dressing that he thought about how good she would look standing in his bedroom, in only her underwear getting dressed alongside with him. He smiled at the image his mind conjured. In her underwear, she would look good standing anywhere.

"What is it?" he asked, pushing away his provocative thoughts.

Judith shrugged. "I don't know. A tree sculpture? But it's pretty, isn't it? I think your aunt would like it."

Carlos couldn't be sure about that. His aunt had a fondness for potted plants, but he couldn't quite make out what the thing was supposed to be. Though he had assured Judith a gift wasn't necessary, she had insisted they stop so she could buy his aunt something. Now they stood in the novelty shop, staring at the unique plant-like thing oddly pulsing colorful lights through its stems. One thing was certain, it was an attention grabber.

They finished their purchase and made the short drive to the banquet hall.

Inside the decorated space, staff in plain black uniforms bustled around, the name and logo of the catering company on their breast pocket the only indicator that they were affiliated with the venue. The buffet tables were currently being set up and a makeshift dance floor had been formed in the back, near a set of large stereos and a sound system. Several round tables were covered with white tablecloths with small colorful flowers in glass vases at the center of each.

Carlos found his uncle and Tristan standing near one of the larger tables at the center of the room.

"Good. You two made it," his uncle greeted as they approach. He grabbed the bags from Judith's hand then pulled her into a hug.

"Looks like you have everything under control," Carlos said, placing the wide box on the table. He glanced again around the room, which had been nicely decked with strings of white lights hanging from the ceiling and spirals of silver and black balloons decorating every corner of the large room. Everything was simple yet elegant.

"I know," Gil said. "I just wanted to make sure you got here in time. It's important that the family show up tonight. Rosa would like that."

"What's this?" Tristan asked, looking curiously at

Judith's gift.

"It's Rosa's birthday present," Judith said. "It's a lamp sculpture. I wasn't sure if we should wrap it or not."

"No need," his uncle assured her. "Let's take it out of the box and put it on the front table."

"I still have the rest of the party favors in my car," Tristan said. "Mind giving me a hand, Carlos?"

"Any news?" Carlos asked the minute they made it outside.

"Yeah," Tristan said. "But you're not gonna like it."

"Why? What is it?"

"I was able to trace a Laurie Fiori at the old restaurant Judith used to work at but she split Vegas a few days ago."

Carlos frowned. "Do you know where she went?"

Tristan shook his head. "Back east, I'm guessing. But it doesn't matter because we can't prove shit and going after her would be a waste of time. For one thing, she could decide not to say anything even if we had her. And for another, the only way to force her back here is to go through the legal channel. You know, filing charges, sending warrants, the whole bit."

"Fine, let's do it."

"Yeah, then we would have to drag Judith through the same process. Sorry to say, but her hands aren't clean in this either. If we want anything to stick on this woman, we'll need her accomplice so to speak."

"Who? Judith? She's not—"

"I know," Tristan interrupted. "But no one forced a gun to her head and made her do it. In the eyes of the law, she's just as culpable. And right now, it's basically

Judith's word against hers."

Carlos cursed. He didn't want to implicate Judith just to catch a woman who probably wouldn't give up anything. It was too big a risk and she had too much to lose if he did. That brought them back to square one.

He cursed again.

"What the hell do I do then?" Carlos asked, running his hand through his hair in frustration. "Carrone isn't going to let this go and I have to get Judith out of this mess."

When they reached his SUV, Tristan popped open the trunk and handed him an envelope.

"Maybe this will help," he said. "It's information about the restaurant, particularly the owner. When you said Laurie may have had a thing going on between them, I did some digging and you won't believe what I found."

Frowning, Carlos pulled out the documents and sifted through them. "What am I looking for?"

"The restaurant, Mia Bella, is owned and managed by a company called Diamante Enterprises. And the owner, or rather *owners*, of that company are women. Izabella and Rachelle Silva—a mother-daughter duo."

"Okay, so Laurie wasn't sleeping with the owner." *Maybe.* "Where does that leave us? Or are you saying these women put her up to it?"

"What I'm saying is that this is all one hell of a coincidence."

Carlos frown deepened. "How so?"

"Diamante Enterprises recently became an investor for Royal Courts," Tristan explained. "I pulled all the other names of those on the payroll there. I find it odd that Laurie, the woman connected to this whole thing, was once an employee for a company that only months ago became an investor for Royal Courts. It's either one hell of a coincidence or your boss got in bed with the wrong people."

Carlos stared down at the documents. This was good. Exactly the kind of proof he'd wanted to bring to David and now he had something more tangible to bring him—besides Judith. Whoever at this company was behind this had scoped out the most vulnerable employee, with the most access around Royal Courts, and landed on Judith. Maybe being the executive assistant to the co-founder and CEO had always made her a target, and the bastards got lucky in using her past against her.

"Thanks for this, man" Carlos said, stuffing the documents back into the envelope. "This really helps."

"There's one more thing." Tristan handed him another envelope, this one with more weight to it.

Carlos reached for it. "What's this?"

"The other favor you asked me for," Tristan said.

Carlos stared down curiously at it before it dawned on him. "So you found them?"

His cousin nodded, but his mouth was set in a grim line. "Yeah, I found her parents, but unfortunately they're both dead."

Carlos released a heavy sigh. He'd wanted to do this for her the moment he'd seen the look on her face when she'd told him she had tried to find her birth parents. There had been a faint yearning there, one she hadn't managed to mask. Now he didn't know what to do with this information.

"Are you going to tell her?"

Carlos looked at his cousin. "I don't know." He didn't like the idea of keeping this from her, but neither did he want to bring her unnecessary hurt. She had enough of that in her life. "Any updates on Tate?"

Tristan shook his head. "Nothing new. He's still in California, doing what he's supposed to. How was your week playing house."

Carlos knew what his cousin was doing and he let him change the subject. "Nice. You should try it sometime."

Tristan chuckled and began unloading the party favors from his car. "I would but I'd hate to disappoint the ladies."

They headed back to the banquet hall, carrying the boxes of party favors that still needed assembling. Carlos instantly spotted Judith with his uncle near the glowing tree sculpture, a frown marring her pretty face. The thing looked bigger and brighter than it had at the store. It was the prettiest yet gaudiest thing in the room and the pulsing lights only drew more attention to it.

"Good God," Tristan muttered. His words had traveled.

His uncle turned to them and shot Tristan a glare. The look on Gil's face dared them to say anything about the flashy gift.

"It's not too much, is it?" she asked them anxiously.

They all shook their head in unison.

"I told you it's lovely, *cariño*," Gil said, patting her hand. "Rosa will love it."

Carlos couldn't help the smile that tugged at his

lips. He wasn't the only one with the affliction of wanting to protect her feelings. It was those eyes. And that smile. Something in them brought out the urge to keep her safe.

He thought of Kenneth Tate and the muscles in his jaw tightened as the fury smoldering inside him began to boil. How any man could hurt a woman like that was beyond him, but to think the woman he loved had suffered that kind of abuse—that kind of physical and emotional trauma—was enough to send him into a rage. For the first time, he was glad Tristan hadn't given him the bastard's location.

Shoving the violent thoughts aside, Carlos focused on the woman before him, letting her lightness and warmth soothe away his rage.

Between him and his family, he'd make sure she only knew joy—and no one would ever hurt her again.

****

Quite a crowd had turned out to celebrate Rosa Delgado, both young and old, and Judith was glad to see the big smile the surprise party had put on the older woman's face. The best part of the evening had been the actual surprise. Just thinking of the random, un-unified chorus of 'happy birthday'—in both English and Spanish—and the lone '*Feliz Navidad*'—almost made Judith laugh again. Their friends and family had a great sense of humor.

But as much as she was enjoying herself, she had stolen away to one of the empty tables at the far end of the room, needing a moment to herself. Watching the crowded dance floor, and witnessing the carefree laughter and fun, brought on an unexpected flood of resentment and nostalgia. If there was one thing she missed after the accident, it was dancing. Though it wasn't as if she'd been forbidden from ever entering a dance floor, dancing just wasn't the same for her anymore. She missed how she used to move, how she used to let the rhythm transport her someplace else for a while, as she let her body take over.

No, it would never be the same…

"Having fun?"

Judith turned to Carlos and her heart warmed at the sight of him. Despite the fatigue that was settling in, she was enjoying herself.

Carlos pulled up a seat beside her and she slipped her hand into his. He gave it a gentle squeeze.

"My aunt really likes your gift," he said. "It makes it easy for her to get all the attention without doing a thing."

Judith laughed. She'd noticed the looks some had given the sculpture and knew this was his way of saying her gift was a bit flamboyant but she didn't care. Rosa seemed genuinely delighted by it and that was all that mattered.

Carlos fell silent for a moment, then said, "I'm going to see Carrone tomorrow."

She tensed, but he squeezed her hand reassuringly.

"Tristan was able to find a connection between Laurie and the casino and I just set up a meeting with him to go over everything." He paused before adding, "I need to bring you with me so you can explain your role it in to him. Carrone values transparency and the only way to get him on your side is to be upfront with him."

She nodded stiffly, forcing her anxiety aside. She'd known this moment would come and she would have to resign herself to it.

"What did Tristan find?" she asked.

"Another name. This one a company and apparently one of Royal Courts' investors. We just need to know who from Diamante Enterprises wanted—" She tensed at the name and his tone grew sharp with concern. "What is it?"

"Nothing," she reassured him. "I just remember seeing that company name on Mr. Kristensen's calendar one day. He had a meeting scheduled with them the day after I received the envelope." The name had stuck with her because she remembered thinking her semester of Italian had come in handy because she understood that *diamante* meant diamond.

Carlos was silent for a moment. "Do you remember if there was anyone specific he was meeting with?"

She shook her head solemnly, wishing she could give him more. "I don't even know what the meeting was about. I could only see what was on his calendar. I never actually set up his meetings."

"It's okay," he said, squeezing her hand again. "This is a start. Once I bring this information to Carrone, maybe he can shed more light on all this."

Judith hoped so. She wanted desperately to put this all behind her. Maybe she could release some of the regret and anxiety in her.

Then that would leave only the quiet panic that wasn't too far from her sanity. The not knowing what Laurie or the people she was working for had done with the information of her new identity, or if Ken had access to that information, was frightening.

They spent another hour at the party until Carlos, who must have sensed her weariness, called it a night. They said their goodbyes to Gil and Rosa then made their way through the crowd and toward the exit. The party was in full swing as people gathered on the dance floor. Though some people were also on their way out, more continued to pour into the lively banquet hall.

Carlos had a firm hold on her hand as they walked into the cool night air. They ran into a couple that appeared to be friends of his and she immediately recognized the big, tattooed man from the photo in Gil's home. She vaguely remembered Tristan mentioning Gil training the large man to becoming a mixed martial arts prizefighter.

Judith glanced at the beautiful woman with the bright red lipstick at his side and waited for the men to introduce them. Neither did. Instead, Carlos told the couple where they could find his uncle and aunt and she couldn't help the annoyance that came over her when he referred to her gift as the "big, flashy thing" that they wouldn't miss.

As she and Carlos made their way to his car, Judith let him know that she didn't appreciate his underhanded insult. At her glare, Carlos lost his grin. Just a little.

"Okay, I apologize for insulting your gift," he said, chagrined, though he didn't seem all that bothered by it. In fact, he didn't seem all that affected by her annoyance with him. If anything, he appeared a bit pleased with it.

"Why are you still smiling?" she snapped.

"Because you're angry with me."

She frowned. "And you're happy about that?"

"No, I'm happy that you're telling me how you feel. And that you're feeling comfortable enough to finally show me your temper."

She rolled her eyes. "Oh, I have a temper. I just know how to keep it under control."

He looped his arm around her shoulders and pulled her to his side. "But that's the thing, *muñeca*. I want you to lose your control with me."

She wrapped her arms around his waist. "I don't think you realize how much I already have."

They made it to her apartment and like before, he walked her to her door. For a moment, they stood in her living room, staring at each other. She didn't want him to leave and he obviously didn't want to go.

"So," she began, "will you pick me up to—"

"Come home with me."

His abrupt words took her by surprise and she gaped at him.

"Now? Tonight?"

"Yeah," he said with a shrug. "You could stay with me for a few days. While we get this whole thing strengthened out at Royal Courts."

"But I have Prince…"

"Bring him."

She was silent for a moment. "Carlos, I won't leave if that's—"

"I know," he said, shaking his head with a short laugh. "Maybe I should just be more blunt. I *want* you to come home with me. I want to make love with you tonight and tomorrow night and the night after that.

Then I want to hold you while we sleep. What do *you* want?"

She couldn't deny her elation at the thought of spending another night with him. She had come to treasure those quiet moments and she wasn't going to deny herself that pleasure. A wide smile spread across her lips.

"I want that too."

She didn't have much to pack since everything was already in various luggages and bags. She quickly threw in some fresh clothes and supplies in a large, old suitcase and dragged it out of the bedroom. "Do you want to head down with these?" she said, handing him the luggage and another bag with Prince's things.

He took the suitcase and shoulder bag from her. "That's it?"

She nodded. "I just need to find Prince and get him in the tote then we'll meet you downstairs."

"Don't be long," he said, pulling her in for a quick hug.

It took less than a minute to track down her stubborn cat, but much longer to convince him to leave his comfortable perch from under her bed. A little bribery in the form of treats—a handful of them—finally got him to come to her. She clutched him to her as she reached for the tote bag.

She wasn't surprised when the knock came at the door just as she began to place Prince inside his makeshift carrier. "I'm coming, I'm coming," she muttered. She swung the bag over her shoulder and rushed to the door. "Carlos, I—"

The words abruptly froze on her lips when she saw

who stood at her doorway. The blood drained from her body and the edges around her vision dimmed.

She was going to be sick.

"Hello Abby."

chapter 16

The thing about fear was that it eventually evolved. So much so that one became numb to it.

That was the stage she was in right now.

Judith took a step back, vaguely surprised that she could still move, as Ken came into the apartment and quietly shut the door behind him.

The bag slipped from her arm with a soft thud. She barely spared Prince a thought as he dashed behind the sofa.

Her heart pounded in her chest, but she never took her eyes away from Ken. The grin on his handsome, light brown face stretched the angry scar that slashed across his left jaw. He seemed bigger too, broader around the shoulders. She hadn't seen him in five years, since the night of the accident, and she absently wondered if the mark had been a product of his decision to end their lives that night.

"I've missed you, Abby."

She had dreaded this moment for so long, wondering what she would do if she ever had to come face to face with her worst nightmare. Fainting had come to mind. Hysteria had also been a thought.

She did neither.

"You need to leave, Ken." The strength of her voice surprised her. "Now."

Ken sighed and came toward her. She took another step back.

"I know you don't want to see me," he said. "You haven't come to visit me in five years, even after I sent you all those letters. You never responded to any of them."

She shook her head, not at all fooled by his solemn expression. She knew what lay behind those earnest brown eyes and deceptively calm tone. It certainly wasn't remorse.

"I didn't get them."

"Because you moved and changed your name."

He said it as if she were to blame for breaking the communication between them. As if she had no right or reason to purposely avoid him.

"How did you know I was here?"

His smile was laced with satisfaction. "I told you I would always find you, Abby. And I did. You're my soul mate and don't forget that."

He raised his hand to her face and she flinched and took another step back. His twisted with anger.

"See, that's that the kind of shit that pisses me off," he snapped. "I want to touch you, but you won't let me."

Bile rose in her throat. "You need to leave," she repeated, keeping her tone calm, not wanting to agitate him. "I was on my way out and I can't—"

His face hardened and he ran his hand over his short cropped hair. Her back stiffened at the small action. He was getting agitated.

"I've been waiting three days for you to get back. Where are you going now?" He looked at her sharply. "Who the hell were you with?"

She knew better than to respond to that. "You can't be here, Ken," she said calmly, trying to remain firm without aggravating the situation. Once she got him out of her apartment, then she would let herself feel something. For now, she would keep it all bottled inside her. "Isn't part of your parole to stay...stay in California?"

He didn't appreciate that reminder. "Is that why you changed your name?" he asked, eyeing her closely. "You didn't want to see me anymore? You thought that would keep me from finding you?"

He rubbed the back of his neck again and shivers of dread moved down her spine.

"I...I'm glad to see you're doing okay, Ken, but you really have to leave now. Before someone finds out you left—"

"*Stop telling me to leave*," he snapped, his hands balling into fists. "I'm not going anywhere. Not without you."

She could only stare at him, her mouth growing dry.

"Five years I thought about you," he whispered. "Only you. And now you can't even pretend to be happy to see me."

Her eyes were trained on his hands. "I-I am happy to see you," she lied.

"Bullshit. You won't even let me touch you." He set his jaw as his brown eyes bore into her. "Do you have a new boyfriend, Abby?"

She didn't know what possessed her to blurt out that response, but she wanted him to know that truth. "Yes."

She should have been prepared for his violent reaction, but she wasn't. As quick as a snake, he came at her and grabbed her by the throat. Pulled at his hand, she bit her lip to keep from crying out. Though he didn't apply any pressure, he refused to release her.

"No one is taking you away from me, Abby. Not again," he said harshly. "Remember that."

Suddenly, the front doorknob rattled, followed by firm knocking. "Judith?"

Carlos.

Her heady relief was abruptly replaced by horror when Ken released her and drew out a small gun. The sleek, black weapon was the most chilling thing she'd ever seen. Her eyes locked on the deadly weapon and her voice was lodged in her throat.

"Who's that?" Ken snapped.

"No!" The strangled shout escaped her when he began advancing toward the door and she rushed to stand between him and the door. She couldn't let anything happen to Carlos.

"*Judith?*" The single word came again through the door, and was filled with so much worry, it tore at her. "Open the door, *muñeca*."

Ken's eyes snapped angrily toward the door. "Is that the new boyfriend?" The eerie calm in his voice frightened her like nothing else could.

"T-that's just my co-worker," she said slowly.

Ken's lips tightened as if he were deciding whether to believe her or not. "What does he want?" he asked, still staring at the door.

She shook her head, knowing the best way to keep Carlos from harm was to lie. "I don't know."

He glanced down at her, his eyes still blazed with angry suspicion. "Get rid of him."

She nodded jerkily then, on barely steady legs, she went to the door. "Mr. Moreno, please go away."

Long silence filled the air.

"Judith, what's wrong?" Carlos asked, his sharp tone muffled through the closed door.

"Nothing. I don't want you here." She kept her focus on the door and added sharpness to her voice to mask the trembling creeping into it. "Now leave me alone. *Please*."

"Open the door and say that to my face." There was a challenge in his tone that said he wouldn't leave until she did just that.

Judith glanced at Ken, debating whether she should do it. The gun in Ken's hand twitched at his side, but there was a growing agitation in him that increased her own. If she opened the door now, nothing would stop Carlos from coming in. And then what? Watch him get shot? Her heart was now lodged in her throat, but she had to find a way to convince Carlos to leave.

"Come on, baby. Please open up."

She winced at the anguish in his voice, and tears blurred her eyes. She didn't dare glance at Ken. "No, I won't," she snapped forcefully, her voice catching. "Can't you understand English? I don't want you here.

Cazador aquí. Do you understand that?" She hoped with everything she had that he did. "Now go away!"

Silence once again fell on the other side of the door. Carlos said nothing else after that and she dimly wondered if he'd truly understood what she'd meant by those words.

She closed her eyes, briefly—whether in relief or despair, she didn't know. She continued to face the closed door, distinctly aware of the monster breathing behind her.

In that moment, she felt more alone than she'd ever felt in her life.

****

Carlos had never known fear quite like this.

He pushed away from the door and reached for his cell phone. Calling the police could escalate the situation, and the lights and noise would likely aggravate Tate. Carlos closed his eyes, thinking of what was going on inside that apartment—and thinking of the last case his cousin had worked on that left a mother and her two year old son dead.

He couldn't let that happen to Judith. Carlos ran his hand through his hair and called the one person he could trust.

"Tristan, he's got her," Carlos said without preamble as soon as he answered.

"Carlos? What the hell are you talking about?"

"That son-of-a-bitch Tate has her," Carlos snapped. "The guy who was supposed to fucking be in California!"

"*Jesus*," Tristan breathed. "How? Never mind. Where are you?"

"At her place. I need your help to get her out of there. Hurry up and bring your gear!"

"Carlos, listen to me. You need to calm down if you want this to all end well. Now tell me exactly what's going on."

Carlos clenched his teeth. He didn't have time for this, but the last rational part of his brain said his cousin was right. He needed to calm down.

"He's got her locked in her apartment. He probably has a gun on her or something because she refused to open the door." There was no doubt in Carlos' mind that the man had a weapon with him. He had tried to kill himself and Judith before. There was nothing or no one that could stop him from trying to do so again.

Carlos released a frustrated breath. "*Damn it*, Tristan. Where the hell are you? I need to get her out of there."

"I'm in my car, not far from you now. I'm going to call my team and we'll get her out. Just don't do anything until I get there." Tristan paused then asked, "Have you spoken to her since?"

"Not since she told me to leave." Glancing at the closed apartment door, he blanched. "What if he..." Carlos' gut twisted at the thought and he clenched his jaw to keep the bile from rising.

"Don't think about that," Tristan snapped. "I'm on my way. Just hang tight."

As the minutes passed, Carlos thought of several ways he could get to Judith. But each one led to her potentially getting hurt if he failed. He watched the apartment door as if he could burn holes through it.

What was that bastard doing to her?

****

Judith blinked away the wetness from her eyes and stepped away from the door, keeping a good amount of distance between her and Ken.

"Okay, Kenny, he's gone," Judith said slowly, using her old nickname for him to calm him. "Please. Could you put the gun away?"

"Why did he call you, '*baby*'?"

Her stomach tightened, but she simply shrugged. "I don't know."

"I don't believe you," he said, his eyes watchful. "I think you fucked him. Did you fuck him, Abby?"

The rigidity in her body kept her legs from buckling beneath her. She was prepared to fight back if he slipped into one of his rages and came after her. She wasn't ready to die and would fight him with every fiber in her being if she had too.

"Kenny, it's just a word," she said, trying to soothe him so he forgot about the gun he held in his hand. "It means nothing."

Ken's face hardened and he took a step toward her. "Do you like having sex with him? Can he make you come like I can?"

Disgust and disbelief rolled in her stomach, but she forced herself to stand her ground. She wouldn't give him the satisfaction of letting him intimidate her or see her fear. The old Abby would have succumbed to her terror by now. But not now. Not Judith.

"Would you like something to drink?"

She surprised them both by the unexpected question, but she wanted any excuse to get away from him. She started toward the kitchen, but he grabbed her arm. His hand was like iron manacles and she hated that he was touching her.

"No," he said, dragging her toward him. "What I would like is a kiss."

Judith stiffened. Nausea threatened to rise again. She could pretend that she wanted him, that he didn't sicken her, just to soothe whatever neurotic desire he had for her. But what if he demanded more? She knew without a doubt, she wouldn't be able to go through with it. She would rather die than let him touch her again.

"I don't want to kiss you, Kenny," she said, her mind racing to think of anything she could to stall him. "N-not with that gun in your hand."

He frowned and looked down at his hand as if he'd just realized he'd been holding it. He laid it on the end table then reached for her again.

"Okay, now give me a kiss." Wrapping his hand around her neck, he pulled her to him. She flinched as he pressed his mouth firmly against hers. His lips were eager and searching over hers, trying to elicit a response from her. It didn't.

"Abby," he groaned against her mouth. "I've missed you."

He forced his tongue between her lips and she jerked away, clenching her teeth and fighting the urge not to gag. She glanced at the gun on the table. She needed to get to it. She had never held a gun before, but she would do whatever she had to convince him to leave her apartment—to leave her alone.

"Kenny," she began slowly. "It's too soon. Please, I need time to—"

He released a frustrated sound. "Enough time has passed. I've waited a long time to see you again. It was the only thing that kept me sane in there."

Her heart thumped in her ear. *But you aren't sane.* "Then why did you come here with a gun? Did you come here to see me or scare me?"

He frowned. "I came here because I love you, Abby. I don't think you appreciate how much I do." Something in his expression changed and tightened with resolve. "The gun is for my protection. I told you I wasn't going back and I meant it. I just came to get you and then we can leave here for good."

Oh, dear God. Did he come here to finish what he started? She didn't want to die.

"Ken, please." She couldn't keep the earnestness from her tone. "Please don't do this."

He ignored her as his eyes ran down the length of her. "You're going to marry me, Abby. Like you should have a long time ago."

A mix of relief and dread washed over her. He hadn't come to kill her, but he was truly insane if he thought she would willingly bind herself to him. The more she glanced at the gun, the farther away it seemed.

"But first," he said, his eyes still travelling down her body. "I want to make love to you. It's been too long."

Before she could react, he grabbed her shirt and began tugging it over her head.

"*No!*" She wrenched free of him and the telltale sound of fabric ripping was loud in the room.

He cursed, grabbing her by the hair and jerking her back to him. She cried out at the stinging in her scalp.

"*God damn it*, look what you made me do," he snarled vehemently.

Cool air rushed down her neck and inside her shirt and she vaguely realized that the collar of her shirt gaped open from where it had torn. Her chest and black bra were exposed and she frantically tried to cover herself while tugging the hand behind her head.

His grip tightened and she winced.

"Abby, don't fucking pull away from me. I didn't punish you for fucking someone behind my back, but don't push me. I'm this close to losing my fucking temper."

But she couldn't go through with it. She couldn't stomach the thought of having him inside her. In that moment she realized she would have to kill him or die trying.

"Okay, Kenny, I'm sorry," she said calmly, trying to placate him. "I didn't mean to. Can you please let me go now? My head's hurting."

He was rigid behind her, but he slowly released his tight grip on her hair. As soon as he released her, she jerked away from him and reached for the gun. He cursed and grabbed for it at the same time.

She was quick but he was quicker.

The taste of failure was bitter in her mouth as he held the gun in his hand. The blow that came next was jarring but not unexpected. His fists connected with the side of her face and a sharp cry escaped her as white sparks flashed behind her eyes. She managed to stay on her feet, but intense pain began to spread through her face.

She tried to clear her head, to orient herself, but she

wasn't allowed the time. Ken grabbed her arm and began dragging her to the back of the apartment, muttering insults and curses at her. Judith panicked as he continued toward the bedroom. She knew if she went in there with him, she would not come out alive.

"*No!*" she shrieked, tugging at her arm and trying to dig in her heels but he was stronger. He always had been.

But she was determined and she continued pulling at her arm and pounding on his back, all the while screaming for him to let her go.

****

Carlos' world froze at the sounds of Judith's screams.

It was as if someone had wrenched out his heart and the only thing that mattered was getting to her. Everything became a blur, and suddenly he was through the door and in her apartment.

His eyes quickly took in the scene before him. From the tall, wild-looking man pointing a nine millimeter directly at him and his other arm clasped around Judith's neck. But it was the black bruise forming on the side of her face and the blood trickling down her cut lip that stole his attention. Her shirt was torn in the front and her eyes were glazed over with terror and pain.

He lost it.

With a violent snarl, Carlos charged toward the man, ignoring the gun leveled at him. Ken's eyes widened as Carlos continued toward him with violent determination. Ken turned the gun on Judith, jabbing it at her side.

Carlos froze.

"Stay right there," Ken snapped, his face contorting with fury and disgust. "Is that him, Abby? Is he the one you've been fucking?"

Judith didn't respond. She just continued staring at him with a mixture of relief and regret. Carlos tried to tell her with one look that everything would be okay, but he didn't know if he succeeded. The terror and rage burning through him made it impossible for him to think straight.

Carlos tore his eyes away from Judith. The gun at her side could end her life in an instant and if he wanted to stay calm, to redirect the man's anger, he couldn't look at her.

"Look man, I know you don't want to hurt her. Why don't you just keep the gun on me?" Carlos took a careful step toward them.

Ken swung the gun toward him. "I said stay right there."

Carlos threw his hands up. "Okay." At least now he had the man's attention.

Ken still had the advantage, but Carlos was relieved the gun was no longer directed at her. He didn't want to do anything to set him off the deranged man.

"Shut the door."

Carlos did as he said, never taking his eyes from him or the gun. Now he just needed to get close enough…

"You can stop right there."

Carlos stopped. "Look, why don't you let Jud—Abby go? She's hurt and scared."

"Fuck you," Ken snarled. "Don't you tell me what to do with my fiancée. You think I'm fucking stupid. I know you've been fucking her. Did you make her come?"

He took his free hand and slid it down her breasts. Carlos' jaw tightened and he forced himself to stay right where he was. He just needed Ken to take his eyes off him for a second then he would lunge. But the man held his gaze as he continued running his hand down to her crotch.

"I could make her come. All the time." He unsnapped her jeans and slowly pulled the zipper open. "Let me show you."

Judith cried out as he teased fingers on the edge of her panties.

"Son-of-a-bitch!"

"Don't you dare come any closer," Ken snapped, bringing the gun beneath her jaw.

Panic stopped him mid-stride and Carlos instantly glanced down at Judith. Her eyes were staring straight ahead, as if she was distancing herself from what was happening.

And what was about to happen.

A frustrated growl burst through Carlos as Ken's hands disappeared into her pants. But there was an excitement in the man's eyes that made Carlos' blood curdle. His light brown cheeks were flushed slightly and he placed a lingering kiss on her hair.

"*God damn you,* let her go," Carlos barked. "She doesn't want this."

"Yeah, she does." Ken jerked her back against him and she winced.

Carlos' blood boiled.

"She always wants me," Ken murmured into her

hair. "I'll show you how much she wants me."

****

Judith mind was numb.

She was locked in a nightmare that she couldn't wake from. A nightmare she had pulled Carlos into. He didn't look at her as Ken slid his hand inside her panties and a jolt of disgust coursed through her, but she tried to lock it all inside her.

Except she couldn't anymore.

She couldn't let him destroy what little of herself she had left. She couldn't let him shame her in front of the man she loved. And in that moment, she forgot the gun, forgot her fear and disgust. She just wanted to get away from him. Her body became stone as his fingers slipped inside her panties, touching her, rubbing her.

Something in her snapped.

With a sharp cry of outrage, she jabbed her elbow as hard as she could into his abdomen. Ken grunted and she pushed away from him.

Carlos didn't hesitate.

In a blur, he flew across the room toward them. Ken barely had time to raise the gun before Carlos was on him. Judith watched as the two men struggled for control of the gun.

Hate like she never felt consumed her and without thinking, she flew on Ken's back, beating and clawing at him with all her pent-up rage.

Ken tried to shake her off him while still holding on to the gun. Everything was a blur and she tried with all her might to hold on, to inflict as much pain as he'd done to her. She managed to dig her nails into his neck and break skin. He yowled then jerked back violently as she scraped him raw.

With one hard swing, Ken threw her from his back and she bounced against the wall, her head connecting hard with the hanging mirror. Glass shattered all around her just as the gun went off.

The sound was deafening and a sudden chill ran through her body as she fell to her knees and onto the shattered glass, numbly wondering where all the blood had come from.

****

The gunshot was loud and distinct in the small apartment.

It was as if someone had wrenched out his heart and he stopped breathing. Carlos didn't remember moving, only that he was now straddling Ken and ramming his fist into his face.

There was a dull buzzing in his ear as he brought his fist down, again and again. But he felt nothing, he heard nothing.

Something wet sprayed across his face but still he didn't stop. Not even when strong hands grabbed his arms and began pulling him away from the now still body.

With a vicious growl, he wrenched free, but was immediately thrown on his side and locked into a submission hold.

"*Damn it, Carlos!* Calm down. You're gonna fucking kill him."

It took a moment for Tristan's voice to pierce through his rage. That's exactly what he wanted. He wanted to kill the bastard. But a glimpse of Judith, knelt across the room, stilled his bloodlust and he briefly shut his eyes as immense relief washed over him.

She wasn't dead.

"Get the hell off me, Tristan," he growled, tugging on the arm around his neck.

Tristan hesitated but eventually released him. Carlos shoved away from him and started toward her then froze, paralyzed by the blood on her face. Her wide eyes stared up at him, dazed.

The look on her face jarred him as he helped her to her feet. He couldn't speak.

God, baby, I'm sorry.

He had promised he wouldn't let anything happen to her and he had failed her.

Tristan came up beside them, cell phone in hand. A low groan came from Ken and they all turned to look at the man who still lay on the ground. For the first time Carlos saw the damage he'd done. Blood covered the man's face and shirt, and the swelling around his eyes began to force them shut.

But it wasn't enough.

Judith dug her nails into his forearm as another groan came from the man. Incredible rage filled him at her distress, and it propelled him to action. The gun was a few feet away from his body and Carlos calmly walked over and picked it up.

"Carlos?"

He couldn't be sure who had called out to him, keeping his gaze down on the son-of-a-bitch who had terrorized his woman, who had tried to kill her. Images of Judith bruised and bloody, of the crushed and twisted car, of her fighting for her life in the hospital, filled his head.

He remembered the way she trembled against him when she told him about that night, the way her voice trembled when she confessed her fear of this bastard. And he couldn't shake the rage or the helplessness of watching that son-of-a-bitch put his hand inside…

With icy calm, Carlos raised the gun to the man's head.

"*Carlos!*"

Judith's scream jolted him out of his deadly resolve. But only enough for him to realize he didn't want her to see this.

"Tristan, get her out of here," he said over his shoulder, unable to look at her without his fury consuming him.

"Carlos," Tristan began, taking tentative steps toward him. "I can't let you do this. Now put the fucking gun down and let me call this in."

He glanced at his cousin, vaguely registering his shock and the cell phone poised in his hand. Carlos shook his head.

"I have to do this," he said, returning his attention to the man whose bloodied face glared up at him with cold, hollow eyes.

Tristan was at his side now. "No, what you need to do is go to Judith. Go to her, man. She needs *you* right now."

Carlos turned to her and sucked in his breath.

The horrified look on her face as she stared at him was his undoing. He handed his cousin the gun and went to her. To his immense relief, she didn't flinch away from him when he gently pulled her into his arms. He never wanted to see that look on her face again.

He never wanted her to look at *him* like that again.

chapter 17

His head felt heavy.

Carlos rested his head in his hands as he sat in the hospital waiting room. He was only down the hall from Judith's room, but he was eager to get back. It had been a long night last night, but he hadn't left her side since. Unfortunately, he'd been forced out while she gave her statement to a detective. With the situation the way it was—an illegal weapon with his prints on it and Tate in the neighboring hospital being treated for his injuries—the officer would not allow them to be together while she gave her account of what happened.

He realized he hadn't left the hospital since they'd brought her in last night. Carlos glanced at the time and cursed. He pulled out his cell and dialed David Carrone.

As soon as the man answered, Carlos said without preamble. "I won't be meeting with you today."

There was a brief pause before David responded. "What happened?"

"I'm at the hospital with Judith."

Carlos told him about her attack last night—just enough to fill him in on her situation without going into detail about her past. He also explained Judith's forced involvement with the break-in, and what Tristan had found about their latest investment company, Diamante Enterprises.

"Shit," David muttered.

"What?" Carlos had planned to tell him all this at their face-to-face meeting today, but it couldn't wait and quite frankly, his concentration was on far more important matters.

"I met with one of the owners last night," David said. "Rachelle Silva. Evidently she needs my help and I never thought to link her company to the break-in."

Carlos frowned. "Help with what?"

David released a heavy sigh. "It's a long story. I'll fill you in when you get back." He paused before asking, "When will you be back in?"

"I don't know," Carlos said. "I'm not leaving her."

Carlos knew his boss had suspected something between them and if his latest actions only raised a few suspicions against him, Carlos didn't care. He'd already been prepared to resign. It would be up to David to decide if he wanted him to finish out the month.

"Look, I understand Judith must have felt backed into a corner," David said. "And I hope she pulls through. But you have to understand that if it turns out the company was compromised in any way from what she did, you won't be able to protect her."

Carlos clenched his jaw. "She's already been through enough, Carrone. If you need to pin this on someone, then pin it on me."

David was silent for a moment. "Well then, until we get this mess straightened out, I guess I'll just have to rip up your resignation letter."

Carlos ended the call, and for a minute he wondered if he'd just been duped into keeping his job at Royal Courts. He shook his head ruefully. Guess he had.

"She still in there?" Tristan asked, taking the empty seat beside him.

He nodded. Silence fell between them. He knew his cousin was shouldering a lot of the guilt for what had happened last night. Carlos wanted to be mad at his cousin for not monitoring Tate better, but Carlos knew that wasn't fair of him. His cousin had gone above and beyond for him these past few days and he couldn't take that for granted.

"About last night," Tristan began.

"If you're going to apologize," Carlos interrupted, "Save it. It wasn't your job to babysit Tate. You stopped me from killing a man last night so whatever guilt you're still carrying, let it go. I'm carrying enough of that for both of us."

It had been Kenneth Tate's parole officer who had exaggerated his visits with Tate on his reports. The man, who blamed his case load on the mishap, hadn't even realized Tate had left California a few days ago. Apparently the now terminated PO had been prioritizing his cases by convictions—the bigger the crime, the more attention he paid the criminal. Unfortunately, Kenneth Tate and his conviction hadn't warranted much of his attention.

A heavy weariness began to settle in him and Carlos rubbed his hand over his jaw. He was grateful that last night hadn't resulted in any fatalities. From Tate's hands—or his. The look on Judith's face when he'd held that gun in his hand was burned in Carlos' memory. He hated that she had seen him lose control like that.

****

"How's your shoulder?"

Carlos squeezed her hand. Judith didn't think he'd let go of her since they'd arrived at the hospital. And the few times he had, he hadn't gone far.

"It's better."

She sat on the edge of the hospital bed, chilled in just the thin gown they had given her to wear. He had stopped rubbing his shoulder so the medicine the nurse had given him must have helped. His knuckles, however, were still red and bruised.

Now that the shock from last night had worn off, Judith could think again. She barely remembered the report she had given the detective that morning. Thankfully, Tristan had taken care of most of it so everything after had been a formality. Apparently, they had Ken in custody at another hospital, while he recovered from his injuries. After he was released, he would face additional charges along with his parole violation.

"How's Prince?" She had worried about her poor cat all last night, scared that the stray bullet had hit him and no one had known.

"He's fine," Carlos assured her. "Tristan brought him to my place and I'm sure he's enjoying having the place all to himself."

Relief washed over her and she smiled at the thought.

"How are *you* feeling?" Carlos asked.

Judith smiled reassuringly at him, placing a hand on his chest, feeling the steady heartbeat there. "Better."

She was lucky to have found him and to know his love. Having him in her life shined a light on a life that had been dimmer than she'd been willing to admit. Until last night, when she'd been faced with the possibility of never seeing him again, she hadn't realized how much Carlos truly meant to her. He fought hard, but loved harder.

Looking up at his strong, tired face, she placed her hand on his cheek and kissed him again. She wanted to tell him what was in her heart, but the lump in her throat was too big.

"Carlos, I...," her voice broke.

Warmth and understanding flashed in his dark eyes as he looked down at her. "I know, baby," He placed a light kiss on her lips. "I love you too."

She tightened her grip on his hands, not wanting to ever let go. She still couldn't believe she was alive. That she was still *here*—with him. Last night, when she'd heard the gun go off, she'd been sure it had hit her—that she would bleed to death on her apartment floor.

But she hadn't.

She hadn't even been hit. The extent of her injuries had been the scalp wound she had gotten from hitting the mirror. Though it had been stitched, the doctors had wanted to keep her overnight for testing and observation, to make sure she hadn't suffered any trauma from the head injury.

Before they had performed the tests, they had asked her standard medical history questions and she had to disclose her birth name so they could pull up her past medical records.

Now, she and Carlos waited for the doctors' to let her know if she would be released today. She had enough memories of nights in the hospital. It would make her smile that much bigger if she could leave tonight.

Carlos, however, didn't share in her relief. Guilt and fatigue etched across his face. No amount of her reassuring him that it wasn't his or Tristan's fault didn't seem to ease his burden.

She accepted that last night had been necessary. She had been running from her past, afraid of what would come—of what it might do to her—if she was forced to face her fears. Now that she had, she realized she was a fighter.

Ken had tried, but failed, to take her life again and for the past five years she had functioned as if he had. He may have changed it, but he hadn't taken it. And for the first time, Judith felt as if she'd finally reclaimed it.

She had faced her demon and survived. Twice.

"Ms. Bell?"

Judith turned to the door. Her doctor and another friendly face in white scrubs entered the room. Both women appeared young though the second doctor had a maturity about her that said she may be older than she looked.

"How are you feeling?"

"Ready to go home."

Her doctor nodded. "Well your results came back and as far as I can see, every thing's fine, so we can certainly make that happen."

Judith shoulders sagged in relief.

"However, there was something that came up in your results that we wanted to discuss with you." Her doctor glanced at Carlos. "In private."

What reprieve Judith felt before vanished at the doctor's words. How could everything be fine if whatever she needed to speak to her about sounded so…ominous? She turned to Carlos. He was tensed beside her—and he didn't look happy about the doctor's words either.

"Do you want me to leave?" he asked her, ignoring the doctors standing across from them.

Judith turned to the women. "Is it okay if he stays?"

They shared a look, but her doctor shrugged. "It's up to you."

Judith squeezed Carlos' hand. Whatever the doctor had to tell her, she wanted him near. His presence was a calm comfort to her.

The younger looking doctor took a step toward her. "At our hospital, it's policy to run all standard tests, including pregnancy, for our female patients. Now, before we ran your tests, you informed the nurse that you weren't pregnant, but your test results show that you are."

Judith gaped at the woman. "Are you sure? We've only been—" She blushed, not ready to go into detail about their sex life. "How is that possible? They told me I couldn't have children."

The woman pursed her lips and nodded. "The urine test and hCG levels confirm that you are, but based on your medical history, the surgery to your pelvic region weakened your cervix." She paused, glancing at Carlos again. "The surgery didn't make it impossible for you to conceive, but it made it highly unlikely for you to carry a fetus to full-term."

Judith couldn't get over the shock. This wasn't what she'd expected. She glanced at Carlos but his expression wasn't one of astonishment or disbelief as she'd expected. It was of fierce possessiveness. But then, he had only just learned of her condition. She'd spent five years living with the idea that she would never be able to carry a life inside of her. Now the doctor was telling her she had been given this miracle?

The younger doctor gestured to the other woman. "This is Doctor Jan. She's a specialist here at the hospital and she has taken a look at your files and can better explain it to you."

"Ms. Bell," the other woman began, "there are several options for women in your condition."

The specialist proceeded to tell her about the harm a weakened cervix could cause her and the baby. She explained the procedure, a cervical cerclage, which would reinforce the cervix, but still leave her at high risk for losing the baby within her first trimester. Even after the procedure was performed, it still did not guarantee that she would have a successful pregnancy.

The casualness in the way the woman outlined the possible risks and complications annoyed Judith. The woman further drove home her point with numbers and statistics, yet none of that could take away from Judith's elation.

She was pregnant. With Carlos' baby.

Judith understood the doctors' were only trying to present her with the realism of her situation, to force her to be practical, but she had something far more stronger on her side.

She had hope.

"The possibility of a premature rupture of the fetal membrane is quite high even during the second and third trimester," the specialist said. "Though the decision is ultimately yours, Ms. Bell, it is my professional opinion that you terminate the pregnancy, while it's still early."

Judith sucked in her breath. "*No*." She wanted to shout the words again, but clenched her teeth to keep from doing so. She had just learned of their baby and now the woman was telling her to get rid of it?

Judith's hand unconsciously went to her belly, as if she could shield it inside her by the mere touch.

She was just given a miracle. She wouldn't willingly destroy it. No matter what.

"Judith, maybe you should take some time to think about this," Carlos said.

She glanced at Carlos, surprised. Was he thinking she should go through with it?

"Carlos, I'm *not* aborting it."

He squeezed her hand. "And I don't want you to," he said strongly. "But I don't want you to risk your life trying to keep it either." He cupped her chin and held her gaze. "I won't lose you."

"This is only a suggestion to spare you from a

potential miscarriage or stillbirth," the specialist added. "You could lose the baby tomorrow or next week or six months from now. And the greatest harm isn't just physical. If you fail to carry this baby, the emotional and mental harm would be tremendous."

Judith stared at the woman and, for the first time, detected a weary bitterness of someone who spoke from personal experience.

"My emotional and mental state wouldn't be any better if I voluntarily destroyed it," Judith said with an easy calm and finality she hoped would make them understand. "I'm not aborting my baby."

With her other hand still clasp in Carlos', she took their hands and placed it over her belly. Five years ago, she had to listen to doctors tell her she would never be able to have a baby. But they were wrong then and they could be wrong now.

Miracles were possible and her baby was proof of that.

She was going to have their baby.

****

Several days after her release from the hospital, Judith received the news that had left her numb with relief.

Ken was dead.

Officers had found him in his cell, a sheet wrapped tightly around his neck. He had ended his life. He'd left no note and no warning.

She couldn't be happy about that. There was nothing to celebrate for anyone dying. Death was permanent. Final. But the relief that had passed through her over the news was unmistakable.

She was finally free of him. He'd said he wouldn't return to prison and he had fulfilled that promise. She'd never have to face him again. She'd never have to testify, to recount everything that had happened that night in the apartment, or that night, long ago, when he'd sent the car careening over the rail.

He was gone.

It was over.

chapter 18

Three weeks later...

Judith's sharp cry pulled Carlos from his sleep.

She pushed at his chest and cried out again. He stared down at her, the low distressed sound tugging at his heart. He turned on the bedside lamp. The light usually helped to calm her when she woke.

"Judith, baby." He kept his tone low. "Wake up."

Her eyes flew open then widened as they focused on him.

"It's just a dream, m*uñeca*."

She lay rigid beside him, her eyes haunted. "I'm sorry I woke you."

"Don't be. You don't have anything to be sorry about."

It'd been weeks since the incident with Tate and even after his death, she had been plagued with these occasional nightmares. They didn't come often, but when they did, they were enough to bother her—and worry him.

He laced his fingers through hers and brought them to his lips. "What were you dreaming about?"

She shook her head, tears welling in her eyes.

"Tell me, baby."

She stared at him silently for a moment. After a while, she smiled softly. "I was dreaming about us," she murmured. "At the ranch house, eating chocolate, and drinking apple cider. And this time my chicken tamale casserole was perfect."

His lips quirked at the image. He needed to tell her one of these days how much he hated chicken tamale casserole but not tonight. Tonight, he wanted to slay whatever demons still lingered in her mind and haunted her dreams. He wanted her to share it with him so that he could carry some of her pain and stress, but she clearly just wanted to forget so he would let her. For now.

"Were we naked?"

She laid her hand on his cheek and slowly ran her fingers along the trim hairs on his jaw. "Yes. Very. In the big bathtub at the back of the house. There were red rose petals scattered everywhere. And about three big candles."

He lazily rubbed his hand down her back. "Only three?" he teased.

She smiled softly. "Okay, maybe six."

They fell silent for a moment, both wide awake. He was glad that her happy memories included him, but nights like this, he didn't know what to do to take away the darker ones that still plagued her.

He felt helpless and he hated that. Hated it as much as he did the panic that filled him every time he thought of her and the baby.

Though their baby growing inside her thrilled him like nothing he'd ever experienced, Carlos couldn't pretend that the risks she was taking in carrying their baby didn't exist. So far, she and the baby continued to do quite well, but he still found it difficult to share in her blind faith and optimism that everything would be okay.

He was terrified. For her. For their baby.

He, however, didn't let her see it. At least he tried not to. He wanted to shield her from any worry or doubt that may come from his fears. He needed to shoulder the burden alone and be strong for her.

Like she was doing now.

Carlos froze as it dawned on him that was what she had been doing. Trying to shield him from her pain and fear so that he wouldn't lose it. They hadn't spoken about Tate since they'd received news of his death. While Carlos was content to imagine the bastard forever roasting in hell, Judith still struggled to put it all behind her. Something she was trying to do alone.

If Carlos wanted her to be vulnerable with him, to share her pain and fears with him, he had to stop keeping his own from her. No matter how much he wanted to shield her from any more hurt, he had to trust that they would be stronger without any more barriers between them.

"I asked Tristan to find your birth parents," he said quietly, still rubbing her back. The silence that followed was so long he almost wondered if she had fallen asleep again.

"Did he?" she finally asked. There was a certain

alertness, a hopefulness, in her tone that tore at him.

"Yes," he admitted. He tried to put the words in a way that wouldn't sound harsh. But in the end, there was no perfect way to tell her. "They're both deceased." She stiffened against him. "Your father died a long time ago, a few months before you were born. And your birth mother passed a few years ago."

She was as still and silent as stone. Carlos tightened his arms around her.

"I have the file if you ever want to know more about them. I wasn't planning to tell you, at least not tonight, but I didn't want to keep something that important from you."

She nodded but said nothing for a while before she finally confessed, "I think I wanted to find them just to ask why. Why didn't they want me?"

He'd once asked the same question of his own father, a man who'd abandoned him and his mother before he could even speak and her words tugged at a deep feeling he'd long since learned to let go.

"I can't imagine getting rid of our baby," she continued, "and a part of me hopes that it had been hard for my birth mother to give me up." She ran her fingers along his chest, absently tracing the outline of his tattoo. "But I'm starting to realize that it doesn't matter. Not really. I was fortunate enough to have been adopted by my mom. We were a family of two, but she was always there for me."

Carlos placed his hand over hers and squeezed it. "And now you have me and my family. Don't ever forget that." His aunt and uncle always made him feel as one of their own and he wanted Judith to know that she never had to feel alone or unwanted again.

She took his hand and placed it over her middle. "And soon, we'll have our own."

He gently rubbed her belly, fierce love and possessiveness once again assailing him every time he touched her there. He looked into her eyes when he finally confessed, "I'm scared. For you, for the baby."

It hadn't been that long ago that he'd tried to convince her that fear wasn't a sign of weakness, yet he'd worried that the words would take away from his manhood. But they didn't. Every night he told her he loved her. And by sharing some of his fears with her, by allowing himself to be this vulnerable, he hoped he was showing her how much.

Her brows pulled together and she tightened her hands over his. "I know," she whispered. "I'm scared too, but my heart tells me everything will be fine. We'll both be fine. I know it and I'll make sure of it."

He knew she would. She followed everything her doctor told her and was taking it easy as they'd ordered.

"There are nights that I dream about holding our baby," she added, staring at his chest. "We're both together in bed, looking down at her while she sleeps in my arms. I can't quite make out what she looks like, but in the dreams, I know it's a girl and she's beautiful. She's perfect."

Carlos blinked, his throat tightening from the powerful emotion her words brought up. He could picture it clearly, a baby girl with tiny dimples, that was a blend of them both. It rendered him speechless.

After some time, she spoke again. "But there are

nights when I dream of Ken and in those dreams he's taking me away from you and the baby, and I'm alone again. With him."

His arms tightened around her. "No one is taking you from me," he murmured. "He's gone now and you don't have to be scared anymore."

Carlos couldn't keep the hard edge from his voice. He still remembered her pain and shame when she told him about her past. Still remembered the terror in her from that night in her apartment. And the blood on her face… He closed his eyes, trying to rid himself of the images, but those were memories that would probably never leave him.

"I know I shouldn't be relieved anyone is dead, but I am," she said quietly. "I'm glad he's dead."

Carlos said nothing, not knowing how to respond to that. He felt the same way, but he would neither encourage nor reproach her for it. Those were her honest feelings and he was just glad she was comfortable enough to share them freely with him. She was opening herself to him again and that was all he cared about.

She and their baby were now part of his present and his future.

He leaned back and tilted her chin until her gaze met his. "I love you, Judith. And I want you to marry me."

She glanced away but he understood. He told her he loved her every night and only recently, she'd been able to return the words. But the damage Kenneth Tate had done wouldn't be fixed overnight. She had been engaged when she'd endured much of her abuse and Carlos didn't want her to associate their union with what she'd experienced from that bastard's hands.

"I know you've been through a lot, but I want you to be my *wife*, not my baby's mama or my girlfriend. I want you and our baby to share my name."

She stared up at him searchingly. "Carlos, you know I love you and I'm happy with the way things are now. We don't need to be married to be a family."

Keeping his movements slow and deliberate, he leaned down and kissed her brow, then the tip of her nose before he moved to the underside of her jaw.

"I'm not asking you to marry me, *muñeca,* because 'no' is not an option." He traced his finger along her lower lip. "Anything worth having is worth waiting for, right? So I'll wait. However long it takes, I'll wait. And when you're ready to become my wife, I'll be here."

Her lips trembled, but she smiled at him through unshed tears. Before they could fall, he brought his lips down to hers and kissed her—kissed her with all the affection and tenderness he held for her, until there was only lightness and love that filled her memories.

epilogue

"Are you ready yet?"

"Yes!"

Carlos came up behind her and gently wrapped his arm around her middle.

"No you're not."

She caught his eyes from the reflection in the large bathroom mirror as she slid on her earrings. "Okay, I'm *almost* ready," she clarified, flashing him a quick smile.

He grinned and moved his palm on her lower belly, pressing the soft chiffon dress against her small bump. "How's my baby doing?"

She placed her hand over his and leaned against him. "Fine."

"Yes, you are," he said, a wicked gleam in his eye. He placed a quick kiss on the side of her neck. "And how's my other baby doing?"

Judith shook her head, but couldn't help the small laugh that escaped her. "She's also fine."

They stared at each other for a moment in the

mirror as he gently massaged her slightly protruding stomach. They didn't know if they were having a girl or a boy, but it became a habit for them to refer to their growing baby as *she*.

Judith had purposely chosen the red, floor length A-line gown, knowing it would conceal their growing baby. According to her doctor, she wasn't out of the woods yet so she and Carlos wanted to wait another month or so before they made a larger announcement.

"We don't have to go," Carlos offered.

She patted his hand. "I know, but I want to. Besides, *you* still work for him and I can't hide from the man forever."

Carlos' worry for her having to face David Carrone again was touching, but she had to remind him that it was unnecessary. Coming back to the casino resort had been a long time coming. Three months, in fact. And from the charity dinner invitation David extended to her and Carlos, he obviously wasn't holding what she'd done to his company against her. Apparently he'd understood her situation and focused his efforts on the blackmailer instead of her. But Judith couldn't continue to hide behind her excuses of fear and blackmail. Tonight, she would get a chance to face David Carrone and apologize for her actions.

"Okay," Carlos said, looking at her intently. "But the minute you start feeling tired, you let me know."

She nodded to ease his worry, but that wasn't going to happen. Though she hadn't seen the project through completion, being able to see the end result of the new Queen's Palace made her a little giddy with excitement. But the past few months, Carlos had been overly worried about her and the baby, and to alleviate some of her "exertions", he'd reserved a room for them at the resort so she would have a place to prepare before the gala and to rest after.

Judith was going on faith, and a fierce intuition, that she and their baby would be just fine. However, her constant reassurance that she felt great didn't stop Carlos from asking her every chance he got. He was more anxious than she was about the pregnancy and she wished she could do something to ease his worry.

She understood his concern, however. The doctors had warned her that she would lose their baby within her first trimester, but she hadn't. The doctors' many warnings had created an overprotection and panic in her, Carlos, and the immediate family who knew about her pregnancy. But the procedure to close her cervix had been completed without any complications and their baby grew safely inside her. She felt better, and stronger, than she had in a long time.

She turned in Carlos' arms and gave him a quick hug, then helped him fasten the small gold and ruby red cufflinks Gil had given him, which he'd given to Carlos for "encouragement."

Once Judith finished securing them to the cuffs of his black dress shirt, she stepped back and admired him as he slipped on his charcoal gray suit jacket. He wore a matching vest underneath with a black tie that blended well with his dark shirt. He looked beautiful—the embodiment of style and sophistication—and he was all hers.

"You know, if being sexy were a crime," she began, trying to contain her grin, "I'd lock you up and throw away the key."

He laughed, his eyes taking on that familiar glint. "We're locked in here now," he said, resting a hand lightly on her waist. "Why don't we make the most of it?"

She smiled at that. She had recently been cleared to have sex, and though they were still as hot for each other as before, he held himself back for fear of hurting her. And she was starting to miss the passionate beast that lay dormant inside him.

"Well," she drawled, placing a hand on his chest, "if we had the time…"

His eyes flashed brilliantly. "Oh, we have the time."

She ran her fingers down his lapels. "Hmm, but do you have the energy?"

His eyes widened, then he laughed again. She liked to play their silly game of who could come up with the silliest pickup line. The fun part for her was the delight in his eyes when she managed to one-up him. Seeing him happy made her happy.

It hadn't been overnight, but she had finally found peace. There was an inner joy in her that was flourishing—a joy she hadn't felt in a long time, but had managed to attain these past few months. Though part of it had come from knowing Ken was permanently out of her life, a bigger part of her newfound serenity came from having Carlos in her life, and having his unconditional love.

He had brought back joy and love into her life—sharing his family with her and giving her the chance to start one of her own. She loved him for everything he was and for all that he'd given her.

She'd planned to wait until after the gala to ask him, but suddenly she wanted him to know how much he meant to her.

Reaching for his hand, she clasped it in hers and held it tight. She ignored his questioning gaze and blurted out what was in her heart.

"I love you, Carlos."

His eyes darkened. He lifted her hand and placed a soft kiss on the back of it. "And you know how much I love you."

"I know," she said. "But I want you to know how much you mean to me, how important you are to me. The moment you came into my life, I started to really smile again, and laugh." She let out a nervous giggle. "I tried hard to protect it, but you still came and stole my heart. And I'm so glad you did because I know now what I would have been missing." A small quiver invaded her voice on her last words but she couldn't help it. "I love you, Carlos Moreno. Will you marry me?"

Something fierce yet warm flashed in his dark eyes. It was filled with a love so intense, she reveled in it.

"That's my line," he growled playfully, then pulled her into his arms for a slow, tender kiss.

They pulled apart, breathing raggedly and grinning at each other like besotted fools. She ran her thumb over his lower lip, removing the faint smear of her red lipstick.

Taking her hand in his, he lifted it, palm open, and ran it over his chest. "Feel that, *muñeca*? Do you know what material this is?"

She bit her lip. "Let me guess," she said, smoothing

her hand over his chest. "Husband material?"

"Damn right." His dark eyes flashed with love and amusement before he swept her in his arms for another kiss—one that literally stole her breath.

♥

THE END

ENJOYED THIS STORY?

If you enjoyed reading this story, please share that with others so they can enjoy it too!

Rate or review this book at your purchasing site or favorite review site (i.e. Amazon, Barnes & Nobles, Goodreads, etc.). Honest reviews are always helpful!

Recommend this book to your family, friends, reader groups, or book clubs.

Share this book with others by spreading the word on your favorite social media site.

Thank you!

ABOUT THE AUTHOR

Lena Hart is a Florida native currently living in the Harlem edge of New York City. Though she enjoys reading a variety of romance genres, she mainly writes sensual interracial romances with a flare of suspense and mystery. When Lena is not busy writing, she's reading, researching, or conferring with her muse. To learn more about Lena and her work, visit LenaHartSite.com.

BOOKS ALSO BY LENA HART

Because You Love Me
Because You Are Mine
Because This Is Forever

The Queen Quartette series:
His Flower Queen
His Bedpost Queen
Queen of His Heart
His Diamond Queen

Anthologies:
For Love & Liberty

2/5/15 — Wrinkled pages noted B.S.

Made in the USA
San Bernardino, CA
06 October 2014